AF620919

WE BECAME WILD

WE BECAME

WILD

H.D. CARVER

A NOVEL

NORTON YOUNG READERS
AN IMPRINT OF W. W. NORTON & COMPANY
INDEPENDENT PUBLISHERS SINCE 1923

This is a work of fiction. All incidents and dialogue, and all characters with the exception of some well-known historical and public figures, are products of the author's imagination and are not to be construed as real. Where real-life historical or public figures appear, the situations, incidents, and dialogues concerning those persons are entirely fictional and are not intended to depict actual events or to change the entirely fictional nature of the work. In all other respects, any resemblance to persons living or dead is entirely coincidental.

Some real places, including portions of the Pacific Crest Trail and surrounding areas, have been artistically adapted for storytelling purposes. These descriptions should be understood as fictional rather than literal representations of the actual geography.

Copyright © 2026 by H.D. Carver

All rights reserved
Printed in the United States of America
First Edition

Quotes from *Wild* by Cheryl Strayed (Alfred A. Knopf, 2012).

For information about permission to reproduce selections from this book, write to Permissions, W. W. Norton & Company, Inc., 500 Fifth Avenue, New York, NY 10110

For information about special discounts for bulk purchases, please contact W. W. Norton Special Sales at specialsales@wwnorton.com or 800-233-4830

Manufacturing by Lakeside Book Company
Book design by Hana Anouk Nakamura
Production manager: Delaney Adams

ISBN 978-1-324-12497-9

W. W. Norton & Company, Inc., 500 Fifth Avenue, New York, NY 10110
www.wwnorton.com

W. W. Norton & Company Ltd., 15 Carlisle Street, London W1D 3BS

Authorized EU representative: EAS, Mustamäe tee 50, 10621 Tallinn, Estonia

10 9 8 7 6 5 4 3 2 1

To Gregg, Finn, and Lila,

for everything.

And to the ones who need it as much as I did.

WE BECAME WILD

Few places in this world are more dangerous than home.
Fear not, therefore, to try the mountain passes.

—John Muir, *The Mountains of California*

0

VAL

Afterward, they'd all say she went up there to die.

They. The collective hive-mind that existed within the walls of high school and in phone screens, who didn't know anything about her but would post RIP with broken-heart emojis in their stories and whisper about her motives. *Why the hell else would she have climbed up on that ridge alone in the middle of the night and didn't you know Tristan cheated on her it makes total sense yeah I heard her mom committed suicide too it all adds up that girl wanted to end it poor thing so tragic just before graduation too.*

Val slipped in a wash of loose dirt and stumbled up the rocks toward the top of the ridge. One hand still clung to the plastic bottle she nabbed from the party, the other bracing her. Sweat and dirt formed a muddy paste against her palm. She wasn't trying to die. She was trying to find some fucking quiet and solitude. Trying to escape the buzzing and noise and chatter of the party she never wanted to go to. Trying to commune with nature because she understood how to do that a hell of a lot better than she understood how to commune with people.

If she were being honest, she was also trying—at least a little—to make Tristan worry about her, hoping he'd regret cheating on her. Thinking about it made her eyes sting. She smashed the sleeve of her hoodie against them. She didn't want to cry, not about him.

The breeze kicked up a whisper of moisture from the low clouds off to the west, like the night air was holding back tears too. Like it shared her pain. Val closed her eyes and breathed in the feeling. This was why she loved nature. It gave her the sense that she was connected to something bigger, something that understood her.

She took a long pull off the plastic bottle. The cheap liquor singed her throat like fire, but she swallowed it down, letting it glow in her belly. It was stupid to drink on the ridge, but it was also stupid to walk around feeling like her heart had been carved out with a pickax, and the booze was effectively numbing that feeling, so she went with it, downing another gulp. She clenched her teeth against the burn so she wouldn't cough and tried not to think about Tristan.

She dropped down onto the dirt and thought about the rocks instead. She picked one up, turning it over in her hand, sharp-edged, volcanic. She knew its name, only she couldn't recall it now. The alcohol swishing around inside her head had stolen it from her.

"Fun fact," she said—speaking aloud to the night and the moon and the party, and most of all to Tristan, because he hated when she recited facts—"this mountain is only a third of the height it used to be. Millions of years of wind and time have shrunk it."

There were probably a lot of people who found her constant fact-spewing annoying, but Tristan was the only one who'd been a real dick about it, calling the habit obnoxious, saying she sounded like a little kid vying for attention. The memory made her cheeks hot. She took another pull from her bottle. "Fact!" she shouted now, the effort burning her throat. "Fourteen million years ago, this whole place was sea floor! Did you know that, Tristan?" She was sure, actually, that Tristan didn't know. He was the dumbest guy she'd ever dated—fact. She wanted that to make her feel better, but it didn't.

The house with its party was far off now in the distance below her. She could still tell which one it was from the crisscrossed lights strung all over the backyard. Val leaned back against the slope behind her. The rocks still held heat from the day's sun, but she imagined it was from the heart of the mountain itself, remnants of the ancient volcano that made it. She pressed her cheek against it, wanting to feel its pulse. "Andesite," she said, finally recalling the name of the rock. Her head spun from the alcohol, a child's top just before it went out of control.

Another tendril of mist rolled in from the backside of the ridge, little bits of the marine layer that stretched inland.

"Fact," she said to just the moon now, shining through the haze, because she was done shouting at Tristan, "ten thousand years ago, this was Chumash land." The moon already knew that, she supposed, but she didn't think it minded her saying so. She pressed her back harder against the mountainside, thinking about what it had seen, about the women thousands of years ago who'd touched it, who'd walked this very spot, sweating in the heat of the sun, children on their backs. It made her feel less alone, less motherless.

Val knew everything about this place—she knew about all kinds of things and places—because when the rest of the world slept, her mind whirred and whined and kept her awake, always hungry, so she fed it with history and science and facts until it was so stuffed that it overflowed out her mouth and onto people who didn't give a shit, like Tristan. When Val used to have a mother, that mother would teach her and guide her and fill her with words and knowledge and advice and love. Now, she had Netflix documentaries and the internet and books. And stories of women who weren't her mother but who she wished could be.

Like Cheryl Strayed.

Val had memorized her words like they were her own personal scripture. Her book, *Wild*, became Val's bible, the outdoors her church. Val was going to follow in her footsteps, leaving home to live for months on the Pacific Crest Trail after graduation. A secret pilgrimage.

She tipped the bottle to her lips again and watched the amber-gold liquor slosh against its plastic walls. Something on her leg burned. She took her phone from her pocket and pointed its light over the swath of skin that stung like a thousand bees had attacked it. (Fact: There were still no messages from Tristan.) Her light lit up an army of tiny cactus spines embedded in her shin, iridescent white, beautiful. Val liked how they looked jutting out from her skin, like she'd grown her own armor. She pinched one of the spines and yanked, her eyes watering with the pain of it. They were the opposite of the tears that had come earlier, born from strength instead of weakness.

The tip of the spine was smeared with her blood. She smiled at it, at how ruthless and unyielding nature was. How it didn't second-guess anything or say sorry for protecting itself or even feel bad when someone drowned in its floodwaters or burned in its fires. Nature just existed, no apologies.

She wiped the spine along the mountainside, adding her blood to the rocks and the stories they held, the journeys of centuries of women who'd walked here before her. Those women would have told her that shit-boys like Tristan didn't matter. That she was bigger than all of this. She stood and scrambled onto the outcropping just another few feet above her, but she felt miles higher standing up there, splaying her arms. She felt invincible. She felt like nature and the moon, like a god looking out at her kingdom. Existing, no apologies.

Only, she was cold. Gods didn't get cold.

The view below her had become obscured. The low clouds were rolling in from the coast in earnest now, climbing up the mountain behind her and tumbling down the slope at her feet. Her hair stuck against her face in the mist that grew thicker by the second. That was another thing about nature—it was fickle as hell.

Val shivered. She tried to find the godlike feeling again, to re-enter the moment that had passed too quickly, but it was gone. The clouds moved fast, coming in great billowing sheets, blotting out the lights below and the world around her, even the moon. She blinked her eyes, trying to clear them.

She was surrounded by nothingness.

The moisture soaked her shirt, raising goosebumps along her arms. An acutely human feeling washed over her as her teeth began to chatter from the cold, stealing even the memory of invincibility from just moments before.

She needed to get off the ridge.

She made her way down the scramble she'd climbed to get to the outcropping. The rocks, now wet and slick, matched her skin.

She slipped and smashed her chin, getting a mouthful of dirt and grit and blood. She slowed her pace, resolving to be more careful. But in the mist, her mind swimming with booze, she was lost.

She stepped, and the ground beneath her was gone.

She dropped through nothingness, her mind searching for a fact. In the end, she couldn't be certain what did it, the booze or the mist, or just nature, existing. No apologies.

PART I
THREE SISTERS

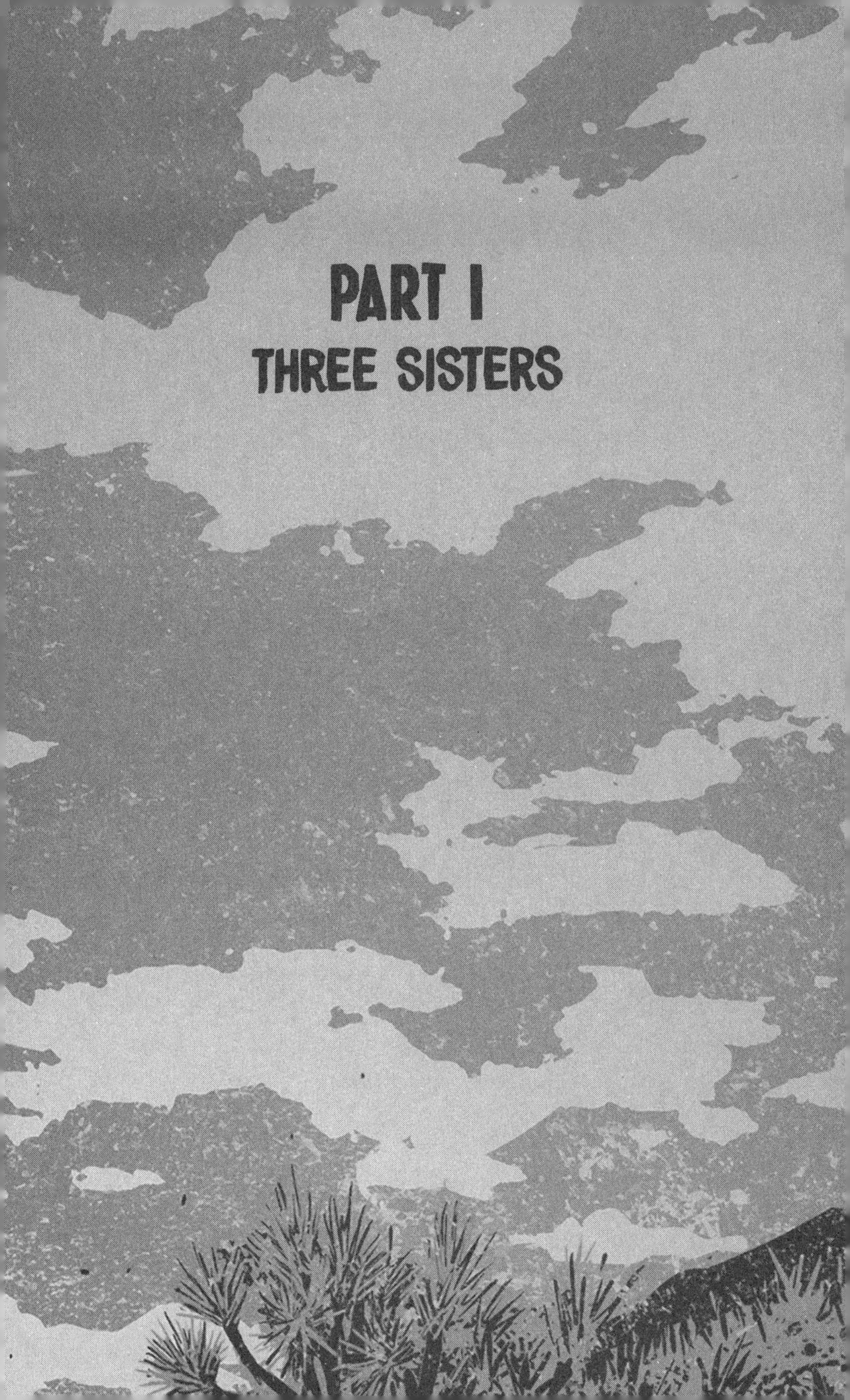

1

LOTTIE

The sun was an asshole. It flooded the shed, lighting up everything that had been hidden by the dark just hours ago. Gabe was curled next to her. *Nestled.* Their skin stuck together with moisture left from kisses. She could see every detail of him now, lit up in high-def by the asshole sun—the sleepy crust in the corners of his eyes, the little rings of gray muck trapped in the pores along his nose.

Don't get grossed out don't get grossed out, the words rang through her mind like a prayer and a wish. But Lottie wasn't the kind of person prayers or wishes came true for. Already, the revulsion was setting in. She knew it would come. It was like a default setting that couldn't be changed, like God or the Universe or whoever created her crossed the wires in her brain, giving her a knee-jerk, if-I-even-look-at-you-I-might-puke reaction to *after*. It wasn't usually much of a problem—most guys tended to want to get dressed and get out as quickly as she did.

But Gabe wasn't most guys. He was Val's—*don't you dare screw with him, I swear to God, Lottie*—brother. The one who offered Lottie rides to work even when her shift started an hour before his did. Who quietly slid over half his burrito when she showed up at the lunch table without food.

Gabe.

He said he loved her last night, whispering the words between panted breaths. Lottie hoped he didn't mean it—guys sometimes got sentimental in that moment, right before—but she knew better. Even if she didn't, there was no mistaking that the way his arms still held her now had nothing to do with sex and everything to do with whispered words.

Regret swelled inside her.

But the truth was this: She'd known last night that she was making a huge mistake.

And also this: She loved every minute of it. It was like standing on the yellow line in the middle of a two-lane highway, a rush that blotted out everything else. Time stopped. The world went black. There was nothing but the feeling of that moment.

Some deep-buried, idiotic part of her had even hoped that breaking Val's cardinal rule might actually piss her off enough to wake her from the dead. That she'd come back just to kick Lottie's ass. But hope was as pointless as prayers and wishes.

Lottie closed her eyes and tried to imagine a scenario where this might turn out okay. She couldn't conjure one. Her mind offered up excuses for what she'd done instead—they were both just drunk and Gabe was the unfortunate one who got caught in her crosshairs.

But the truth was this: She hadn't been that drunk, despite her efforts.

She and Messina had gone in hard, starting the night off with a drinking game, huddled together in a shadowed corner of the deck, watching the party rage around them. The game was simple—a drink every time someone mentioned Val. Those assholes at the party never even knew her name a month ago—now she was all anyone talked about. *It's so sad. I can't believe it happened so close to graduation. Yeah, I heard she was only going to community, but still, so sad.* Lottie and Messina downed their beers in minutes.

"I'll be right back," Lottie had said, lifting the empty cup from Messina's hands and wandering off to find the keg. She found Gabe instead, tucked away in his own dark corner, avoiding the crowd. Her brain warned her not to do anything stupid, to fill the cups and go back to Messina—a fresh scab had barely formed over their wound of a friendship. But Lottie hated being told what to do, even when it came from her own mind.

She watched Gabe. He didn't look like himself, glaring out at the party with a quiet fury, like he didn't care if the whole world went up in flames. Gabe cared about everything—especially Lottie. But he didn't give her a second look as she passed. Maybe that was what did it, the sudden feeling of insignificance blooming inside of her. She wanted to obliterate it.

She dropped the empty cups into the grass, along with any thought of Messina, and closed the distance to Gabe. She pressed against him like she was trying to bruise her insides. Like if she tried hard enough, she could absorb him right through her skin. Like maybe all the goodness inside him could heal all the fucked-up stuff inside her. She liked how he pressed against her the same way, like maybe there was something good in her too.

Truth: There wasn't.

If there had been, she wouldn't have ended up here in this stupid shed in the first place—she would have stayed with Messina. *Shit*, she thought, remembering that Messina had stolen her stepdad's minivan to get them to the party, something she'd only agreed to after Lottie swore up and down that they'd be back before he got up for work. They were nowhere near home—the bougie, rich-kid parties were always south or inland, up in the hills. She didn't know where her phone was, but it had to be getting late, and Messina's fucker of a stepdad was an early riser.

She needed to get up and find Messina and get the hell out of here. But she didn't move. Because if she moved, Gabe was going to wake up. If she moved, he was going to look at her and talk to her, and she wouldn't know what to say. But none of that was really the truth of it.

The truth was this: If she moved, she was going to have to break his heart.

2

MESSINA

Fucking Lottie. She wasn't picking up her phone. Messina weaved in and out of rooms looking for her, stepping carefully around passed-out people and . . . fluids. Her pant leg was splattered with purple-tinged vomit from the girl three rooms ago who'd puked right as she passed. Messina could still smell it.

A memory of Val whispered at her. *Fun fact: Did you know that when you smell something, you're actually breathing in millions of tiny particles of that thing?*

Messina blew all the air out of her lungs with a hard breath and tapped her thumb and index finger together in an OK motion again and again until she got a good one.

The house was a giant maze with endless rooms that led to walk-in closets that morphed into bathrooms bigger than her living room. It could take hours to find Lottie in this place. She didn't have hours. She rounded a corner and found herself in a huge room with arching windows. She knew she wouldn't find Lottie here. Whatever Lottie had done last night, it wasn't the kind of thing done in front of windows—she'd be hidden away.

Messina had been stupid to think Lottie would stick around

long enough to actually be a friend—wishful thinking. She'd been even stupider to let Lottie convince her to take out Jeffucker's van. By the time they got back now, he'd be awake, waiting for her.

"You're.fine.you're.fine.you're.fine," she whispered to herself.

She rounded a corner and saw a girl who'd for sure overheard her whispers, staring at her with a *Here comes Crazy* face. She didn't know which was more embarrassing—being overheard talking to herself or being overheard lying to herself. She was not fine. Not at all.

Fucking Lottie.

The logic in Messina's head said she should just leave. That she should've left last night. But the last friend she left at a party wound up dead. Anyway, Lottie was all she had now. Beggars and choosers and all that.

Messina felt watched, like the eyes of everyone in the house were on her, even when she crossed through empty rooms. It was a sense she always had, being watched. She could sit alone in the dark of her closet with the door closed and still feel it. *God is always watching.* Jeffucker had jammed the words into her head over and over like a never-ending song on repeat.

Messina didn't believe in God until Jeffucker came along. Even now, she knew God wasn't real—because no god would let innocent people get blown to bits in wars they didn't start, or let child molesters walk around pretending to be normal people, or let someone like Val die at seventeen—but knowing something and believing it were different things.

Jeffucker hadn't brought religion with him at first, when fate spewed him into the lives of Messina and her mom. He found that later. But receiving God's grace didn't affect him the way it did other people, the way it turned them nicer and softer and more forgiving. It did the opposite. Messina had never understood the term *righteous anger* until Jeffucker found the Lord. Now, she understood it plenty.

She moved through another room, past sleeping people piled on a giant sofa. She refocused her thoughts on her search for Lottie, checking faces and body shapes for one that resembled her friend. None did.

Fucking Lottie.

The puke spot on her pants clung to her skin. She could feel it soaking through her leg, a stranger's bacteria leaching into her body, wreaking havoc. Her brain countered that this wasn't logical, but that didn't help anything because Messina's fears weren't bound by logic or any other rules.

Facts about microbes bounced around inside her head, little leftover bits of Val that had lived on, even though the rest of her was gone. *Did you know people are made of more bacteria than human cells? Fun fact: We're only 43 percent human—the rest is microbes that affect everything about us, even the way we think.* Messina clung to them, even as they spun her mind into a panic, too afraid to let them go, scared she'd lose the only pieces of Val she had left.

She dragged her fingernail along the back of her scalp until it reached the scab hidden beneath her curls, just above where her neck met her hairline. She picked along its edges, slipping her fingernail beneath it until it came away red. She felt a rush of relief. She put the blood-smeared fingertip against her tongue, erasing the evidence.

She was in an office now, overflowing with leather furniture and leather-bound books. She hated leather—dead cow skin. This whole room was a museum of cow carcasses. The smell of it filled the air. Messina lifted her shirt collar over her nose, trying not to breathe in the particles.

"You're fine," she whispered. She lifted a silver pen from the desk and rolled the cold, heavy metal around in her fingers *you're.fine.you're.fine.you're.fine* until it was hot from her touch. She tucked it into her bag next to Val's copy of *Wild*—she carried the book with her everywhere now, just like Val had. She looked behind the desk and the leather sofa and chairs—no Lottie.

She widened her search to the backyard. She was so lost in her frustration that she almost stepped on a guy—naked, his jollies hanging out all over the place—who was definitely going to wake up with a sunburned dick. She gave him a wide berth as she went around him. She hated seeing dicks. They were horrifying to look at, like raw fucking bratwurst. If she were being honest, she didn't like anyone's private parts, not even her own. She'd have preferred for everyone in the world to exist only from the waist up.

The brat-dick visual got burned into her mind like a sunspot, and she flicked at the air, trying to get rid of it. "You're.fine.you're.fine.you're.fine."

Watching eyes burned her skin. She looked up and saw Tristan, wearing a look that made her skin crawl. She wanted to charge at him and unleash the anger.rage.windstorm inside her, but she didn't. Because Messina wasn't the kind of person who did things like that. She was the kind of person who only thought about doing them.

She dropped her shoulders and clung to the fence at the edge of the yard, stepping around a plaster gnome, trying to become invisible. Sometimes she convinced herself she was. She slunk past a couple in the grass, watching them from behind. Flirting looked so easy for other people—fingertips on an arm, a little smile—but it was a foreign language Messina didn't speak, something based on instinct and impulse. Lottie practically breathed it. She had a charm that felt like magic. People always liked her when she wanted them to—even if they'd heard awful things about her. She could make them forget with an easy smile.

That wasn't the case for Messina. Her brain didn't work like other people's, always twisting things around, whipping up windstorms inside her. It made people uncomfortable. The more she tried to fit in, the more people avoided her. Like they could sense her desperation.

She reached the gate marking the end of the yard, ready to give up her search, when she saw a shed tucked behind a vine-covered lattice. She stepped alongside it, standing up on her toes to peek through the high window, hoping not to encounter another brat-dick situation, and saw Lottie twisted up on the floor with some guy. She looked desperate, a wild animal caught in a trap.

It wasn't until the guy turned, his arms tightening around Lottie, that Messina understood why.

Fucking Lottie.

3

LOTTIE

None of it was real. Gabe's pulse ticking beneath the skin of his neck, the sick feeling in her stomach, the smell of *them* congealing in the air. It wasn't real. It was a movie of Lottie's life that she was watching from the audience. She zoomed out, seeing herself from above, hair askew, lying next to a big plastic kayak. The thought brought a wave of numbing relief over her. Until Gabe opened his eyes, his smile coming at her full force, brighter than the asshole sun. He touched her shoulder in the spot where other guys avoided the burn scars along her skin and pulled her in close. She twisted away, trying to hide her cringe, and felt his body go tense against hers.

"What's the matter, Lottie?" She hated the sound of her name coming off his lips that way. It wasn't how he normally said it. It was soft, like it had been coated in powdered sugar and feelings. She was saved from answering by the shed door swinging open, even more sunlight flooding in. Gabe whipped up the tarp they'd been using as a blanket, covering Lottie's body in some kind of effort to protect her honor or something. He hugged her tighter, pressing things she didn't want to think about into her abdomen.

She couldn't see who'd just discovered them around the

blinding sun, but her first guess was the parents of whoever's house they were at, come to ask what in God's name they were doing under that tarp. She blinked the sun-sting from her eyes, and the shape in the doorway became immediately recognizable. Messina's body language was so sharp and rigid, it read like she'd been pasted together from glass shards. She stood silently, haloed in the sunlight, taking in the sweaty-tarp, brother-fucking situation that was Lottie.

Lottie wanted her to be pissed. She wanted her to yell and say how Lottie had been a shitty friend and how she deserved every bit of the mess she was in now, but Messina didn't do any of that. She stared at a camping light hanging in front of her, like she didn't even want to look at Lottie. She flipped the lamp's switch on and off again.

"Get dressed," she said, her eyes still on the lamp. "We should've left an hour ago."

Lottie started to sit up but got caught halfway as Gabe clung to the tarp around them. She was like a mouse stuck in a glue trap, just about ready to tear off her own arm if she thought it would get her out of there. "I'll be there in a sec," she said.

Messina turned without a word, leaving Lottie alone with Gabe and her swelling regret. She squirmed out from Gabe's grasp and the cover of the tarp, not thinking twice about modesty. It was something she was born lacking, the way some people couldn't taste the PTC paper in biology class. She found her shorts on the floor in a heap between a pair of mountain bikes, phone dead in the pocket, and hiked them into place as fast as she could. Her underwear had gone AWOL.

Gabe followed her lead and put on his clothes. He held the shed door open for Lottie, rubbing his other hand over his mess of ink-black hair, like it was doing anything to tame it.

A pair of guys lying in the grass nearby snickered as Gabe and Lottie emerged from the outbuilding, tousled and squinty-eyed. Gabe shot them a look like he was defending Lottie's honor again and took her hand. She whipped it away. Gabe's feelings got stuck all over his face, caught halfway between hurt and confusion. The sadness of his eyes made Lottie sorry, but it didn't make her give her hand back.

"What's wrong?"

She shook her head in a lie. "It's just hot out. Makes my palms sweaty."

Gabe looked at her like he didn't believe her, but like he'd give anything to be able to. Lottie looked away and stared down at the grass. It was lush and green—freshly watered despite all of California being in a drought.

They were forced to alter their course through the yard around a passed-out guy, naked and sunny-side-up in the grass. His dick was turning red in the sun. Lottie felt bad for him, even though a little bit of her was glad she wasn't the only one having a rough morning. She nabbed a sun-bleached cushion from a nearby lounge chair and tossed it over his middle. Gabe's smile blazed again. Jesus, it was giving her retinal damage.

"What?" The word shot out of her, harsh, raw.

"Nothing . . . you're just nice."

"I'm not." Truth: She wasn't.

They picked their way around patio furniture littered with

bottles and cans. Butts and roaches floated in the half-drunk beers warming in the sun. Something—that itchy feeling she got when someone was watching her—made her turn. Tristan—Val's ex—was on the retaining wall above the pool, slouched deliberately, like he was waiting for things to become interesting. Eyes on Lottie.

He only ever looked at things one of two ways—like he wanted it, or like he'd already had it. Lottie had seen both now, but she didn't let herself think about that. He exhaled a cloud of vape, its sweet cinnamon stink drifting on the air, and shot her a knowing grin that made her turn her face away, a second too late.

She grabbed hold of Gabe's arm, letting the feel of him—all muscles and skin and warmth—fill her, using him as a forcefield to block out the memories that clawed at her mind. She steered them in the opposite direction, away from Tristan. They were halfway through the house before she realized she was still clinging to Gabe's bicep, hundreds of miles of swim practice stored up there beneath his skin. He smiled down at her, ten thousand watts. *Fuck.* She'd made it so much worse. She didn't know how to cut him loose now.

She towed him out front to the street where Messina waited inside Jeffucker's burgundy minivan. Gabe looked down at Lottie, his eyes all full of devotion and morning goo-crust. Something inside her sensed the impending kiss. Before she could react, his lips were on hers, hopeful and exhilarated like a bird as it flew right into the side of a glass building.

He pulled away, confused. His eyes searched hers, full of questions—each one a different version of *What did I do wrong?*

Lottie flicked her gaze down to her shoes.

"See you at work?" Gabe's voice was unsteady.

"I guess so," she said, still staring at the ground. Gabe hovered for another moment before he turned and walked back toward the house. Lottie only looked up once she was sure he was gone. She climbed in next to Messina, trying to remember the rules from last night: *1. No mud in the van, 2. No trash in the van, 3. Don't move the mirrors in the van, 4. Don't touch anything in the van . . . Ad infinitum.*

Messina's entire world was comprised of rules. She shot Lottie a weird look, making her wonder if she'd accidentally broken one of them.

"That was like watching a unicorn get bludgeoned to death," Messina said, turning the key as Jeffucker's van coughed to life. Lottie knew now that the look wasn't because she'd broken a rule—it was because she'd broken Gabe.

She dropped her head, letting it come down on the dashboard with a hard thud, the pain weirdly soothing. She did it again. *Thud.* Maybe it would knock loose the memories of last night. Gabe's face—*thud.* The look in his eyes—*thud.* His words, "I love you." *Thud. Thud. Thud.*

Messina's silent irritation was a tangible thing in the air.

The truth was this: Messina hated spectacle and display.

And this: Lottie was nothing but spectacle and display.

Thud. Thud. Thud.

"Dude, you'll set off the airbag." Messina's hand jutted out in front of Lottie's forehead, catching it just before it hit the dash again. "Ew, you're leaking." She held up her fingers to show Lottie the smear of blood there.

Lottie touched her forehead with her own fingers, recalling the zit-scab she'd been messing with before the party, the one she'd slathered in cover-up and forgotten about.

Messina dug around in her bag and pulled out a bottle of sanitizer that she squirted into her hand before hitting the gas so hard that Lottie flopped back in her seat. She held the bottle out to Lottie, offering her some. When Lottie shook her head, Messina motioned to the glove box. "Tissues on the right."

Rule number fifty-two: No bleeding in the van.

"I'm sorry about last night." Lottie grabbed a Kleenex and pressed it against her forehead as they sped out of the neighborhood. "I shouldn't have left you like that."

"It's cool," Messina said. But it wasn't the truth.

The truth was this: Lottie was a shitty friend, and they both knew it. She just didn't know how to fix it. She pulled down the visor to see if the bleeding had stopped. She looked like a wreck, only worse. Like the shit left behind on the freeway after the wreck is cleaned up, all the pieces of glass and plastic that are smashed up too small to bother collecting. Blood wept from the open crust of her scab. She flipped up the visor and mashed the tissue against her skin harder.

She glanced at Messina, who somehow looked like a goddess at seven a.m. after an all-night party—not a single curl out of place. A little twinge of envy pricked at Lottie. She wished she could be that way, the opposite of a wreck. The kind of person who carried sanitizer in her bag and didn't sleep with her best friend's brother. That's just who Messina was—clean, sharp-edged, put together. At least on the outside, which was the part that mattered.

Lottie was none of those things. She was chaos, slipping from one disaster to the next. A liar and a shit-friend. Her label warned *Caution: Flammable.*

Then there was Val. The daring one. Brilliant. Obnoxious. Manic. The one with a wild spirit who couldn't be caged. That used to be the truth, but it wasn't anymore.

Now the truth was this: Val was the dead one.

And also this: She was dead because of Lottie.

"She was supposed to die in a mudslide."

Lottie had said those words inside her head a hundred times since Val's death. It hadn't occurred to her how alarming they might sound until she said them out loud to Ms. Sipes, school counselor for students with last names beginning L–R, four weeks earlier.

She'd raised her eyebrows at Lottie. "I'm sorry?" Lottie had probably sounded like a sociopath saying it like that. "What do you mean 'Valerie was supposed to die in a mudslide?' "

It had been her third appointment with Ms. Sipes. She'd called Lottie in every day since Val's death became known to the school. Lottie had always wanted a therapist, like the ones in shows that were cool and easygoing and had funny retorts whenever a client said something mildly worrisome. But Ms. Sipes did this thing where she'd watch Lottie in silence with a frown hanging on her face for minutes on end. It was unnerving. TV therapists never did that shit.

"I don't mean it like that," Lottie said.

"How do you mean it?"

"I mean we used to talk about it, how we'd all die. Together."

The concern on Ms. Sipes's face didn't diminish. "We live in La Conchita," Lottie added. "Val, Messina, and me. We just all figured that was how we'd go."

There came the nod of understanding. La Conchita was infamous, a tiny coastal neighborhood that someone decided to build below an unstable mountain. Ten people died in the last big mudslide—killer beach views though.

It wasn't strange to Lottie that they'd spent so much time pondering their own deaths when they'd grown up in a place that was actively trying to kill them—it was a bedtime story they told each other whenever they slept over at Val's. She'd been the one who kept them glued together—"the three sisters"—even as things were strained between Lottie and Messina, their friendship rotting like a bad marriage they both stayed in for the kid. They still always ended up at Val's when the rainstorms came, squished into her bed and tucked beneath the warmth of her old quilt. They'd huddle and talk about how when the mountain came down, they'd all be buried in the mud, just like that, eternally bonded. It seemed weird, but the idea of them being together forever, even in death, gave Lottie a sense of comfort.

But Val died alone.

The thought burst open inside Lottie, a flash of cold and pain so intense that her mind checked out completely. When she came back, Ms. Sipes was staring at her again. "Lottie?" Her mouth was stuck in her signature frown. "Were you having another one of your episodes?"

Episodes. That was what Ms. Sipes called it whenever Lottie mentally checked out. Lottie thought it was funny because that's what it felt like sometimes—episodes of a show Lottie was watching, but also somehow starring in. The bad bingeable kind where there's too much drama, and you're rooting for the main character but she keeps fucking stuff up and making life harder for herself. You want to love her, you really do, but damn if she doesn't make it hard.

"Is this something that started when Valerie passed?"

Lottie hated when people called it that—Val hadn't passed, she was dead. All the way. Because of Lottie. She wondered if the doctor-patient privilege thing existed within these walls, if she could tell Ms. Sipes the truth about Val's death without her blabbing it to anyone else.

The truth was this: Val's death had been ruled an accident, which was right—Lottie knew she hadn't jumped. But it was also this: Lottie was the reason Val was up on that ridge in the first place.

Ms. Sipes took a long sip from the straw of her giant cup and watched Lottie. She'd asked her a question, but Lottie couldn't remember what it was.

"Do you feel like these episodes happen when you're under pressure or stressed?"

The truth was this: They came whenever her feelings got so intense she felt like she might die from them. Like they were drowning her and stabbing her all at once.

Lottie tried explaining it in a way that didn't sound crazy. "I guess so? But it's kind of all the time. Like whenever things happen that I don't like, or when I feel dumb or someone's shitty to me. Or after I kiss somebody I shouldn't, or when I do something wrong and wish I hadn't. It's like the camera just zooms out, and I'm watching it instead of being there."

It felt nice to talk about it. No one had ever asked her about how her brain worked or why it did certain things. Lottie let out a long breath through her lips, feeling the relief that came with letting out secrets, even if they were only crumbs.

Ms. Sipes's frown went deeper, carving fresh lines into her face. The relief Lottie felt vanished, and she wished that she hadn't told Ms. Sipes anything at all.

"Have you ever heard of something called dissociation?"

Lottie nodded, like she knew what that meant, but Ms. Sipes explained it anyway. *To disconnect, separate. To split off from your mind.*

"I think you should consider getting real counseling, Lottie."

"Isn't that what this is?"

Even her eyes frowned at that. "This is school crisis counseling. It's being offered to any student who feels affected by Valerie's death. It's not meant to be long-term . . . or for other issues." She dug in a drawer and slid a paper across the desk.

Lottie scanned it. It was a list of local therapists, all with addresses that were followed by suite numbers. Not the free kind—that was what Ms. Sipes meant by *real* counseling. That was what *real* always meant—expensive. Foods made of *real* ingredients, furniture made of *real* wood. Lottie's entire existence was the plastic imitation of a real life.

"Most of them will accept some form of insurance," Ms. Sipes said.

But insurance was another one of those expensive things that only existed in a *real* life. Lottie didn't even have the fake, plastic version.

4

GABE

Your heart's going to break, no matter what you do.

That's what Val told him the last night they sat on the rooftop together, months ago. She'd woken him in the middle of the night, like she sometimes did when all the words and books and films and sticky notes in the world weren't enough to slow the spinning in her mind.

"Let's go up on a mountain," she said, like always. Gabe heard her in that far-off way you hear things in your dreams. She shook his shoulder. "Gabe, come on. Let's go up on a mountain."

He rubbed his eyes and tried to make out the numbers on his clock. 3:13 a.m. He didn't want to go up on a mountain. He wanted to sleep. But he knew why she was here, even in the dark, unable to see her wild eyes. He knew she was having one of those nights. She was already dressed, ready to go.

"How about the roof instead?" he offered, picking up a hoodie from the floor and pulling it over his head.

Their dad hated it when they climbed up on the rooftop—risk of falling, too high—so they kept it secret. They could see the ocean from there, on the other side of the 101. It was easier to ignore the freeway at night, when the traffic was low. They could hear the waves between passing cars.

They sat in silence together for a long time, watching the moonlight dance on the water.

"I think I used to be a tree in another life," Val said, and Gabe smiled because if anyone else had said something like that, it would have sounded crazy, but when Val said it, it seemed perfectly reasonable. "Like a redwood or giant sequoia, one of the ones that's been here for a thousand years. I think my bones have tree memories."

"What do they feel like?"

"Like time. Like there's this other version of me that existed somewhere before the one in this body. Some bigger, truer version of me that was rooted to the earth. With a thousand years of wisdom inside her. The *real* Val."

Sometimes he loved hearing what it was like on the inside of her mind. Sometimes it scared him.

"I know you're in love with Lottie," she said then, and it caught him off guard, a sudden shift from tree memories. But that was how Val's mind worked, leaping from planet to planet with ease because entire universes were contained inside it. "She can't love you back, you know. Your heart's going to break, no matter what you do."

He didn't say anything. There was nothing *to* say. She'd just stated a fact, and they both knew it was true. It didn't change anything.

They stayed up there for hours, Gabe shivering in his too-thin sweatpants and bare feet, Val in a thick jacket and hat, because she knew better how the early morning moisture could chill you all the way down to the core. He wondered how many times she didn't wake him, when she climbed up on the roof or on mountains alone, without him. It made him worry.

Gabe blinked away the memory and watched the road, heading away from the party and back toward the 101. A smoke plume billowed up along the horizon. New fires had been sparking every week, late bouts of Santa Ana winds fueling the flames. L.A. and Ventura Counties had both been under a red-flag warning for half the month. Gabe pulled to the right and slowed as a firetruck passed him, lights and sirens blazing.

The first fire of the season had sparked a month ago in the Santa Monica Mountains the night Val died. It burned ten thousand acres in two days. In his mind he'd drawn a connection between the fire and his sister, even though there wasn't one. He still couldn't help thinking it. That the fire had been nature's way of grieving Val, that it was raging and inconsolable at the loss of her.

Maybe that was just the way his brain was trying to make sense of all the things that didn't make sense right now. He still felt messed up for thinking it. It was the kind of thought he kept inside now, because he only would have shared it with Val. She wouldn't have thought he was crazy or messed up for having it. She would have understood it.

She would have understood about last night with Lottie, too. Even though she'd warned him about her a thousand times, she wouldn't have reminded him about any of that or told him how he'd been stupid or that he should've known better. She'd have smashed him in a too-tight hug and asked him if he wanted to go up on a mountain.

It was her solution to every problem, convinced that nature

could heal everything and that nothing seemed as bad when you looked at it from up on a mountainside. Gabe didn't always feel like climbing a mountain, but he knew it was her way of trying to comfort him, her own version of buying him an ice cream sundae after he'd had a shitty day.

He would have given anything to do that with her now.

5

MESSINA

She tore a chunk off the scab at the back of her head. Blood and pain wept from the wound. Messina closed her eyes feeling the hurt of it bloom over her, pulsing. She was still in the van. Its engine idled in the driveway. Messina idled in the driveway. The clock screamed at her—7:44—but she didn't move. Her brain looped on images of what would happen if she went inside. Of what would happen if she didn't.

She was fucked either way.

It didn't matter that her mom was home. She never did anything. She'd be tucked out of sight, stuck in her own faraway game of make-believe, convincing herself that she didn't know what went on beneath the roof that was theirs once, but now belonged to him.

Messina and her mom had been happy Before. Messina knew that, even though she couldn't really remember it. Just like she knew she hadn't always been afraid, even though she couldn't remember that either. The things she remembered were small. Details that burned in her mind like dying stars in a black sky—a smile on her mom's face, her sunflower perfume, how she'd tell Messina again and again about the day she was born because Messina never stopped asking to hear it.

The story hadn't been told in years now, but she could still remember the last time, or a memory made up of all the times before, pieced together like a puzzle. How her mom would pull her onto her lap, the stubble along her legs tickling Messina's skin. She'd tell Messina how the Santa Ana winds were blowing on the day she was born. How when she was in labor, the winds were so strong that they knocked down a hundred-foot palm tree right into the hospital where she was giving birth. She said the first thing Messina did wasn't to cry like all the other babies—instead, she reached up and grabbed some of the wind and captured it forever, and all that strength and power were still blowing around inside her to this day. Even as a kid, Messina knew it wasn't real, but she still believed it. Knowing and believing were different things. Sometimes she could still feel the wind blowing around inside her, only now it got stuck in her head, whipping up thoughts and worries, making a mess of things. She wanted it to make her strong again.

When she was done with the story, her mom would squeeze her in a giant hug. Sometimes she'd do it so long and hard it scared Messina, and all the breath would go out of her. Sometimes she'd hug her like she was trying to fill up the big hole inside herself that Messina couldn't see but still knew was there—the same kind of hole that, years later, she would recognize in Lottie. Messina wanted to be able to fill that hole in her mom, but she never could.

Her mom had sometimes tried to fill it with other things. That was how they ended up with Jeffucker.

It was too late to hope he'd still be asleep. The van was parked at the wrong angle, slanted, so there was no hiding that she'd taken it. She hated parking—last night she made Lottie do it for her.

Messina's hands gripped the steering wheel. The engine still whirred, almost as fast as her mind. The Santa Ana winds raged inside her, thrashing and howling. But she didn't move.

Shadows from leaves in the tree above her danced over her skin. Even the leaves could move. The wind blew, they answered. They didn't question it. But Messina was frozen. The raw skin at the back of her skull throbbed. Blood was seeping into her hair. Her winds continued their war cry as the clock changed.

7:50

He'd be awake. Waiting for her.

7:52

Righteous anger.

7:53

Her mind whispered. *R u n.*

She was desperate to obey it. She'd been trying to leave for years, ever since Jeffucker slammed into her life like a bullet, cutting a hole right through its center. She'd gotten as far as a packed bag and the entrance to La Conchita about a hundred times, but never any farther than that. It was always the same. The panic would come, and she'd freeze—sometimes for hours. Eventually, she always turned back.

She'd been running away the first time she met Val—or trying to, anyway. After school, seventh grade. It was just starting to rain. It was the kind of warm day where the moment the first drop of rain hit the pavement, the smell of the air changed to something completely different. Messina was half a block from her house, hunched on the bench outside the beach access tunnel that led beneath the freeway and out of La Conchita, stuck and hopeless, her bag beside her. She knew she wasn't going anywhere. She'd pulled up the hood of her jacket so her face was shielded. Tiny raindrops tapped against it. She closed her eyes, inhaling their scent.

"It's petrichor."

She opened her eyes. A girl stood next to her, uncomfortably close. Like she'd just appeared out of the ether. She had eyes that were too big for her face that made her look like a baby animal in a cartoon. Messina had the sense that this girl was an even stranger creature than she was.

"What?"

"The rain smell." The girl blinked sprinkles out of her giant eyes. "It's called petrichor. It comes from the bacteria in the ground."

The girl wasn't wearing a jacket or carrying an umbrella or anything, even though she looked like she could afford one—not like Lottie, who you could tell with a single glance didn't own a rain jacket or much of anything else. This girl was just letting the rain fall all over her, soaking the shoulders of her purple T-shirt. On its front was a circular symbol with lines fanning out from the edges. Messina didn't know what it was, but it was the kind of thing Jeffucker would have called Satanic.

"It's not really true, right?" she said, still talking, as if Messina had given any indication that she wanted to participate in a conversation. "The sign." The girl motioned to the huge, infamous sign at the entrance of the neighborhood.

WARNING

THE LA CONCHITA COMMUNITY IS A GEOLOGIC HAZARD AREA. COUNTY OFFICIALS ADVISE AGAINST ENTRY.

It went on for ten lines, stating that based on previous landslides, the towering hillside above their homes was due for catastrophic failure. It was a lengthy message, punctuated by red and black lettering, occasionally bursting into all caps to say things like **AT ANY TIME AND WITHOUT WARNING** and **ENTER AT YOUR OWN RISK**.

The girl went on. "I mean, I know it's *true*," she said, putting air quotes around the word, "or else it wouldn't be there, but is it true like how there's a warning on the window of every fast food place here that chemicals inside are going to cause cancer? Like the kind of warning California gives everyone about everything? Or is that mountain over there actually going to fall on us?"

Messina didn't need to look at it. Her mind drew up the image she'd seen so many times in perfect detail, the mountain behind them carved out in the center from the last mudslide, like someone had taken a giant spoon to it. She looked at the girl. Raindrops collected along her cheeks and forehead. She seemed oblivious to them.

"It's weird here," the girl said, "even without the creepy sign. I've never seen a neighborhood that has two-story houses right next to metal ones on cinder blocks."

Messina wondered how someone so observant couldn't see the simple fact that the rules didn't apply in this place.

"My dad moved us here to help my mom's depression. She loves the ocean." The girl's honesty made Messina uncomfortable. She felt like she was hearing information that shouldn't be shared with a stranger, or even a friend. She didn't even know this girl's name.

The girl finally wiped a hand across her face, squeegeeing the water off.

"I'm Val." She stuck her squeegee hand out at Messina in the nice-to-meet-you handshake way. Messina stared at it until it dropped. She wasn't trying to be rude, she just didn't like touching strangers, but she didn't want to say that, so she didn't say anything. She was always doing that, seeming mean or rude, even when she didn't mean to. It was like she spoke her own alien language and had her own alien customs, and everything got lost in translation when other people tried to understand.

The girl—Val—didn't seem bothered. She kept on, like it hadn't even happened. "I just moved here. My brother Gabe, too. He's ten months younger than me. You'll see him around, but *don't* get a crush on him. He was all my old friends ever wanted to talk about."

She said "old friends" in a way that implied Messina was her new friend. Like it was something that had already been decided when Messina wasn't looking. But Messina didn't need a new friend. She had Lottie, who was enough—too much sometimes—even though they weren't friends exactly. They were something different, something more desperate. They'd leaned on each other so hard their organs had fused.

It was only a week before she and Lottie decided to let Val in. They had no way of knowing her mom would die a month later by suicide, or that before she'd even unpacked any of her boxes, Val had littered half a wall of her bedroom with sticky notes. Or that she'd love them harder than anyone in either of their lives ever had. They only knew that they could see something inside her that looked like something inside of them. Like a kind of sixth sense that picked up internal bleeding, their wounds calling out to each other like beacons in the darkness. A shared understanding of pain. Once it was decided, their bond was instant. Val called them sisters.

Messina let go of the steering wheel now, her fingers stiff, and took Val's book from her bag. She knew it couldn't help her. But knowing and believing were different things.

The book should've been given to Gabe with Val's other things, but Messina had stolen it from her locker before the custodian could clean it out. She only meant to keep it for a little bit, but when she found Val's plan inside—her permit to hike the Pacific Crest Trail this summer—it felt like she'd meant for her to have it, like she was talking to Messina from beyond, trusting her to keep her secret.

Messina ran her fingers over the raised letters of the title—*Wild*—and put the book up to her nose, inhaling its scent. It smelled like Val. Like daring and sweat and frenzy. And a little like rain. The rain smell was a part of why Messina thought the book was magic now, why she thought Val could use it to talk to her. That sounded dumb, but it wasn't—at least not inside her head, which was where Messina liked to keep things.

She pressed the book against her chest, trying to hear Val, asking her what she should do. She was terrified to go inside. Even if by some miracle Jeffucker was still asleep and she'd somehow make it through this unscathed, that place had become worse than a prison to her. A place where she was afraid to breathe, where portraits of Jesus (not the friendly version) watched her from every room, where her door wouldn't shut now because it still hung sideways from when Jeffucker tried to rip it from its hinges. The unstable hillside above La Conchita made sure no one's home there was safe, but Messina's had become something truly dangerous.

A sound outside the van made her look up. Through the dirty windshield, she watched the front door of the house fly open. Jeffucker's eyes locked onto hers. *Righteous anger.* Her heartbeat slammed in her ears, deafening. Val's voice came too, booming like thunder, even louder than her heart.

Run, it said.

6

GABE

DON'T TAKE RISKS! PROTECT YOURSELF TO AVOID INJURY!

Gabe stared at the safety protocol sign in the storage closet. It was always there, but today it felt like it was tacked to the wall just for him, a bad joke. He'd spent half the morning replaying how it had all gone down with Lottie and what he could have done differently. The sign laughed at him. It told him he'd known the risks. It told him this mess was his own damn fault.

Gabe's dad was in risk-assessment. Gabe had no idea what he wanted to do in life, but he knew that wasn't it. Still, he must've had some kind of statistical gene in him or something, because he could make sense of his dad's charts and stat sheets like Mozart looking at the pages of a symphony. The irony of his dad's job was that he'd moved them to La Conchita—low risk, he'd told them, because of how far their home stood from the slope and the original landslides. *And look at the views!* But what he hadn't calculated was the risk of it not pulling their mom from her depression. And the risk the weight of her death posed for the rest of them.

Gabe tried not to think about it. What he thought about was how stupid he'd been at the party last night. How he'd already done the math a thousand times, weighed the risks—he knew Lottie, her history. If he'd created a risk assessment matrix, the square with Lottie's name would have been a deep and terrifying shade of red. SEVERE RISK VERY LIKELY. Gabe knew it was going to end exactly the way it had, yet he'd gone willingly (more than willingly, to be fair) every step of the way.

His sister used to talk about this parasite that had been discovered in wolves. It altered their brains so they were more likely to engage in risky behavior. They'd later found it in humans too. Maybe he'd been accidentally exposed to it. That would have been a good explanation. More convenient than the truth, anyway, which was that his heart had filled up with hope. Hope that made him toss aside the risk and dive in head-first. Hope that made him think maybe it wouldn't just be hooking up. Hope that made him imagine that his love for Lottie might fill up the gaping hole through her middle she thought was invisible. Hope that made him think she might fill the hole of grief inside him too.

But hope wasn't a variable that could change the odds.

He felt asinine thinking of it now, the way it overcame him, clouding his reason. He wished he didn't still feel it twitching inside his chest, mostly dead, but not quite.

"Gabe, qué estás haciendo? Did you get lost?" Javier called from the kitchen.

Gabe wasn't sure how long he'd been standing in the storage closet, but he was sure Javier had sent him to get napkins several minutes before his leg had fallen asleep. He shoved aside the crate of avocados and dug out the napkin boxes from the shelf. He filled the dispensers, then went out front to put up the umbrellas and wipe down the outdoor seating. He tried to pretend he couldn't hear the couple standing directly in front of him shouting at each other.

Man: See Jules, look, it says so right there, "World's safest beach."

Gabe knew without looking that he was pointing to the sign taped to the window of the taqueria. Carpinteria was just a little over five miles from La Conchita, but the shift was drastic from the little neighborhood that was sure to kill you to the tourist town that boasted *World's safest beach! Bring your kids!* The signs had been all over town for as long as Gabe could remember, painted on shop windows, hanging over the streets.

Woman: But what does that even *mean*?

Man: It means you can relax and let Tyler have a good time.

Gabe flicked his eyes up at them, just long enough to catch a glimpse. He assumed Tyler was the little kid standing between them, making the plastic shark in his hands chomp at their legs.

Woman: I'm not taking parenting advice from a taco shop.

Man: They're all over the place, Jules. Look, there's another one right there.

Woman: So what? Who decided it was the world's *safest* beach? What's the criteria? Low crime, extra lifeguards, low incidence of drowning?

Something scratched at Gabe's arm. He looked over and found the plastic shark with its open mouth wedged onto his forearm. He made an *Oh no!* face at the kid, pretending to try to wrench himself free of the shark's teeth. The kid cracked up.

"Excuse me," the man said, waving at Gabe to get his attention, like he hadn't already been dominating it.

"It's true, right? The sign?" He pointed behind him at the

banner stretched out across the street: **COME AND ENJOY THE WORLD'S SAFEST BEACH!** but Gabe wasn't seeing the sign. He was looking past it, to Lottie, pedaling up the street in the sun. The dying shred of hope fluttered in his chest, its wings so sharp they left spots of red blooming against his shirt. Gabe tried to tamp it down and hold on to his logic. He looked back at the man, still pointing his finger at the sign. "The world's safest beach—it's true, right?" the man repeated.

But it wasn't true. The ocean didn't care whether it drowned you, not here or anywhere else. The signs were meant to bring tourists by filling them with the promise of safety. By filling them with hope.

But hope was a lie.

7

LOTTIE

She should've asked Gabe for a ride. That SUV packed with beach gear had nearly taken her out at the intersection. But even Lottie knew it was fucked up to ask for a ride from someone she couldn't even stand to look at.

The pavement sizzled as she rode, her sweat soaking into the orange polo she worked in. It already smelled like al pastor when she'd put it on this morning—now it was going to smell like old meat with sweat and lavender deodorant rubbed all over it. A foul smell to match her mood. She was worried as shit about Messina. Lottie knew she'd fucked up huge this morning by making her late. There'd been nothing but radio silence since then, even though Lottie had called and texted about a hundred times. She'd even walked to Messina's house to see if she was okay, but she turned around before she made it to the door, for fear of making things worse if Messina was in trouble.

Lottie didn't know many specifics about what went on within the walls of Messina's home or even too much about Jeffucker—aside from the indisputable fact that he was a shithead—but there was one concrete fact she had about him: Last year, he'd slammed his fist into the back of Lottie's head, thinking she was Messina.

She'd been sitting on the bench by the beach access tunnel in La Conchita, wearing the jacket she'd borrowed from Messina, hood pulled up against the wind, when Jeffucker struck her so hard it sent the whole world spinning off its axis. She couldn't see straight. There'd been no warning, just *bam*, fist on skull. As soon as he realized it was Lottie, he apologized in a panic, telling her that Messina was late getting home, and he'd been stressed out looking for her. He was embarrassed, saying he was sorry over and over.

But the truth was this: They both knew he wasn't apologizing because he'd hit her. He was apologizing because she wasn't his stepdaughter.

Val had asked Messina once, point blank, if he'd hurt her. Messina told her to go fuck herself, and that was the end of it. Val had seemed so hurt by Messina's reaction, but Lottie understood—not what Messina was going through, just that there were things that felt safer locked away. Things that were so messed up you were sure if you tried to put them into words, they'd grow claws on their way up your throat and shred your insides like a cheese grater before you could even get them out. It wasn't something Val understood. She talked about everything—her thoughts, her facts, her mom's death and depression—even when no one wanted to know. She didn't have any secrets. She wanted Lottie and Messina to be the same way, but they couldn't be.

Lottie leaned her bike against the wall outside and went in through the kitchens. She tried to ignore the jagged voice in the back of her head that whispered that maybe Messina wasn't in trouble—maybe she wasn't speaking to her because she knew what Lottie had done. But that was impossible. No one knew.

A combination of al pastor and waffle cones hung in the air, making her empty stomach growl and churning up memories of Val, the countless hours they'd spent working shifts together. Lottie breathed through her mouth, trying not to smell the air, trying not to remember things. But everything here was a memory. This was the last place she wanted to be.

Her insides felt raw, chewed up like hamburger meat.

"Qué pasa, Lottie?" Javier said, giving her a wave, his hand stained red from the al pastor paste.

"Not much," she lied. She was an open wound. "You good?"

"Sí, nada nuevo."

She'd almost cleared the kitchen when Javier called to her again. "Hey." She turned. Concern hung on Javier's face. "You sure you're okay?"

It was a simple kindness, checking on her, noticing something was wrong. But it pricked at her eyes as if it had been something vicious. A million feelings welled up inside her at once, all threatening to spill over. She nodded at Javier, forcing her mouth into a smile, her hand in a thumbs up, and turned away just as her tears broke the levy. She darted into the break room and wiped her face before anyone could see, trying to steady herself for the day of work ahead. And for Gabe.

Lottie and Gabe technically worked in separate shops, but all that separated Lu's Artisan Ice Cream and Javi's Beach Tacos were the different colors painted onto the concrete floor, a faded orange-brown on the side of Javier's place, and bright white on the side of Lu's. Lottie knew Gabe was already here—his rust-eaten truck was out back—but she still got a gut-punch at the sight of him out front, talking to some couple and their kid. The unwanted disgust rose up in her like nausea, along with the knowledge that she was the worst person ever. Lottie, destroyer of things.

She searched the rack on the wall for her timecard, finding it tucked beneath Gabe's. Lu's might have served bougie, artisan ice cream, but they still used an old-timey punch clock that they shared with the taqueria, the kind with paper cards. Lottie dropped her card in and heard the deep *thwack* of the stamp. June 16 stared out at her in fresh ink. It was less than a month until Val's birthday.

Lottie shook off the thought and stuck her card back into the rack, away from Gabe's. Val's card had finally disappeared—someone threw it away, probably. The thought of it had her eyes burning again. She wished she'd thought to take it home. She didn't know what she'd have done with it, but she hated the idea of it lying in the dumpster beneath rotting bits of uneaten tacos and old ice cream cups. Her chest went tight. Her mind zoomed out wider and wider until she felt far away, until she could breathe again.

She put on her apron—crusty with days-old ice cream because she'd forgotten to wash it—and started hauling the big containers out of the walk-in freezer. It was a two-person job, but Lu wasn't here yet, and she still hadn't hired anyone to replace Val. Lottie already felt a strong dislike of whoever might be brought on to take her place.

The first few buckets were easy enough, only half-full, but the mint chip needed replacing. Lottie stepped on the lowest shelf in the freezer and grabbed the rim of the bucket, edging it off the high shelf above her head. Her plan was to pull it out and bring it down slowly. Instead, it tipped toward her all at once and crashed to the floor, cracking the lid. Gabe popped in out of nowhere, coming to the rescue.

"Let me help you." He scooped the bucket up off the floor like it was filled with helium instead of forty pounds of ice cream.

"Thanks, I've got it," Lottie said. It sounded rude, but Gabe propped the bucket onto his shoulder and walked out to the serving freezer like he hadn't heard her. Lottie stormed after him. It felt good, having something to do with all the reckless energy inside her. "Will you stop? I don't want your help!" She was half-shouting. Javier and Miguel looked on from the kitchen, but she didn't care. She wanted them to see—she wanted everyone to see—that this was who she was. That she was a mean and shitty person who didn't deserve to have everyone treat her so goddamn nicely all the time. Gabe looked at her, his eyes full of the same hurt they'd worn this morning, only more tired now.

"Fine. Have fun." He stalked across the painted floor to the taqueria.

Good, Lottie thought, glad that he was finally starting to understand. She was so sick of everyone giving her these looks like she was better than how she was acting—she wasn't better. Everyone pretending she was just made her feel more ashamed.

She dragged the next bucket from the walk-in freezer, working herself into a full-body sweat. She was determined to get it into the serving freezer by herself if it killed her. She wrestled it up, wedging it onto her hip. She was pretty sure she did some damage to her internal organs, but she got the bucket in. She wiped her forehead and surveyed the rest. Lavender Lemon and Strawberry Cheesecake still needed full replacements, but there was no way. She stuck Out of Stock cards in their spots and took a rag to a spot of hardened fudge on the counter like it had personally wronged her. Lu's fudge was indestructible—NASA could have made rockets out of it.

A few feet away, Gabe worked, clearing out the old salsa bins, ignoring her, just like she was ignoring him. They'd played this game when they were younger too, pretending the other didn't exist. Only then it had been because they both wanted the other's attention.

Outside, a group of kids crowded around the door, noses pressed up against the glass. They stampeded the second Lottie unlocked it, and she began the automatic work of scooping cones and sundaes and wiping down sticky tables and chairs. It was an easy rhythm—quick, mechanical. Too busy for thinking. She wished she could do it forever. Gabe was less than ten feet away from her, but they could've been on different planets.

8

MESSINA

A horn blared. Messina jerked the wheel, swerving the van back over into her own lane. She blinked the sleepiness from her eyes and batted her hands against the steering wheel, trying to keep some part of her moving to stay awake. She hadn't slept since before that stupid party.

The ocean looked angry, waves churning it into a froth, like it was so hungry it was foaming at the mouth, waiting to swallow up one of the cars driving above it on the towering cliffs. She tried not to look at it, but it pulled at her tired eyes. She flicked them back to the road. She hated this stretch of highway, the way it filled her mind with thoughts of falling and drowning.

She drove against the midday sun, exhausted. She'd stopped earlier in the morning to try to sleep, but all she managed to do was crouch in the backseat and stare out the windows from a different angle, too afraid of being discovered to close her eyes. Now she was driving northbound again. She'd been going in circles, trying to figure out what to do. *This was why I never left*, she thought, furious at herself. *Because I have no place to go.*

Another horn screamed at her. She needed to stop, to figure out a plan, to sleep. Her signal click-clicked as she exited and pulled into the parking lot of a shopping center.

She'd never been braver than the moment she drove off, leaving Jeffucker in a red-faced fury screaming at her in the driveway. She'd never been so stupid either, stealing his van. What the hell had she been thinking? She hadn't thought—that was the problem. She'd only run. Now, she was an idiot driving around in a stolen van with no place to go, no plan for what to do, and next to no money. She didn't even have extra clothes.

The Fucker had probably called the cops and reported the van stolen the moment she drove away in it. She was going to end up in jail or juvie or wherever they sent seventeen-year-olds who were convicted of grand theft auto. Or worse, she'd be taken back to Jeffucker. She would have googled the potential outcomes of her actions if she hadn't smashed and dumped her phone, for fear he could use it to find her. She knew at least that running away would end with her being detained and returned home—that bit she'd looked up years ago. It was another reason why she'd never left—the danger of getting caught and making things even worse was too great.

Jeffucker's little wooden cross dangled from the mirror in front of her. She yanked it down, breaking its string, feeling a shock of relief. It was immediately followed by panic that she'd just doomed herself. She hastily tied it back, making a new knot in the string. It stared at her, knowing what she'd done—*He's always watching.* She drew a little cross in the air with her index finger, hoping to undo whatever curse she'd just put onto herself.

She was sweating. She'd turned off the engine to save gas but forgot to roll down the windows. She took a tissue from the glove box and sopped up some of the wetness along her forehead, trying to calm her mind long enough to assess the situation.

The only viable option she'd thought of was such a longshot that it was as good as useless. The entire plan consisted of a name—Anna Collins, an old friend of her mom's who worked at a community college in Brookings, Oregon. Messina knew little else of her, aside from the kindness she'd once shown her when she'd come to their house for dinner. Anna spent the meal asking Messina about herself and suggested that she visit her on one of her summer breaks—something Jeffucker never allowed. But Messina clung to the promise of the offer all the same. The idea of it had been a life preserver, keeping her afloat for years now.

She had no idea if Anna Collins still lived in Brookings or worked at the community college, or if she was even still alive. She knew even less about what Anna would think of having Messina show up on her doorstep asking for help. *Hi, we met once. Can I live with you?* It was beyond ridiculous. At this point, she didn't even have enough gas money to get to Oregon.

She knew what she had to do, but she couldn't get her mind to accept it. "There has to be another way," she said out loud, arguing with herself. But there were no other options.

She raked over the possibilities again. Stay here, in this parking lot with no food and no money and hardly any gas left, until either the cops came or she was raped and murdered. Keep driving until she ran out of gas and got stuck roadside until the cops came or she was raped and murdered. Or go back to La Conchita.

She screamed at herself and pounded her fists against the steering wheel, accidentally honking the horn. A couple passing in front of her looked up, alarmed. She looked away, trying to pretend it wasn't her who'd honked.

"Fuck." She exhaled the word. "I don't want to go back."

She shook her head. It was the only way. If she left now, she could get there while the Fucker was still at work. Any longer trying to decide, and she wouldn't survive the homecoming.

She pulled a pen from her bag and scribbled a short list of what she needed onto the back of a receipt. Clothes, cash, toothbrush . . . *And no fucking stolen van.*

She screamed at herself once more and turned the key in the ignition. She looked up at the highway sign in the distance. She'd never made it this far from home before.

She couldn't believe she was going back.

9

LOTTIE

She spent her shift beneath the surface of the ocean, deep down where it was quiet, where she couldn't hear the rumble of the waves above. Sounds, voices, even her own thoughts were muffled. Other things were magnified. Like the pattern of tiny blades the frost made in the freezer, and the crack in the mirror behind her, and the way the lettering was rubbed off the CASH button on the register. It all set off memories that drifted around her like schools of jellyfish, stinging if she came too close.

The crack in the mirror behind the counter was from two summers ago, before either she or Val worked there. They'd met some guys on the beach—just Lottie and Val, because Messina was grounded again—who'd had a thermos of rum and some bottles of Coke. Val and Lottie had spent the day in the sun getting drunk and flirting with the guys just enough to keep the booze coming. Thoughts turned slippery and hard to hold onto. They were careful to watch each other, sharing glances embedded with questions like *Are you okay?*—both making sure the other wasn't getting too sloppy.

Lottie didn't like how the blond guy would smile at Val with his too-white teeth and put his hands on her knees. Or how he'd make a jerk-off motion to his buddy, just out of Val's eyeline, when she'd stare out at the sea and talk about the sand or why the ocean was salty. Lottie spit in his Coke when he wasn't looking and smiled at him when he was.

The vibe shifted as the sun sank, going chilly like the air. Lottie said they had to go meet some friends, but as they walked up the beach toward the path, she could feel the presence of the guys like a shadow. She and Val ducked into Lu's just as she was about to close the shop. Lu let them stay until the guys lost interest. Lottie and Val offered to help her clean as a thanks, though neither of them knew what they were doing. Val wiped stuff down while Lottie mopped. Bits of sand kept falling from her legs, adding to the mess. She was behind the counter, trying to get at some schmutz under the freezer, when she took out half the syrup bottles and smacked the mirror with the mop handle.

Lu wasn't even mad. She helped Lottie restack the bottles (plastic, thankfully) and said the crack in the mirror was hardly even visible. Lottie was sure Lu was only pretending not to be pissed about it, but the next day when Lottie passed by on her way to meet Val, Lu stuck her head out the door and asked if she wanted a job.

Lottie was surprised to look up and find Lu beside her now, her tattooed arms scooping cones right alongside Lottie's. She wondered how long she'd been there.

"You can clock out after your side work," Lu told her.

Lottie gave her a thumbs up. She still felt half-underwater. She worried if she tried to speak it would come out as gurgly bubble sounds.

She grabbed the checklist and started her side work, which was just a nicer thing to call all the gross stuff she had to do at the end of her shift, like wiping ice cream smears off the windows and cleaning the bathroom. She always saved the bathroom for last because it was the worst. She didn't know why the hell so many parents took kids out for ice cream who were clearly lactose intolerant.

It took her forty-five minutes to work her way down the checklist of duties. When she finally emerged from the bathroom, soaked in sweat and God knows what else, she found Gabe waiting for her in the break room. Cornered. She turned around and stared at the schedule on the wall, like she didn't know her shifts by heart. She was acting like a child, but she didn't care. It was the only way she knew how to deal with being in the same room with him right now.

Gabe let out an audible sigh.

"I'm off in five if you want a ride home," he said to her back.

The silence that followed was so miserable Lottie could hardly stand it. It sat there between them so long it began to sour like old milk.

"You're serious." She could see the frustration on his face, even with her back turned. His voice painted a full visual, like bat-sonar. "You'd rather pedal in the sun and car exhaust for half an hour than ride in the truck with me for five minutes?"

She didn't answer. She was too chicken-shit.

He came up beside her, visible in her peripheral vision. "What happened between last night and now?"

More silence. She wondered when she'd gone from being just a shitty person to an actual Demogorgon.

"Lottie," there was a gutting desperation in his voice, "did I do something wrong, or . . . did I hurt you?"

She didn't know where the anger inside her suddenly came from. She just knew she hated that question. She hated Gabe for asking it. For even thinking it. "God, Gabe. No, you didn't *hurt* me."

"Then what? What happened? Lottie, please . . ."

Please. The word hung there in the air between them, asking for an answer, a scrap of compassion, anything. But Lottie couldn't muster it. She didn't know how to say that this was just the way it was. That she was messed up. That every time he looked at her, she felt like someone was holding a pillow over her face. That yes, she'd rather pedal home in the sun and exhaust than get into the truck with him for five minutes. It would only come out cruel and covered in spikes if she tried to explain.

She could feel his eyes trying to pry an answer out of her. She still didn't look at him, but his curls and shoulders and feelings were taking up too much space. Her peripheral vision was overflowing with him.

She turned to go, catching a glimpse of Gabe's timecard—it was nestled against hers again, half covering it. The tiny thread holding her together snapped. She whipped her card out and rounded on him.

"Will you stop putting your timecard on top of mine? It's smothering!" She jammed it into another slot and stormed out of the break room, running face-first into Fox Girl. Lottie had never bothered to learn her name. The bike garb she always wore had foxes printed on it. Today's outfit was a blinding yellow and pink so intense it vibrated.

"Sorry." Lottie put herself in reverse, trying not to make eye contact, but it was too late.

Fox Girl's eyes found Lottie's like magnets. She was Val's favorite customer. Not quite a regular, but she came in every other month or so after she'd ridden in some days-long mountain-bike race, and she'd sit at the counter and take down a family's worth of ice cream while she recounted her crazy adventures to Val—about run-ins with bears, or getting so dehydrated that she couldn't see straight, and nearly dying from a lack of electrolytes, all like it was great fun. Val would sit there listening, practically salivating with excitement. It bugged Lottie, though she couldn't put a finger on why, aside from having to scoop everyone's ice cream while Val fucked off and listened to Fox Girl's stories.

The last time she came in, Val had still been working. And breathing. Lottie could see it on her face that she hadn't heard, her eyes scanning the shop for Val.

Lottie had been the one to inform all the regulars who'd asked about the other girl who worked here, the one with the blue streaks in her hair. She hated it. Having to answer the questions that came—*What happened? How?*—and wading through the sympathy that followed. For a couple weeks, she'd kept a copy of the local paper that reported on Val's death behind the counter so she could wordlessly pass it over and let the person feel like an asshole for asking, without further involving her.

"Is Val here?" Fox girl said.

Grief slammed Lottie at the sound of Val's name, even though she'd known it was coming. She grabbed a rag off the bar and scrubbed at a stain on a four-top like her life depended on it, pretending not to have heard. She couldn't deal with this right now.

"Hey, it's Lottie, right?" Fox Girl said, stepping a little closer. Lottie could smell the detergent from her biking clothes, light and soapy, like something that had the word *Breeze* in it. It wasn't usually the way she smelled after one of her races. "Is Val here?" she repeated.

Lottie kept scrubbing. "Nope." The word rolled out of her mouth and onto the table like a half-chewed piece of food. Ugly. Rude. She felt a grim little thrill at it. At feeling a shred of control when everything else in her world and in this room felt like it was spinning off its axis. This was easy—anger was easy. Volatile, sure, but at least she knew how to feel it.

"Do you know if she's coming in later?"

Lottie scrubbed. "Nope."

Fox Girl waited. She adjusted the straps on the oversized backpack she was carrying. It was dirty and mud-speckled, highlighting how weirdly clean Fox Girl was today. Lottie pretended not to notice. It was a silent game of chicken—Lottie scrubbing, Fox Girl staring.

"I've got some stuff she asked to borrow—sort of an early birthday gift."

The words stung—it felt too personal, like Fox Girl shouldn't have known they were coming up on Val's birthday. Like she didn't have the right. The table had never been this clean. The varnish was going to start peeling if she kept scrubbing it.

"Do you know if she's working later this week?" Fox Girl asked.

Lottie ignored her. *Scrub scrub scrub.* She was aware of Gabe's footfalls crossing the floor toward them. She felt him step up on her left, shadowing her.

"Val's not coming in later," he said, stepping in like a white knight for the second time today. "She—"

"She's not coming back." Lottie cut him off. She didn't want his help. She was making a glorious mess of this all on her own. "She's gone . . . Peace Corps." Gabe shot Lottie a pained look, like she needed his help more than ever, but she kept on. "She signed up a few months back. Left last week for Zambia. She'll be there at least a year."

"Wow, that's . . . wild. She never mentioned wanting to do that." Fox Girl's brow was a hard line across her face. It looked like *I call bullshit.* Lottie dug her heels in.

"Yeah, well that's probably because you weren't really that close to Val." She was being properly horrible now. It felt good, like all the pent-up shit inside her was finally being released. Gabe was nudging at her shoulder, urging her toward the break room, urging her to stop talking, but she was a runaway train flying off the rails, wheels ablaze. "I mean, just because you'd come in here and try to impress her with your stories didn't really mean you were actually friends. Aren't you a little old to be hanging out with teenagers anyway?"

Gabe nudged her again, harder. Lottie gave in and began shuffling toward the back of the store, Gabe right behind her. "Excuse us for a sec," he said over his shoulder. Always polite, always kind. Always Gabe.

He spun to face her once they were out of sight. The motion reminded Lottie of when they'd goofed off for an entire shift last fall, one of those strange days when both shops had been slow. They'd spent it trying to make each other laugh with stupid dance moves and acting out scenes from bad movies. Gabe didn't look like he was in the mood for fun now.

Lottie spoke before he had a chance to. "Look, I know you think I'm acting like an asshole, but—"

"No, I don't," Gabe said. His dark eyes were unreadable. "I think you're acting like a *monster*."

Lottie stared at him. A part of her was relieved that he finally saw it. Only now, she didn't want him to. This was different—this wasn't about her, it was about Val. Gabe was supposed to understand.

"You've got no right. Zambia? What the actual fuck, Lottie?" He was looking at her like he had no idea who she was, like he was exhausted, like just being here in this world was taking every last bit of his energy. Or maybe it was Lottie taking it.

Shame welled up inside her, and she hated Gabe for making her feel it.

"Val's dead, Lot." She flinched at the words. "It's never going to feel better, so could you please just accept it and let the rest of us move on?"

Fox Girl rounded the corner, ignoring the **EMPLOYEES ONLY** sign. "Sorry," she said, though her face said the opposite. She shrugged off the backpack and dropped it onto the floor between them. Something inside it clattered. "You two seem to have your own stuff going on here. I'm not trying to intrude—I just want to make sure this stuff gets to Val before her trip."

"Her trip?" Lottie asked, forgetting her lie.

"For the PCT." The way she said it, without a hint of question, as if it were indisputable fact, shook Lottie. She knew the PCT only from Val and the book she carried around. It was a hiking trail—the Pacific Crest Trail—that spanned the country from Mexico to Canada. Val talked about it the way stans talked about celebrities.

"... Or Zambia?" Fox Girl looked at Lottie, like she was waiting for her to say something.

Lottie's mouth was glued shut. This wasn't real. She looked at Gabe. He looked like he was in the middle of the world's worst brain-freeze.

"Can you just let her know it's here if you see her? I told her I'd bring it by." Fox Girl turned to go, not waiting around for a response this time, but she stopped short when she reached the door. "Hey, tell her to be careful—conditions are dicey out there."

Lottie's pulse was everywhere. It was shaking the ground.

No, this wasn't real. Because if it was, it meant that Lottie had taken even more from Val than she knew. It meant she'd taken her dreams too.

"What a fucking nutso." Lottie threw her apron on the hook and stormed out the back door.

Gabe followed her. He was holding the stupid pack from Fox Girl. Its contents clanged as he tried to keep pace with Lottie. "She's not nutso, Lot." Lottie kept walking. She wasn't listening to this. "Lottie, stop."

She didn't stop. She climbed onto her bike. "That chick is either batshit or a liar, because Val was going to spend this summer like every other one, with M and me watching old VHS movies and going to the beach."

He caught up to her, grabbing hold of her handlebars so she couldn't ride off without going over him. She had half a mind to try.

"She's not crazy or a liar. She's telling the truth."

Lottie's heartbeat swished in her ears like ocean waves trying to pull her under.

"Val was going to go. But it—that—happened before she could."

Lottie squeezed the handles on her bike so hard they threatened to snap off. "Why are you saying that?"

"Because it's true."

"She told you?"

Gabe shook his head, mashing his teeth together. "I don't think she told anyone—except the lady with the backpack, apparently."

"Then how do you know?"

"I—" He stopped short, shoving his hands into his pockets, like he didn't want to say. They stared at each other in a standoff.

"Gabe."

He let out a rough breath through his lips, his eyes on the pavement. "I've been reading her journal. I wasn't trying to invade her privacy or anything. I just miss her. It makes me feel like she's here."

No, Lottie thought, rejecting the idea. Val might have been obsessed with the PCT and that damn book but it was just another one of her fixations. One of her projects that filled up notebook after notebook and then got shoved aside when something else came along.

"She said something about it," Gabe said. "About leaving for the summer and being alone on the PCT—I don't remember exactly. But I don't think she was going to tell anyone until after she was gone."

Lottie didn't believe him. Val would never do that—she didn't keep secrets.

"All this is in her journal?"

"Yeah."

"Show me." She abandoned her bike and wrenched open the door of Gabe's truck.

10

MESSINA

A Highway Patrol cruiser slid up behind her. Messina's hands clenched the wheel. Even when she wasn't doing anything wrong, seeing a cop in the rearview made her forget how to drive. Her arms went wobbly. Images of faceless men in uniforms dragging her off to jail, or worse, back to the Fucker, swam through her mind.

Red and blue flashed in her mirror. Messina flipped on her turn signal with a shaking hand and merged right.

The cop zoomed past and flew down the freeway.

She let out a breath she didn't know she was holding—it flew out of her with a strange sound, like when a glass hits the floor but doesn't break.

She watched the clock as she sped south, back toward the lion's den. She'd have at least an hour until Jeffucker got home from work. Something in her gut twisted, urging her off the freeway just before her exit. She stopped at Rincon Point, trying to muster her courage.

"You're just scared," she said, holding tight to her own fingers so she wouldn't pick at the fresh wound at the base of her skull. But she wasn't convinced it was just fear. That feeling, the one in her gut, felt like a warning.

She left the van behind. She was only a mile or two from home. She walked on the bike path. Her party outfit—black jeans and top—didn't have her blending in with the families and tourists on the paved path, all in weekend beach clothes, while she stalked between them.

Adrenaline rose in her veins as she neared the La Conchita tunnel. "He's not there," she whispered to herself. "You're safe." She nearly laughed out loud at those last words to herself, a complete lie. She'd never been safe, and every cell in her body knew it. She wondered where this other voice in her came from sometimes, the one that tried to calm her and tell her that she was okay.okay.okay. Probably from the part of her that needed a mom, she thought. As much as she wanted to cling to its assurance, she knew she couldn't trust it to keep her safe. *Just like a real mom.*

The sun hit her skin as she passed out of the dark shelter of the tunnel. It burned, like God's eyes. *He's always watching.*

She sprinted the half-block toward her house but caught a flash of dirt-colored hair and stopped short. She darted behind a low palm, heart hammering in her chest. Jeffucker was at the neighbor's house—the twenty-somethings who rented—standing porch-side, close enough Messina could hear his booming voice, demanding to know if they knew anything about where she'd gone, demanding to know if they'd seen her or the van.

Of course he isn't at work. She thought the words in a yell, berating herself. *You stole his car!* She turned and pressed her back against the trunk of the low tree hiding her. She couldn't breathe.

She closed her eyes, wishing she could disappear. She clawed the raw skin at the back of her head, blood smearing onto her fingertips and in her hair. She didn't know how long she stayed like that, long enough for the blood on her fingers to dry. When she turned and squinted through the slits in the palm leaves, he was gone.

She bolted down the street toward Lottie's, running in a low crouch like a hunted animal trying to make itself a smaller target. Every sound made her jump. She ducked around the back of Lottie's trailer and banged on the door, hoping Lottie was home. Hoping Maggie wasn't. No one came but Grimace, the feral neighborhood cat Lottie decided to adopt and make her own, who scuttled out from under the trailer at the sound of her.

He rubbed against her leg, giving her a look like, *Are you going to let me in or what?*

Messina tried the door. It was locked, but she dug the spare key out from under the broken plastic pot on the porch. Weeds had long ago strangled whatever once lived in it. Grimace darted inside as soon as the door opened, Messina following behind him. She turned the lock and let herself breathe.

It smelled like stale cigarette smoke and faded memories. She hadn't been inside in years. Lottie avoided having people in her home nearly as much as Messina did. She tried not to think about the decades of secondhand smoke particles collected in here. At this point, she'd be lucky if she made it to an old enough age to even worry about lung cancer.

Grimace yowled at her. Val always joked that Lottie was the only one who loved him because they were just alike. He mashed his face against Messina's leg, purring. She reached down and stroked the fur along Grimace's back, dirty from lying in the muck beneath the trailer. He leaned into her touch, sticking his butt into the air. Then he bit her.

Just like Lottie.

Messina washed her hands in the sink. There was no soap, and everything here was so thickly coated in a yellow-brown film that even the water felt dirty. Grimace lapped at the tap, so Messina filled his dish. He ignored it, licking droplets from the sink-bottom, his hind legs still on the counter straddling a cigarette burn there. The mark stared up at her, a long-forgotten memory.

It was years ago. The three of them—Val, Lottie, and Messina—had been at Val's all day, doing nothing, but it somehow felt like everything. Messina's mouth tasted like the Cheetos and sour straws they'd binged along with old episodes of *Gossip Girl* because Val's house had all the good streaming services. They'd decided to spend the night there and see how far they could get in the series, but Lottie needed to go home to feed Grimace.

"Maggie will just let him starve."

Messina thought it was weird that Lottie wasn't allowed to call her grandmother something like Grandma or Nan, but she knew better than to bring it up.

They decided to all walk together. They said it was because it was dark out, and there was safety in numbers, but that wasn't really why. Really it was because they were all in love with being together. The lights were on in the trailer when they followed Lottie inside, still talking about who Blair was better off with, when the whole world ground to a halt.

Maggie was on the kitchen counter with her dress half off and her legs wrapped around the waist of a man with his pants down, the muscles of his backside twitching. The girls froze. Messina couldn't stop looking at the forgotten cigarette on the counter, the long line of ash it made. Like her eyes were convinced if they stared hard enough at it, they'd forget the other stuff they'd just seen.

Maggie didn't yell or cover up or anything. Her gaze barely touched Lottie. "Get out of my house," she said and pulled the man in tighter.

It was the first time Messina thought there might be people in the world who had it as bad as she did. She couldn't tell which was worse—being hated, like she was, or completely unwanted, like Lottie. It was no secret Lottie's life had been messed up. Messina knew how she'd gotten the burn scars along her arm and shoulder, that she'd been young enough that she needed to stand on a chair to reach the stove. But this felt worse somehow. It wasn't just the neglect—the ugliness in Maggie's eyes when she looked at Lottie matched the look Messina had seen in Jeffucker's when he was at his worst. It was something Messina didn't have words for, but she knew it well. A look that caused a forever wound. A look that meant *You're nothing.*

The real difference, Messina would later come to learn, between herself and Lottie, was that Lottie believed it.

Exhaustion pulled Messina to the couch now. It was covered in food stains and cat hair and the same yellow film as everything else, but Messina's body was so tired it overruled her mind's objections. She sank into it and let her eyes close. But sleep didn't come. The gas station coffee she'd downed to keep awake while she drove fired through her synapses, even though her thoughts were becoming incoherent. It felt like when she was coming off anesthesia after having her tonsils out as a kid.

She took *Wild* from her bag and hugged it to her chest. Its edges were so worn they were soft like cotton. Val's heart was spilled out in colored ink along the margins of every page. Messina could feel her in it, like she'd poured so much of her soul into the book that some of it had gotten trapped there. She closed her eyes and breathed in its strange rainy-day Val scent, pressing the book against her. It was the closest thing she'd felt to a hug since Val died.

11

LOTTIE

The muddied heap of the pack sat between her and Gabe on the bench seat of the truck, a barrier marking no-man's-land that Lottie had dragged in behind her as an excuse to sit on the opposite side. She usually rode right next to Gabe, sitting in the middle of the bench seat, even when it was just the two of them, never minding if their arms or thighs accidentally brushed against each other.

The truth was this: She used to like it. The way Gabe's skin would flush, and the shadow of a dimple would show along his cheek whenever they touched.

And also this: If he knew what Lottie had done to Val, he wouldn't have wanted her anywhere near him now. He'd have pushed her right out into oncoming traffic.

Something in the pack clanged as they dipped into a pothole. Lottie didn't want to think about what was inside of it. Or if Val had really wanted it. Or what might or might not be in her journal. She stared out the window, sweating. The truck didn't have A/C, and the old vinyl seats were scorching the backs of her thighs. Her window wouldn't roll down all the way because Robbie Clark had slammed his Jeep into the passenger door at a kegger last year, stuck in reverse when he thought he was in drive.

Gabe didn't even get pissed at him. He told Robbie not to worry about it, said it added to the truck's character. Lottie couldn't forgive people like that if her life depended on it. She held on to grudges the way someone dangling from a cliff held on to a rope. But not Gabe. Even now, after she'd been a complete asshole to him all day long, he still looked at her like he wanted her around. Like he was just waiting for her to let things go back to normal. It disarmed some small part of her.

Gabe pulled onto the freeway. The stretch between work and home was pinned between the ocean on their right and the mountains jutting up on their left. The mountains cooked in the midday sun. Even with the constant touch of marine layer, the vegetation there had mostly died. While the little community of La Conchita dreaded the rains, the entire rest of the state was worried about the worst drought on record and all the fires it was causing. Lottie looked away from the mountainside—all its brown-gray vegetation reminded her too much of death—and watched the coastline, full of happy memories, instead.

"Remember when you tried to teach me to surf?" she said, as they passed the beach near the Rincon, where Gabe had taken her for her first lesson.

His whole face turned to a smile at the memory, all the way up to his hairline. "Pretty hard to forget someone attempting to drink the entire ocean."

She laughed. "God, who knew puking up salt water would burn that bad?" It felt good, the laughter. "Hey, I'm sorry," she said, and

Gabe looked at her, eyes brighter than the sinking sun. "I didn't mean to flip out about the timecard thing."

His face dropped a little, and suddenly she felt stupid for saying it, for apologizing about the smallest of things when she'd done so much worse. But that was the only part she knew how to say sorry for.

She turned and looked out the window, embarrassment burning her face. Gabe reached out and put his hand on hers, giving it a squeeze. She didn't pull away.

"It's okay," he said. It felt nice to believe him. "Most of the time I can't even think straight right now. It's like I'm completely numb, you know?" Lottie nodded, even though she didn't know. She felt the opposite, everything hurting all the time, like her skin had been turned inside out. All she wanted to do was turn it off. Her mind, the noise, the thoughts, all of it.

"I didn't even cry at the funeral," Gabe confessed, plunging Lottie deep into the memory—*dizzy/heat/flowers/sick*—the shock just like when she'd fallen off the surfboard, her mouth full of salt water. "It's like I'm going through days like a robot," he said. "Like there's some kind of black hole inside me that's sucking up my emotions. It's scaring me." He gave Lottie's hand another squeeze, but her body felt far away now. "Last night with you was the first time I've felt anything at all since she died . . ." She couldn't hear him anymore. The water was choking her, it was flowing into her nose and ears. Gabe's hand was tugging at hers. She hadn't realized they were in front of his house, in front of Val's house, until Chicken—their half-blind shepherd—jumped up at her window.

She was going to be sick. There was too much salt water inside her.

This was a mistake.

She looked at Gabe. She wanted to tell him she was sorry for everything. But like always, she did the wrong thing. She turned without a word and ran toward home.

12

MESSINA

She woke when the front door slammed. She sat up, not knowing where she was, until she saw Lottie, wide-eyed.

"Hey," Lottie said. The word broke on its way out, like it was cracked down the center.

"Hey."

Lottie stood there, looking like she wanted to say something else, or like she wanted to run at Messina and smash her in a hug the way she would have done once, a long time ago, but she didn't do either. She stayed planted where she was, her face strange, like she'd just been woken in the middle of a bad dream.

Messina rubbed the blurriness from her eyes. Lottie sat down on the opposite end of the couch, leaving a Val-sized gap between them where Grimace popped up and tucked himself into a perfect circle. He narrowed his eyes at Messina while Lottie scratched behind his ears.

"You haven't returned any of my messages," Lottie said.

Messina had thought about Lottie in the time she'd been gone, but mostly in the way that she'd wished for her help. She hadn't considered that Lottie might be worried for her.

"My phone's smashed."

Lottie looked stunned. "Jeffucker?"

Messina shook her head. "Me." She gave her an abridged version of what happened—in truth, there wasn't much to tell. She'd spent most of her time gone just arguing with herself about where she could stay and driving in circles.

"I'm sorry," Messina said, "for leaving without saying bye."

Lottie waved off the words. It stung a little that she wasn't more upset. But then why would she be? Messina had always come back when she said she was running away. There was no reason for Lottie to think this time would be any different. It was probably such an annoyance to her and Val every time she'd made a huge deal out of her plans to leave and then shown up at the bus stop for school the next day. Shame warmed her cheeks at the thought.

"So what now?"

Before Messina could fumble for an answer she hadn't figured out herself yet, Lottie tugged at something under Messina's leg. Val's copy of *Wild* slid out from beneath her.

"Why do you have this?"

The permit slipped out from the book into her lap. Lottie unfolded it, her eyes moving over the words Messina had memorized, *PCT Long-distance Permit, Valerie Sullivan.* Lottie's face turned to grief. Messina hadn't known it would cause her that much pain.

"She was actually going."

"I was going to tell you," Messina said.

The book slipped from Lottie's fingers and onto the floor. "Why did everyone know about this but me?"

Messina shook her head. "Who else knew about—" They both

jumped at the sound of banging on the door. Grimace sprang up from the couch. Messina shook her head at Lottie with a look—*Don't answer that.*

"It's Gabe." Lottie was already on her feet to answer, but Messina grabbed her arm, yanking her back. She put her fingers to her lips and shook her head again.

"It's not Gabe," she whispered, terror clawing through her voice. That knock had slammed against Messina's bedroom door too many times. She knew it in the same way mice recognize the sound of an owl's wings on the air. She dove behind the couch, pulling Lottie with her.

"Messina!" Gravel crunched outside the trailer, moving clockwise as Jeffucker circled. Lottie's arms wrapped over Messina, squeezing tight, sheltering her like she'd done when they hid from him as kids. The stink of their stress and sweat and breath mixed up in the air around them, a strange comfort. It meant she wasn't alone. She knew if Jeffucker burst through the door, Lottie wouldn't leave her side. He'd have to go through her first.

The curtains were drawn, but in Messina's mind, she could see him peeking through the tiniest gap, seeing everything, watching her cower behind the couch in Lottie's arms. *He's always watching.*

He shouted forever.

Footsteps were heartbeats were minutes were hours and the numbers ran through her mind like fire *1.2.3.4.5.6.7.8.9.10.9.8.7.6.5.4.3.2.1.* Her nails drilled into her skin and she couldn't breathe, her eyes welded shut.

Even when the world finally went quiet, she didn't feel safe.

"He's gone." Lottie's words came to her from thousands of miles away, somehow finding her in the cavern she'd built for herself inside her mind, and Messina heard them, but she didn't believe them. Lottie's arms didn't leave her.

When Messina finally opened her eyes, back in Maggie's trailer again, Lottie brushed the sweaty hair off her face. She watched Lottie get up on wobbly legs and move two paces to the kitchen, where she emptied a bag of tortilla chips, mostly crumbs, into a bowl.

"Have you eaten?"

When Messina shook her head, Lottie grabbed another bowl and dumped in half of her crumbs. They scooped the pieces into their mouths with spoons, like cereal. Messina hadn't known she was so hungry until the salt hit her tongue, and the bottom of the bowl came too soon.

Lottie tossed the bowls into the sink and picked up her backpack from the floor. She dumped the books out and began throwing clothes inside.

"What are you doing?"

"Packing." She said it like it was obvious. She had a look in her eyes that reminded Messina of Val. Wild. Manic. "I'm going to take Val on the PCT," she said. "I'm getting clothes for you too. Unless you've got other plans, or you want to go back home and duke it out with that fuckface." She motioned outside the trailer where the echoes of Jeffucker still loomed.

Messina watched her in disbelief. "You're not serious." But she could see in her eyes that she was. Something was driving this inside Lottie—Messina just didn't know what. "That trail is thousands of miles long. We can't walk that."

"Hike, not walk," Lottie said, invoking Val's words. Messina didn't like them coming out of her like that. "And we don't have to do the whole thing, just some. I doubt Val was going to start all the way back at the Mexican border. Anyway, didn't you just say you wanted to get to Oregon to see if this Anna person is there?"

"You want to walk to Oregon?"

"Hike." She lifted up a worn-out pair of runners and looked back and forth between the shoes and Messina's feet. "I don't think I have shoes that will fit you."

Messina rubbed her temples. This was insane. She couldn't believe she was even considering it. She looked at the book lying half-open, upside down on the floor, its cover bent, forgotten in the storm of Jeffucker's rage. Maybe this was why Val had shared her secret with Messina. Maybe it was her way out, her way to really leave La Conchita for good. She'd imagined it so differently—being on a bus for one, but all her money for that was back home under the guard of the Fucker, along with her clothes and everything else. Maybe this was the only way. Maybe it could actually work.

Messina picked up the book, bending the front cover back into the right direction. When she'd first taken it from Val's locker, she tried to read it the way she thought Val would've wanted her to, but she was bothered by the author's voice—it felt too much like Lottie, not Val. Messina found herself drawn to Val's words instead, her scribbled notes that filled the margins, the things she'd circled and underlined, like she'd left secret messages for her. Messina had spent most of her time with the book trying to decode them, to find the meanings in the words Val had hidden inside just for her. It was like the way people read the bible, opening it to a page that felt good or familiar and taking what they needed from it.

She opened the book now, scanning both the notes and text, looking for a sign. She'd seen the words on this page before and didn't like them—*heroin* and *knife* and *sweetheart*. She flipped to another one, far away from those words, at the opposite end of the book. Val's message stared up at her, clear as day. She'd highlighted the author's words in a jarring green—*the Three Sisters peaks.*

"Can I borrow your phone?" Messina said.

"Coffee table." Lottie's voice was muffled, her head half-buried in the closet.

Messina googled Three Sisters peaks. They were located in the center of Oregon, in a place called the Three Sisters Wilderness, ten miles south of a town called Sisters.

Sisters, sisters, sisters.

Messina looked up through the yellowed ceiling, imagining the sky where she thought Val would be, as if to say *Okay, okay. I hear you.*

Lottie dropped a pile of clothes into Messina's lap. "See if any of that will fit you. I know I've got more in the hips than you." Messina smirked at the understatement. Lottie was built like a Woman, capital W, while Messina could have passed for a fourteen-year-old boy from behind.

"What are you looking at?" Lottie bent over her, looking at the phone screen.

Messina pressed her lips together. She didn't like sharing her supernatural beliefs with Lottie—too many eye rolls. But this didn't feel like something she could keep from her, at least not entirely. She held up the page in *Wild* with the highlighted words.

"Three Sisters," Lottie repeated. No eye roll. "It's in Oregon?"

Messina nodded. "I think it's where we're supposed to go." She shook her head. "This still seems so crazy though. Do you honestly think we can walk—sorry, *hike*—that far?"

Lottie slipped the phone from Messina's hands, keying out *distance to 3 Sisters Oregon.* A map popped up with a red arcing line cut across it, tracing a path from La Conchita to the Three Sisters. "Six-hundred and sixty-two miles," Lottie read.

"That's a lot of fucking miles."

Lottie pressed the button on the side of the phone and spoke into it. "How fast does the average person walk?"

"A walking speed of three to four miles per hour is typical for most people."

"If we walk eight hours every day, that's thirty-two miles a day. It's twenty days and change."

It still felt impossible. But the longer Messina thought about it, the more it felt like Val wanted them to do this. Like this had been her plan all along to help Messina leave La Conchita. *Three sisters.*

"Okay. I'm in."

13

LOTTIE

Messina was already complicating things. She could turn breathing into something that required thinking.

"We can't just go. We need to prepare, we need gear."

"I've got some cash saved up," Lottie said, waving her off. "We can hit the gas station on our way out and get some food and water bottles." She kept herself moving, throwing things into bags. If she stopped, she'd have to think about the Truth of it. That she'd stolen the most sacred thing possible from Val. That this was the only way she could think to fix it. That it would never fix it in a million years—because how could it?—but she still had to try.

She threw a wad of extra socks into her bag.

"Lottie."

She ignored Messina. She thought about the pack from Fox Girl and tried to imagine what kind of essentials might have been inside it. It didn't matter though—there was no way she was going to ask Gabe for it. She pulled the flattened Sugar O's box from under her bed and dumped the bills onto the floor. "Twenty, forty, sixty, eighty—"

"Lottie, we *need* a tent," Messina said.

"We can sleep on the ground. A hundred, hundred twenty—"

"No. First, we'll freeze, and second we're not sleeping where the tarantulas can just roam all over us."

Lottie didn't want to admit it, but Messina was right—they hadn't even made it through the night Val wanted them to all sleep on the ground in her backyard to watch a meteor shower without bailing out and running back inside halfway through—but Lottie held firm. She wasn't going to ask Gabe for that pack.

Messina took Lottie's phone, thumbs flying across the screen. "Sleeping bag, whistle, knife, solar charger, water filter."

"What are you doing?"

She turned the phone screen to face Lottie. "PCT checklist."

Lottie ground her teeth together until they made a creaking sound, certain all of this crap was in Fox Girl's pack.

"Stove, fuel," Messina said, still reading from the list. "Bear cannister. What the hell is a bear cannister?"

Lottie didn't know, but she was imagining something like a giant snow globe with a little dancing bear inside. "We don't need all that. You're overthinking this."

"You're underthinking it. Just like you do with everything. It's going to get us screwed."

Lottie kept counting her money, trying to ignore the sting of Messina's words. It wasn't just a jab, it was the truth.

"I've got an idea," Messina said. "I can't believe I'm even thinking it—apparently I'm cool just living a life of crime now."

"What the hell are you talking about?"

Messina sat up straight, hands on her knees. "We steal what we need from the sex shed."

"The what?"

"The sex shed. Where you and Gabe did it. You saw all the outdoor stuff in there. It was like the whole place was sponsored by Patagonia."

The sex shed. Lottie felt like she was never going to stop paying for that mistake. Like life would just keep throwing it in her face again and again. But she was starting to think that Messina was right about needing the gear. All the things she'd encountered on her few hikes and camping trips with Val, from mosquitos to freezing rain and snakes, were beginning to crowd her mind with unpleasantness. Being exposed to the elements was going to have them failing on this mission before it even began.

She couldn't fail—this was too important. She didn't understand it, this plan and whatever warped reasoning her mind had come up with that it would fix things, but that didn't matter. She just knew she had to do this.

She sighed, resigned to Messina's plan. "Fine. But how are we going to get there?"

Messina's face fell. They both knew there was only one way.

14

MESSINA

"Am I close?"

"Yeah, you're good," Lottie said without checking. Messina leaned across her to see out the passenger window. There were miles between the van and the curb.

Lottie was doing her zombie thing again. That was how Messina thought of it—those times when Lottie would drop off mentally, but her body would stay in the present world. She'd been teetering on the edge ever since she saw the book, which frightened Messina. She needed her here, in the present.

Messina's mom did it too—the zombie thing, getting stuck sometimes like Lottie. Only now she'd been stuck for years, a permanent zombie mom. *Mombie.* The scariest part was that Messina understood it. Sometimes, when things were bad, she went *n u m b* just like Lottie and her mom. She couldn't help it. Sometimes it was the only way to survive.

"Hey!" Messina clapped her hands at Lottie. "I need you awake for this."

Lottie's mouth formed a frown. "What do you mean?"

"I mean you're doing the thing where you start just going

through the motions of things but you're not really here." Lottie looked offended, but Messina carried on. "Whatever, I'm not judging. But we're going to get our asses caught if we don't focus here, so I need your brain on."

"Okay."

Messina watched Lottie's eyes flick around, like she was taking in her surroundings. It was weird, like seeing someone come out of a trance.

"You good?"

Lottie looked at her, life in her eyes again. "Yeah."

"Good."

Messina pulled forward, cranking the wheel.

"How am I now?"

Lottie looked out the window. "You're four feet from the curb."

Messina threw it into reverse again.

"I thought when you're trying to steal stuff the goal was to be inconspicuous, not back up fifteen times in front of the same house," Lottie said. Messina took the mild assholery as confirmation that Lottie was herself again. "You want me to park it?"

"*Shhh.*" She put it back into drive and bumped the curb. "How about now?"

Lottie checked. "Your face is on the curb and your ass is in another zip code."

"Fuck it." Messina killed the engine and got out, pressing her hip against the door to close it silently. Lottie's door slammed shut.

"Rule number one," Messina hissed, "don't make any noise."

"Sorry," Lottie whispered back.

She looked like a walking traffic cone in her Lu's shirt, practically glowing in the dark. Messina was the opposite, blending into the darkness. She'd never broken into a place before. She'd lifted things from parties and school and occasionally a store, but this seemed like an entirely different level of crime. It put her stomach in knots.

The night air was chilly, full moon shining down on them like a giant floodlight. They may as well have been doing this in the middle of the day. Messina took in the details of the house—a pair of Teslas in the driveway; the porch light was on, but most of the lights were off inside. She could see the blue-ish flickering of a television from a window downstairs. She hoped someone inside had fallen asleep with it on, but her gut tightened at the thought. A reminder that wishful thinking had never served her well.

She started toward the left side of the house, but Lottie grabbed her arm.

"Shed's on the other side."

Messina was about to argue, when she realized Lottie was right and altered course. The gate was locked, so they scrambled over the fence. A blinding floodlight clicked on over their heads, sending them bolting into the shadows. Messina's heart pounded so hard the world shook. "I think it's on a motion sensor," she whispered as they clung to the darkness. "I set one off the night of the party. Just don't—"

"I know. Rule number two, don't set off the fucking lights."

Once the light clicked off, they skirted the edge of the yard and made their way to the shed. The grass sighed beneath their feet. Noise from the TV spilled out through an open window. When they reached the shed, Messina tried the door, but it wouldn't budge.

"Shit. It's locked," she said, looking to Lottie, who was already making her way in a crouch around the other side, like the rogue asshole in a war movie who gets everyone shot. Messina cursed beneath her breath. "Lottie!" she whisper-shouted. "Lottie!"

She didn't respond. Messina watched in horror as Lottie darted past one of the open windows, setting off another light as she ran. Messina squatted low against the shed. She dug her fingers into its wood paneling, paint flaking beneath her nails. *Fucking Lottie.*

Messina lost sight of her. She couldn't see what was happening on the other side of the arcing light. When it finally turned off, she heard Lottie clamber through the bushes back across the yard toward her, past the reach of the motion sensor this time. She sprang up around the corner of the shed, out of breath, carrying a big plaster gnome, her arms straining against its weight. She dropped it with a thud at Messina's feet.

Fury pounded through Messina's veins so loud she was sure the people in the house could hear it. "How the hell is Rumpelstiltskin going to help us get into the shed?"

In answer, Lottie rolled him around to the side where there was a high window, the one Messina had looked through when she'd discovered Lottie and Gabe. Lottie reached up and jimmied the window open. Then she climbed onto the gnome's face and heaved herself through. A second later, Messina heard the lock click, and the shed door swung open. It was a clever plan. Messina didn't say so—she lacked whatever muscle people used when they gave compliments—but she tried, giving Lottie a little nod of approval as she came into the shed. She wasn't sure she saw it in the darkness.

"Turn on your light," Messina told her. She would have turned on her own if she still had a phone.

"What light?" Lottie whispered back. Somehow, she was already deep in the shed, far away from Messina, who was afraid to step anywhere she couldn't see.

"The one on your phone."

"It's in the car."

"Why would you leave it in the car?" She nearly shouted it. Her sense of caution was being driven out by frustration.

"If you wanted me to bring it, you should have told me."

Messina blew a breath through her teeth to keep from yelling at Lottie. She took baby steps around the shed with her hands out in front of her, trying not to get impaled. Her mind was conjuring up a room full of sharp metal tools, like the kind the Grim Reaper carried. She tripped over one of the kayaks and let out a yelp. A flashlight clicked on, shining in her face.

"You okay?" Lottie extended a hand to her, pulling Messina to her feet. "Found a flashlight," she said, waggling it around, like *see?* sending its beam bouncing around the shed like she was trying to signal to passing airplanes.

"Can I see it?" Messina took the flashlight and aimed it at the floor, but she felt like bonking Lottie on the head with it. She moved around the shed, taking an inventory. She thought she'd feel more guilt—this wasn't like the small stuff she'd lift impulsively or take because she needed it; this was worse. But all she felt was the same sense of unfairness she always felt when she looked at the world, the way it drilled a hole right through her middle. And how taking things from people who had more felt like putting a tiny patch over it.

"God, how does it still smell like sex in here?" Lottie said, her scrunched-up face catching in Messina's light.

Messina froze, mid-breath. "That's not funny."

"I wasn't joking. It smells in here."

"Sex doesn't have a smell."

"It *definitely* has a smell."

Messina exhaled, trying to empty her lungs of the particles. Anxiety and nausea battled inside her, each threatening to overwhelm her. She pulled the collar of her shirt up over her face, covering her nose and mouth.

"What are you doing?"

"Filtering your boink particles," Messina said. Lottie looked back at her like she wasn't speaking English. "Whenever you smell something, you're breathing in particles of that thing. I'm not inhaling a bunch of you and Gabe's sex particles. It's disgusting."

Lottie's face was unreadable. She turned away, toward the shelf. "Sorry for being disgusting." She started collecting things at random, not bothering to use the list Messina had made.

"Start with the backpacks," Messina said. She aimed her light at the back wall where three of them hung on hooks beneath a reflective sign that said *Adventure Awaits*. Lottie took down two, wordlessly passing one to Messina.

"Where's the list?" Messina said. She'd given it to Lottie to hold because the pockets on her jeans were the stupid fake kind, nothing but an extra seam sewn into the material. Lottie pulled out a crumpled wad of paper that used to be Messina's list. It was like she couldn't not ruin things. Messina took it and began collecting the items in order.

"Wouldn't this go faster if we divided the list?"

Messina ignored the question. She needed to make sure they

got everything—there wouldn't be any turning back for her if things got difficult. She resumed her search for a water filter, not entirely sure what one would look like, only that it wasn't going to look like the image of a Brita pitcher she had in her head.

Lottie leaned back against the wall and huffed out a breath. "You know, you'd still be standing outside if it weren't for me, so don't act like I'm such a fuckup that I can't do anything to help."

"I didn't say anything about you being a fuckup."

"You don't have to. It's in parentheses every time you look at me."

Messina ripped the list in half and passed part to Lottie—the half with less stuff, where a third of the items were checked off already—and kept searching through her own portion. It took forever to find sleeping bags. Apparently, the expensive ones were tiny and didn't look like sleeping bags at all but like little compressed turds that a full-grown sleeping bag might crap out.

"Done," Lottie said.

Messina flicked her eyes up from her own list. She was still searching for another down jacket, and she wasn't sure what they'd even need Gorilla Tape for—it weighed a ton, but she added it to the pile. "Double check that you got everything."

"It's fine. I got it all." Lottie creased her section of the list and jammed it into her back pocket, out of Messina's reach. Her insides boiled. She chewed the inside of her lips to keep from losing it at Lottie. She located a second jacket and finished triple-checking her own half of the list. Together, they filled the two packs with the rest of the gear. Messina hoisted hers onto her back. They didn't even have food or water yet, and already it felt like she was carrying a whole person.

"Holy shit, this thing's heavy," Lottie said, lifting her own pack onto her back, too close to the shelf behind her. The base of it shifted, sending an avalanche of supplies to the floor, clang-clattering against the concrete. They both stood frozen as the room went quiet. The only sound left was their breathing, broken suddenly by an alarm. A door slammed outside the house, and the alarm grew louder like it was charging toward them. Messina's brain finally put together that the alarm wasn't an alarm—it was a dog, running at them, yipping.

"Run!"

She shoved Lottie toward the door, both tripping over the guts of the broken shelf. A tiny demon-mutt chased them as they sprinted across the yard, their oversized packs bouncing around on their backs. The dog snapped at them, barking and snarling with murder in its eyes. Messina made it to the fence a split-second after Lottie. She bolted over. Lottie should've been on the ground just ahead of her, but she wasn't.

She let out a yelp of pain from the other side of the fence, spitting a string of curses right behind it. Messina heaved herself back up. Lottie's pack was caught on a post. She kicked wildly as Cujo-mini jumped, attacking her. Messina reached over and shifted Lottie's pack, unhooking her, as they both scrambled to their feet on the other side. Lights were coming on in the house. The two of them sprinted down the street.

They hurled the packs into the van and jumped in. Messina gunned it, popping up over the curb and back down again as they tore out of the neighborhood, tires squealing.

15

MESSINA

Fluorescent lights flickered above them. They put Messina on edge—the flickering felt too much like the flashing lights of a cop car to her adrenaline-soaked mind. She looked out the mini-mart's window and nearly jumped at her own reflection. Going to steal that stuff in the Fucker's van was a stupid idea. She wanted to get the last of their supplies and get the hell out onto that trail where no one could find her. It was the last place on earth Jeffucker would ever think to look for her.

She picked up another bottled water from the shelf—the kind with electrolytes—but set it back down when she saw the price and grabbed a regular one. She already had six of the big ones, and her arms were straining beneath the weight of her basket, but she worried they still didn't have enough. She paced the snack aisle looking for the right trail foods.

She looked over at Lottie, wondering what she was getting. She was on the dried meat aisle. Messina preferred to stick to the vegetarian aisles—the whole idea of jerky grossed her out. Meat was bad enough in its regular form. She didn't like to think about the processes it underwent to become shelf-stable and made into a stick. She grabbed some nuts and protein bars, keeping a mental tally of the cost of it all. She hated having to borrow money from Lottie to pay for it. She hated even more not knowing how she would pay her back.

"Did you get that from Val?" Lottie asked, rounding the corner.

"What?" Messina looked down at the protein bar in her hand.

"The particles thing you said back at the shed. About inhaling them. Did you get that from her?"

"Oh. Yeah." An image of Val flashed through Messina's mind, the way she'd make little gun fingers whenever she'd say *Fun fact.*

"It's funny the way we remember different things about her. Sometimes it feels like she was two different people." Lottie wore a paper towel bandage over her dog wound that Messina had made for her because actual bandages were nine dollars. Tiny blooms of red were seeping through it.

"What kind of stuff do you remember?"

Lottie's eyes turned sad at the question. She pointed to the display of dried noodles in front of them, stacked high with chicken and beef flavors. "Want ramen?"

Messina shook her head. "There's only meat flavors." She took a bag of dried fruit from the shelf while Lottie grabbed an armful of the noodles and threw them in her own basket.

"Jesus, that's a lot of water." Lottie was staring at Messina's basket.

"Please don't say his name like that," Messina said, flicking at the air to undo the blasphemy. It sent shivers down her spine, like when kids would say "Bloody Mary" into the mirrors in the school bathrooms. She got that same sense of impending doom, like someone was coming for her. Jeffucker was adamant about not taking the Lord's name in vain. He hung pictures of him with condemning eyes all over the house once he'd converted, replacing all Messina's mom's paintings of sunflowers.

Lottie rolled her eyes. Messina knew she hated all of her rules and superstitions, but they just didn't need any more bad luck. They could've been arrested back there—they still could be. They didn't need God smiting them now.

"Why can't I say that when you don't even believe in him?" Lottie said. "It doesn't make sense."

It didn't have to make sense. Irrational fears crisscrossed Messina's brain like razor wire. She inhaled through her nose and out her mouth, the way the redheaded therapist on IG had taught her to. She looked at Lottie. *Remember to stay calm and assertive*, she could hear the lady's voice in her head. "Do you think shape-shifting demons or evil beings that take the form of clowns are real?"

"No."

"But you still didn't want to use the beach tunnel for a week after you and Gabe watched *It*, right?"

Lottie stared down at her basket, adjusting her pile of ramen. "I get it. I'm sorry," she said. She gave a weird sort of wave toward the fluorescent lights over their heads, like she was making her peace with Jesus. "But seriously, can we talk about the shit ton of water in your basket? Didn't we get a filter from the shed?"

"Yeah, but that only works when there's water to filter. The trail doesn't follow a river. It goes through like half the Mojave. Also, what if the filter breaks?"

"How do you know all this?"

Messina pressed her lips together, wishing she didn't have to say it. She already felt bad enough about keeping it secret for so long.

"Right." Lottie made an annoyed face. "The book." She walked up to the register, dumped her basket, and asked the guy if he carried cat food.

"Aisle three, bottom shelf in the very back."

Messina stood awkwardly at the register, staring at the counter so she wouldn't have to make conversation with the guy. Lottie returned with a bag of cat food.

"Please tell me you're not trying to bring that cat with us."

Lottie looked at Messina like she was being ridiculous. "It's to keep him fed while I'm gone. I'll put a big bowl out in my room and leave the window open for him."

"You know that cat's feral, right?"

"Only as much as I am," Lottie said. "And I still need to eat."

16

LOTTIE

Part of her wished she were doing this alone. Messina already felt like an anxious weight she was dragging behind her. She kept thinking that if she'd decided to go alone that she'd already be on the trail by now, marching along through the darkness with Val. Though she had to admit, having a sleeping bag and tent were going to make things a lot more comfortable. But the idea of her being alone in it all kept cropping up in her mind again and again. She felt like it would all matter more if she took Val out there on her own.

The truth was this: Lottie desperately wanted it to matter.

And this: Something quiet inside her wanted it to make *her* matter.

She felt it ache deep down in her bones—*mattering*—like something she'd yearned for her entire life, despite the sum of her experiences saying it would never happen. Everything from the towering hillside above La Conchita and the sad glances from the teachers at school to being left to live with Maggie. They all sent the same message.

Streetlamps flew by overhead, blinking orange halos of light at them every few seconds.

“You should have the book,” Messina said. Lottie didn’t respond. She knew a gesture driven by guilt when she saw it—she’d invented them.

Messina dug around in the bag beside her with one hand, not taking her eyes from the road. She fished out *Wild* and plopped it onto Lottie’s lap. Lottie stared down at it, the raised black lettering and worn-out boot on the front cover. She couldn’t look at it without seeing Val. She wanted to throw it out the window and never have to look at it again. But she let it sit there. After a minute, she opened it. Val’s writing covered every space on the page not already occupied by the print. In some places, she’d written overtop of it, sometimes so messy that it was illegible, in other places intentionally neat. It was like seeing inside her mind.

Lottie’s eyes tried to take it all in beneath the passing streetlights, but it was too much—like pieces of a puzzle thrown against the wind. But at the very bottom of the page, Lottie’s name stood out, written in Val’s hand. Beside it was a single line of typeface circled in blue.

I was ravenous for love.

The words stared out at her, condemning. A memory sucked her under.

White lines on the school parking lot. The smell of hot pavement and exhaust and hormones. Lottie’s bus was long gone. She waited, baking in the sun, for Gabe to get out of swim practice so she could get a ride.

“Mitchell.” Tristan used her last name to get her attention. She always fell for stupid shit like that, but knowing it didn’t change the way it felt. Like intimacy. Like a dare. She turned. “Need a ride?”

She should have told him no. Not just because he was Val's boyfriend, but because she saw the look in his eye when he asked.

She answered, "Yes."

Lottie slammed the book shut. Sat completely unmoving, not even drawing breath. She felt exposed and naked, her guts and secrets and insides spilled out all over the car. Beside her, Messina watched the road like nothing had happened. Lottie felt sure she was pretending not to see.

It was there, plain as anything, the truth bleeding through her pores. It was written all over her face.

She's dead because of me.

17

LOTTIE

They left the van crooked, a street over from Messina's house. They divvied up the supplies and shouldered their packs. Lottie was sure she was carrying more than her own body weight in water as she started off down the street to Val's.

"Something's poking me," Messina said. She stopped to adjust her pack, but Lottie kept walking. She was going to lose her nerve if she didn't do this now. She cut through the rows toward Val's house and headed up the driveway. Gabe's truck was gone. Questions of where he was and who he was with swam in her mind. Barbs of greed and jealousy pricked up her spine.

She left her pack on the ground and scaled the tree outside Val's window—her feet knew where to find the notches in the bark by muscle memory. The window slid open with barely any help from her, like it had been waiting for someone to crawl through it again.

The smell hit her first. An afterimage of Val—her leave-in conditioner and calendula lotion and summer sweat, all mingled up with that god-awful raspberry body spray she'd use after the beach. Lottie's brain puked up a scramble of memories spanning a decade, all twisted up in that scent—sleepovers and borrowed clothes and half-true secrets spilled in whispers. Frozen pizzas and shared Cokes and watching old tapes on the vintage VCR, all of it tangled up now with the reality that Val was gone. It ripped a fresh wound through her, and she dropped onto the bed, all the air going out of her at once.

She put her head between her knees. She thought she was going to vomit, but slowly, the urge passed, the ringing in her ears subsiding. Next to her, a pile of dirty socks poked out from beneath the covers at the foot of the bed. Val's feet were always cold, but she'd get hot in the night and kick off her socks beneath the blankets, letting them pile up there until she needed to do laundry.

Her room had been left untouched. Signs of her obsessions were everywhere, just visible in the dark—endless scribbles on sticky notes covering her desk and half her wall, books littering every surface, piles of rocks she'd collected one by one and brought home for safekeeping. She was the only one of them who'd had a chance to get care for the faulty wiring inside her head. Her dad even insisted that she and Gabe get therapy after their mom died. Val went to the sessions and got on medication, but she hated it. She said it felt like having ants in her brain, and it all ended as fast as it started.

Messina clamored through the window, still open on the opposite wall. "What the hell are you doing?" she whisper-hissed through her shirt that she'd already pulled up around her face. Lottie hadn't even thought about the particle thing. She wondered if Messina was afraid of breathing in little leftover bits of Val or if she just didn't want to get knocked on her ass by memory-smells the way Lottie had just been.

"I'm getting Val," Lottie said.

Messina's eyes went wide. "When you said you were taking her, I thought you meant the book."

"The book's not Val."

Val was sitting right above them in a pretty metal urn with yellow hibiscus painted around its surface. Lottie flipped the switch on the lamp beside the bed. It was shaped like a bird—a chickadee, Val called it—and when you turned it on, its belly glowed like it had swallowed a hundred fireflies. It illuminated Val's room with a dim, warm light.

Messina sat down on the bed beside Lottie. Lottie stared at Val's pillow, afraid of invoking more memories if she looked elsewhere. A long, half-blue hair was curled against the corner of it, a little piece of her that was left behind. Lottie picked it up and held it in the air, not sure what to do with it once she had it—she wanted to hug it or Jurassic-Park its DNA back into her friend.

"I bet they're everywhere," Messina said.

She was probably right. Lottie imagined them scattered all over the house—on the cushions of the couch and in the carpet and along the bathroom counter—blindsiding Gabe and his dad when they least expected it.

"That's fucking horrible." It felt unfair, like there should've been a rule that all the leftover parts of you vanished after you died. She put the hair back on the pillow, taking care to get it back just as it was.

Messina reached out and touched it with the tips of her fingers, so gently, like she thought it might shatter under too much pressure. Her lips mouthed something Lottie couldn't read. Something just for Val, probably. Then she looked at Lottie. "So what's your plan?"

"To take her ashes with us while we hike the trail." It was the only way.

"Lot, that's messed up." She didn't say the rest, but it hung there in parentheses *Even for you.* "What if her dad sees they're missing?"

"Gabe said he never comes in here now."

"So Gabe's okay with you just taking his sister's urn out on the PCT for a few weeks?"

"No." Lottie's gaze dropped to the floor. "He'd never forgive me. But he's not going to know," she said, pulling a wadded up Ziploc baggie from her pocket. "I'm only going to take a little."

"You can't do that!" Messina yelled it, her shirt falling down from around her face. Lottie reached out and pressed a hand against her mouth, shushing her. Messina's eyes were wide, panicked. She was doing that thing where she freaked out about some rule only she knew about.

"I'll bring her back. She just needs to make the trip."

"You can't separate her ashes." Messina's voice was rigid and strained, a yell in whisper-form.

"Why not?"

"Because you don't know what will happen. What if she gets . . . splinched or something?"

"M, she's not a fucking wizard." Lottie wanted to laugh, but the fear in Messina's eyes was real. She was bubbling over with it. Lottie could see it, but she didn't know how to help, and she didn't have the patience to try. Her instincts just made things worse.

She did the only thing she knew how—she ignored Messina and grabbed the urn off the shelf.

18

MESSINA

She shut her eyes. It was going to be like that scene from Indiana Jones where everyone's face melted off because they opened the ark. She waited, bracing for the sound of the lid opening, metal grating on metal. All that came were Lottie's grunts. A lot of them. And curse words.

She opened her eyes. Lottie sat on the bed, sweaty, holding the unopened urn.

"It's stuck." She wrestled with it more while Messina watched, glad Val was winning. Lottie's face turned red with effort. Sweat and desperation seeped from her pores. "Fuck," she said, finally releasing it.

Messina wanted to feel relieved, but Lottie's despair was making it impossible.

"I think it's sealed."

"Then let's just leave it," Messina said. "We have the book. Let's just go."

Lottie shook her head. "No. I have to do this. *She has to come.*"

"Why?"

She looked away. "I don't know. It just has to be this way."

She was hiding something. Lottie met Messina's gaze, and for a single, bare second, Messina understood. Not why she needed to bring those ashes, but she recognized the fear in Lottie's eyes. It was the kind of fear that didn't have to follow the rules of logic, because knowing and believing were different things.

For whatever reason, Lottie believed she needed those ashes with them on that trail.

"Give them to me," Messina said.

"What?"

"Give them to me, and I'll be the one to take her. Then Gabe can't blame you."

Messina slid her hand across the bed toward Lottie's. She wanted to squeeze it, to find the comfort that used to be there. But she stopped short, leaving their fingertips just close enough that if they'd been magnets, they'd have snicked together.

Lottie passed her the urn, holding it carefully, like it was a baby. Messina pressed it against her chest.

"Meet me outside."

Lottie started to go but turned back. "M, are you sure you—"

"Go. I'll be out in a sec."

Messina untaped Val's map of the PCT off her closet door, then took a pink sticky pad from the desk and scribbled a note. She had the same kind of feeling she'd felt back at Lottie's when she understood that Val was taking them out of La Conchita to the Three Sisters. She wondered if Val wanted it this way, Messina bringing her urn. She imagined Val had somehow locked it from the inside on purpose, like a child in her room, so Lottie wouldn't be able to split her ashes apart.

The feeling bounced around inside Messina until it became a solid thing, real enough to hold. They were supposed to bring Val. They were supposed to do this together.

Three Sisters.

PART II
WEIGHT

19

MESSINA

She was really leaving. Her brain still didn't believe it, but some part of her kept whispering it. *You're really going this time.*

The dot on Lottie's phone showing their Uber's distance hadn't moved in ten minutes. The shitty cell service where they waited near the front of the neighborhood wasn't keeping up. There'd barely been enough cash in Lottie's account to cover it, and Messina swore she'd pay her back—first for the food, now the ride. At least she'd done something for Lottie now, bringing Val. It felt like it balanced things a little more.

She glanced over her shoulder again, wishing the Uber would hurry. She felt too exposed standing here by the tracks at the entrance of La Conchita, like Jeffucker could be anywhere. Like he was going to round the corner on horseback like a Ringwraith and drag her back home.

She hugged her pack where Val's urn was. The extra weight from it was a lot, but she liked it. She liked knowing that Val was with her, that they were doing this together, helping each other. She heard Val's voice whisper in her mind, *You take me, I'll take you.*

She didn't want to talk to Lottie about it—it was all too woo-woo for her. Val was the one Messina would talk to about mystical stuff. Val had a Mexican grandmother who believed in ghosts, so she never thought the things Messina's mind conjured were weird. At least the parts Messina had shared with her. She hadn't told her about all of it. No one could understand the actual vortex inside her head—it wasn't anything beautiful passed down through culture or tradition; it was a twisted maze of magic and religion, gods and rules, rituals and superstition, built up haphazardly over years from fear and stories and other people's beliefs. Half the time it didn't even make sense to Messina, and she was the one who'd created it.

She looked down at the phone again to check their ride's progress, but Lottie had it open to the map now, the spot they'd found to get onto the PCT. Their nearest entry point was an hour's drive from here, just before the Escondido Canyon exit, where the trail crossed beneath the 14. There was no option on the Uber app to end the ride in the middle of the freeway, so they'd used a fast-food place about a mile further, planning to ask their driver to pull over just before the exit. Messina preferred it that way, no one else knowing where they were headed. She wanted to be as untraceable as possible. She knew the Fucker wasn't going to stop looking for her.

"I wish the driver would hurry up."

"Relax."

"I can't." She looked over her shoulder. She could feel the Fucker everywhere. This was the exact spot where she'd turned back every time, where the fear would always turn so threatening that she surrendered to it.

Headlights exited the 101, turning toward them into the

neighborhood. The car stopped just before the tracks at the T intersection. It idled. Uncertainty vibrated through Messina.

"What kind of car was it again?"

"Blue Honda. James."

Messina squinted, unable to see anything but the car's bright lights. Lottie shouldered her pack and looked at Messina. She didn't budge. "I don't trust it. What kind of driver sees their customers with giant-ass backpacks and stops a hundred feet away?"

"I don't know. Who else is it going to be?"

"A serial killer. Parking alongside the freeway so he can make a quick getaway."

Lottie shot her a look, like she was wondering if she was going to be like this the entire time. "I'll go check," she said. "I'll wave at you if I don't get strangled to death."

"No, stop. I'll come." Whatever was going to happen from here on out, they were together, all three of them. Messina picked up her pack and heaved one side over her shoulder. It was so heavy, she could barely stand upright, but she liked it. She knew part of that weight was Val.

"Hi." A waving hand popped out of the car, followed by the driver as they approached. "I'm James." He didn't look much older than them, early twenties maybe, with shaggy dark hair and a skinny build. "Sorry for not coming all the way up—I saw the sign." He pointed at it. "County officials advise against entry. I figured I should stay back there. I hope I didn't freak you out or anything."

"We're two girls alone in the middle of the night. Why would that freak us out?"

James laughed off her response, but Messina hadn't meant it to be funny.

"I haven't been here before," James said. "What is this place?" He opened the trunk and tried to take Messina's pack from her. She clung to it with a warning in her eyes that made James change course.

"La Conchita," Lottie said, no further explanation. She opened the door to the backseat and shoved her backpack in, climbing in behind it. Messina did the same. The overhead lamp glared, lighting up the inside of the car like a beacon calling out to Jeffucker. Messina covered it with her hand until the doors closed.

The interior of the car reeked of the coconut air freshener hanging from the rearview mirror. Messina put her shirt over her nose and rolled down the window. As they drove away from La Conchita, she turned and watched the mountains in the rear window getting smaller, until they barely existed anymore. She wondered if she was really leaving this time, or if something would bring her back again, like it always did.

"Do you mind the music?" James said. "I can turn it off if you do."

Messina only noticed it then, a familiar song humming through the speakers, the one about leaving. It was one she knew from Val and Gabe's dad playing it on Saturday mornings after sleepovers when he'd drive them to Carpinteria for donuts. He loved all the old stuff.

"Nothing beats rock from the seventies." James turned his head back toward them when he talked. It made Messina nervous. "This guy's great—Billy Joel." Messina didn't think this was Billy Joel, but she didn't say so. Billy Joel was the one with the song about the piano man that Val liked. This was someone else, she thought.

They took the 126 east. No traffic, so they flew. Lottie and Messina huddled over the phone screen, watching their progress. Lottie's hair whipped against Messina's face in the wind. The lights from Santa Clarita faded, and they drove on in the darkness with only scattered lights ahead on the horizon.

The air turned cold and dry as they got farther from the coast. Scattered pieces of Val's facts about microclimates bounced around inside Messina's head. *You can go from a green, fog-covered mountain to a desert that's a hundred degrees in the space of twenty miles.* She couldn't remember why, something about mountains and marine layer and pressure. Even without knowing the specifics, Messina could feel the shift, the way the dry air leeched moisture from her skin. Any minute now, Lottie's nose was probably going to start bleeding from the dryness. Her insides were always on the outside—emotionally, physically, in every way possible—for all the world to see.

Messina looked at her, still in her Lu's shirt and cutoffs. She had on the old sneakers she always worked in. Neither of them had on proper shoes for this. Messina was still in the knockoff Docs she'd worn to the party.

The screen on Lottie's phone flashed with a call. There was no contact name, just a number. But Messina knew it. The order of the digits stared out at her like a threat.

"It's him." There was no further explanation needed. She knew Lottie could hear it in her voice that she meant the Fucker.

"What do I do?" Lottie held the phone out toward Messina like it was a bomb about to explode. Before she could even think, Messina's body acted on instinct. She grabbed the phone and threw it out the window.

The volume of the world cut out as they watched it fly. Sailing into the night like a frisbee.

Lottie's anger exploded. "What did you just do!" It was deafening at close range. "M, what the *fucking hell*?"

"I don't know! Fuck! I'm sorry!" The reality of her action slammed against her. That phone was their only means of navigating, of calling for help. They were lost and fucked and probably dead without it.

"HeyHeyHey! You can't throw stuff out of my car!" James turned around in his seat, face like a pissed babysitter. Messina ignored him. Lottie's fury was taking up all the room in the car, sending panic alarms ringing through Messina.

Lottie's hands squeezed against her own skull like she was trying to pop it. When she spoke, her words came slow and raw. It was more frightening than her shouting. "I can't believe you did that."

The shock of it still rang through Messina too, sickening her. Lottie had saved for eight months for that phone. But the fear exploding inside Messina's chest told her it was the only way, that Jeffucker would never stop hunting her. "I had to." It was barely a whisper.

"No. You didn't." Rage spilled through Lottie's teeth. "You could have sent it to voicemail. You could have *turned it off*. FUCK!" She kicked the back of James's seat.

"Please. Don't. Kick. My seat." James's voice had turned high-pitched. "I'm going to have to ask that you two calm down, or I'm going to end the ride."

Messina could barely hear him. Wind and adrenaline whooshed in her ears—this was all going to be so much harder now. She looked around, trying to get her bearings. They'd been tracking their progress to the trail's intersection on the phone. Now she didn't know how close they were. They needed to stop a mile before the exit.

"I think we need to stop soon," she said to Lottie. "We were close, right?" Lottie didn't say anything. She just stared at her hands where the phone had been. Messina was about to ask James how far they were from the exit when his navigation announced it. *In two miles, take exit nineteen onto Escondido Canyon Road.*

"Hey James, could you pull over?"

"Sure-sure-sure," he said, checking his blind spot as he merged right. "Just let me exit."

"No, I need you to pull over right here. *Now.*"

"Oh." He hurled a collapsible trashcan toward them. It hit the backpacks and bounced onto the floor at Messina's feet as the car veered sharply to the right. "Are you gonna be sick?"

The remaining windows were coming down on both sides of the car as they skidded to a stop on the shoulder of the freeway. Cars zoomed past them, one blaring a horn, its pitch bending as it whooshed by.

"It's okay. Nobody's puking," Messina said, looking at James, who had fully turned around in his seat now. "We're just getting out here." She couldn't tell if James was alarmed at her words or relieved by them. She wasn't sure he could either.

"But we're in the middle of the freeway. They said in training not to let people out there. It's not safe."

She popped open her door. Lottie was already stomping around outside, looking furious, wrestling with her backpack right next to the oncoming traffic. According to what was on the phone before Messina threw it out the window, there was a tunnel below them, an entrance point onto the PCT, cutting right across this section of the interstate. "Thanks for the ride," Messina said, climbing out and yanking her pack along with her.

"But you're not safe!" James shouted at them over the noise of the traffic.

Messina leaned down and looked at him through the interior of the car. "We never have been."

20

GABE

Gabe's truck idled in the driveway. He stared up at Val's glowing window, his mind and heart and insides all trying to reconcile what he was seeing. When he pulled up, his heart had leapt in front of his brain, screaming *Val.* In the seconds it took for his logic to catch up, he felt like he'd lost her all over again.

It must've been his dad, finally entering the room he'd avoided for the past weeks. Gabe exhaled a breath. Most days it felt like he was carrying around his dad's grief along with his own. He needed another minute out here alone before going in. His emotions still felt strung out from being at that party tonight. It was the last place he'd wanted to go, but he'd gone along anyway, just like he did with everything.

His entire life had been just that—going along with things. Un-choices. Inaction. He hated the way it felt when he stepped back and looked at it all, how the decisions that determined his path were never really his. Maybe his dad's whole risk-assessment mindset had gotten into his head as a kid, or maybe it was something else, but whenever he was faced with doing this or that, he did neither. He sat still, trying to decide until it was too late, and the choice was made for him.

He'd joined swim team because his best friend, Marcus, dragged him to the sign-up meeting. Becoming captain was the coach's doing. His job at Javi's had been because his school counselor said he needed work experience for his college applications. Even Lottie. He'd wanted her half his life, but he hadn't chosen to be with her the other night—she'd chosen. Maybe if he'd had the guts to be the one to do it, things would've turned out differently, but he hadn't. He just kept saying okay and going along with things.

The situation at the party tonight, for instance. He didn't choose to go. He didn't choose Merilee Winters. He didn't ask her to sit down on his lap and start devouring his earlobe, but he didn't choose to stop it, either—he just let her do what she wanted and went along, doing what he was supposed to do.

The memory of it felt gross now—not because Merilee had on too much perfume and her lips tasted like waxy Froot Loops, even though he definitely hadn't liked that part. It felt gross because she'd only spoken to him a handful of times. She didn't know anything about him, aside from him being swim captain. And that his sister was dead. Everyone knew that. The most fucked-up thing had been that girls like Merilee suddenly found him more attractive because of it. It tore at something soft inside him. He was certain it would have caused him pain if he could feel anything. But it was like he'd been standing in a bucket of ice water since Val died, his limbs all numb. Except when he'd been with Lottie.

Lottie. She'd bolted out of his truck today like her hair was on fire.

Your heart's going to break, no matter what you do.

He wondered what Val would have told him now.

He looked up at her window, the light spilling out into the night. He cut the engine and pushed open his truck door, steadying himself for whatever state his dad might be in. The house was dark. His dad's familiar snores came from the downstairs couch where he so often slept now. Chicken, who was curled at his dad's feet, raised his head just a few inches before dropping it back down. Printouts of real estate listings were scattered across the coffee table, some circled. Gabe couldn't blame him for wanting to get out of this place. It was saturated with sad memories.

After his mom died, his dad had kept it together for him and Val. He'd put on a brave face every morning and took them to school and therapy and Saturday donut runs and all the rest. He'd kept strong because Gabe and Val needed him to be. But since Val's death, it hadn't been like that. He was barely holding on. And Gabe was faced with the reality that his existence alone wasn't enough to keep his dad going.

He climbed the stairs to Val's room. Maybe he'd imagined the light. Maybe he was losing it.

A warm glow spilled out from the crack under Val's door. He opened it and saw three things:

1. The bird-shaped lamp by the bed was on.
2. A note on the desk said *Don't worry, I'll keep her safe. Back soon.*
3. The map on Val's door was missing, along with Val.

. . . Fucking Lottie.

21

LOTTIE

Her phone was gone. Her brain kept puking up the image of it flying out the window. She tried to zoom out and stop thinking about it, but she kept seeing it fly again and again. A GIF from hell.

She started walking along the freeway, half-hunched under her pack, back in the direction they came from. Maybe her phone was still on the side of the road.

Messina caught her arm. "Where are you going?"

Lottie yanked away. "To find my phone."

"You can't. It's gone."

"I know that, M! I watched you throw the only thing I had out the fucking window. So what do you want me to do right now?"

"I want you to come with me." Messina's voice was quiet now, the opposite of Lottie's, hardly audible over the howl of passing cars. But her eyes were steady. Messina looked back toward James, outside his car on his phone. "I don't know if he's calling the cops or his boss, but if we stay on the freeway, we're going to be found."

Messina took a step off the shoulder into the darkness. She looked back at Lottie. The moon offered just enough light to make it known that they were standing at the edge of a steep downward slope. Nothing beyond it was visible.

James was off his phone. He stalked toward them. Messina took another step. “L, please.”

Lottie blew out a breath and followed Messina into the darkness.

The ground immediately shifted. The slope was so sharp Lottie lost her footing and sank through the chaparral. She struggled against the weight of her pack, trying and failing to get back up. It was all Messina’s extra water weighing her down, given to Lottie to make room in Messina’s pack for Val.

“M!” she shouted.

Messina turned around and scrambled back up the slope to help Lottie to her feet. They inched their way down together.

Reaching the bottom didn’t improve things. They’d traded the last dregs of civilization for darkness. The grass was higher here, and the towering freeway above them blocked the moonlight, casting them in shadow. There was no trail in sight.

“What the hell do we do now?” Lottie looked around them at the nothingness. She was angry and freezing and Messina had fucked this all up, and now Lottie wanted her to fix it.

“The book said there are trail markers.”

“Do you see any?”

Messina shined her light around them. The world was an endless sea of dead grass and sharp underbrush.

“No. But I stuck one of Val’s maps into the book.”

“How is that going to help us if we don’t know where we are?”

“I know where we are.” Her tone was defensive. Messina was

nearly as stubborn as Lottie. "We stopped a mile from the exit. You should get your flashlight out too, while you're getting the book."

Lottie would've just flicked on the one on her phone if she'd had it. Instead, she wrestled her pack off, letting it fall into the brush. It sounded like hundreds of tiny bones snapping. This whole place felt like death. It probably hadn't seen water in years. At least by the coast, the marine layer took the edge off the drought, but not here. Everything around them was brittle and lifeless, just waiting to feed the next fire that came along.

She dug in her pack. Everything useful was buried beneath the lifetime supply of water bottles. "Do we honestly need all of this fucking water?"

"Do you want to trade?" She meant for Val. Lottie didn't want to think about that.

Truth: She was scared to put Val into her pack, to be that close to her. Like proximity to her might reveal things the way the book had. Lottie wondered if Messina had seen the circled words, Lottie's name written beside them. It felt incriminating.

She didn't answer. She dug deeper into her backpack, finding her light and passing the book to Messina. She unearthed a jacket too. At least the top half of her would be warm now. "What do these markers look like?"

"White rounded triangles. They'll say something about the PCT on them."

Lottie moved off in a random direction. The brush clawed at her bare legs. In the edge of her light, she could see Messina tapping her thumb and forefinger together in one of her rituals, making OK signs again and again.

Lottie stretched out the arm holding her flashlight, trying to make its beam go farther. No markers, just infinite nothingness. She reached toward her back pocket, her hand mindlessly checking for her phone there, like a phantom limb. A voice inside her told her she'd still have it if she'd done this on her own. *You'd be whistling and skipping down the PCT by now.*

"We're lost," she yelled to Messina. "We haven't even started, and we're already fucked."

Messina didn't say anything back. She was crouched down, shining her light over her paper map. Lottie stomped over and looked over Messina's shoulder. She let out a sound that was the inverse of a laugh. When Messina had said she had a map, Lottie thought she was serious, that she meant an *actual* map. What Messina was staring at was the poster-map from Val's door. The thing was maybe eighteen inches tall and spanned from the southern tip of California to Washington with the PCT highlighted in green.

"Are you kidding me right now?" Lottie wanted to shake her. "M, there is no navigating with this fuckery of a map. Everything within a hundred-mile radius of us is a tiny black dot." Lottie grabbed the book at Messina's feet, leaving her with the "map," and stormed off through the brush in a direction parallel to the freeway above them.

"Where are you going?"

"How the hell should I know? I'm picking a direction and walking in it. If you've got a better plan, then say it, but I don't see one right now."

Messina didn't say anything back, but Lottie could hear her footsteps clomping along behind her. The darkness around them felt alive. It hummed and skittered with invisible life that raised goosebumps along Lottie's arms. They were going to turn into an urban legend. Two girls stranded and murdered off the side of the freeway.

"Lottie?"

She turned and saw Messina a few yards behind her, shining her light over a rusted metal beam. Lottie added her light alongside Messina's. The beam was part of a huge metal grate that stretched up over their heads. Behind it, surrounded by graffitied concrete, was a massive mouth opening up beneath the freeway.

"It looks like a drainage pipe," Messina said. The thing was enormous, ten times bigger than the tunnel in La Conchita.

A nasty smell seeped out of it, sickly sweet, like rot. It looked like the gateway to hell. "It has to run all the way through, beneath the freeway. Do you think it's the path?" Lottie said, already hating the idea of going through it.

She looked at Messina. She was doing the OK sign with both hands now, still gripping her flashlight with her other fingers "No." Messina's voice was weirdly calm, like something was wrong with her, but it was buried too deep for Lottie to see. She turned away from the tunnel and kept walking.

"Hey." Lottie grabbed the handle on Messina's pack, putting the brakes on her exit. "You can't just shut this down as a possibility without a good reason. It cuts under the freeway. We know we'd at least be going in the right direction."

"I'm sure that's not the way. That tunnel looks like Satan's asshole. Val wouldn't send me through there."

"What does that mean?"

"Nothing." Messina's fingers were going crazy with OKs,

even while her voice still held that same eerie calm. "Where's the book?"

"It's not going to help, M."

"Can I just have it, please?"

Lottie gave her the book. "This is like following the advice of a magic eight-ball."

Messina flipped its pages frantically. Lottie turned back to the tunnel and cast her light over its face again. Decades of graffiti covered the concrete, but standing out from it all was a fresh tag repeating in the same abrasive neon green, like someone had used it as their practice canvas. Lottie couldn't read it. She could just make out a J and an O. She stepped closer and nearly impaled herself on a warped metal post sticking out of the ground at waist height. A rusty piece of metal was nailed to its top, bent at an angle so it looked like half a jagged heart.

"I think I found something."

Messina aimed her light at Lottie.

"It almost looks like a marker if you imagine it straightened out, right? And with smooth edges? . . . And white."

Frustration seeped out of Messina like a stink Lottie could smell. She shined her light over the metal post and picked at what was either a remaining fleck of white paint or the remnants of some bird shit with the edge of her fingernail. It flaked off and fluttered to the ground.

"It kind of looks like a marker, right?" Lottie said again.

"No, it doesn't!" The calm had completely vanished from Messina's voice, replaced by a ragged sound from whatever storm was spinning around inside her. "It doesn't look like a marker, Lot. It looks like a fucking complementary tetanus dispenser!" She kicked its base with the toe of her boot. "FUCK!" Whatever thread had been holding her together, keeping that eerie calm in her voice, had properly snapped now.

The anger Lottie had shoved down ignited.

"No, this is bullshit. This whole thing is your fault, so you don't get to have a meltdown because we're lost."

"How is this my fault?"

"You threw my goddamn phone out the window!" She said *goddamn* on purpose, using it to jab at Messina.

The confusion on Messina's face vanished. Her eyes narrowed into something frightening, even as she drew a little cross in the air. "You're right. I did." Her voice was devoid of the regret Lottie had expected. "Do you know why?"

"Because you're even more fucked in the head than I am?"

The words caught on Messina's face like a slap. A pinprick of regret sprouted inside Lottie's chest.

"Do you have any idea what he'll do to me if he finds me? Or if the cops manage to track me down and bring me back home?"

When Lottie didn't respond, Messina got louder.

"Do you, L? Because I fucking don't. Whatever it is, it's so awful and terrifying that my mind can't even fathom it. So yeah, I threw out your phone. And I'm sorry that it's gone and that it meant a lot to you, but I'm not sorry I did it."

The weight of Messina's words hung there between them.

"Say something," Messina said. "If you're going to flip out, will you just go ahead and do it now? I hate when that shit sneaks up on me."

Lottie stared at Messina, barely an outline in the dark. If it had been light out, she wouldn't have been brave enough, but in the dark, it felt okay. "You've never talked about it."

Messina's eyes found Lottie's. "Neither have you." She motioned to Lottie's burn scars, their tendrils snaking out past the collar of her shirt and up her neck. Lottie had thought so many times about how she would have died if the firefighters hadn't visited the school the week before in their brown and yellow gear, teaching the class how to stop, drop, and roll if their clothing caught fire. She could still remember the way it smelled, her skin burning. The way the fabric of her shirt had melted to her, splotches of green mingling with her flesh. She pushed it from her mind.

"Yours is worse," Lottie said, meaning Messina's situation. Her home life, Jeffucker, all of it. She knew Messina understood what she meant.

"Maybe. Doesn't make yours good."

Despite the darkness, Lottie wasn't sure if she'd ever felt so seen. It was the kind of knowing they'd only hinted at before, in coded words and shared glances. Now it was here, out in the open. They stood there together in the quiet of it.

"I tried once," Messina said, "telling someone. Summer after sixth grade." She dug the toe of her boot into the dirt, forming a little notch in the hardened ground. "There was a counselor at church camp who was always nice to me. After I told her, she said she'd call my mom, and we'd have a meeting when she came to get me at the end of the week. But when they brought me to the office on the last day, he was there, sitting right between my counselor and the camp pastor.

"I knew the second I saw him that I was going to pay for it. But the punishment that came after was nothing compared to being in that room. Every single person in there knew what was happening, and no one did anything. Fucker called me a liar, said I was making it up for attention. I was right there in front of them, asking for help, and they all turned their backs on me. They sent me back home with him."

Messina wiped her sleeve against her face. "It was worse than anything he's ever done to me. That's why I don't say it. I'd rather keep it all in than feel like that again."

Lottie understood. They were the same in that way, in knowing that the world didn't give a shit about them. They'd always been on their own.

Val would have given the perfect kind of comfort in a moment like this. She would have wrapped her body over Messina's and swallowed her up in a hug. She was full of warmth and love and touch. Lottie should have at least reached out and squeezed Messina's hand or patted her shoulder or something, but she didn't know how anymore. That part of her was all twisted up—she knew how to touch someone when she was hitting on them, but offering comfort was something different.

For a moment, they stayed like that, in the silence of their knowing, until Lottie ruined it. She didn't know how she screwed up this time, because she hadn't even realized she was thinking about her phone until Messina looked at her and said, "What?"

"Nothing."

"Don't lie to me."

"I'm not lying. I'm trying not to be an asshole."

Something close to a laugh came out of Messina. "Are you going to tell the wind not to blow too? Come on, you're already thinking it. Just spit it out."

"I just . . ." She stopped talking and chewed her lip. Asshole alarms were going off inside her head. *Stop talking.* "I just still don't think you should've thrown it out the window. It's not like Jeffucker can track you from *my* phone."

She knew the second the words were out that she shouldn't have said them. But there wasn't a retract button to get them back.

Messina's posture sank, like just the act of dealing with Lottie was so exhausting that she didn't have the energy to keep herself upright anymore. She was right. Lottie felt exhausted from herself too. Messina looked at her with tired eyes. "There's no way to be sure he can't trace me."

Lottie fought the impulse to argue again. Jesus, what was wrong with her?

Messina went on. "What if he calls the cops and says we're missing? Are you sure they couldn't convince the company to give up your info? We're both minors—we could be kidnapped or dead for all they know. Do you think a billion-dollar corporation is going to risk the bad publicity of two dead girls for the sake of our privacy?"

When Lottie didn't say anything, Messina looked at her like *Well?* Lottie stayed silent this time. Messina was right.

"That's why I threw your *goddamn* phone out the window." Messina made another cross in the air after she said it.

Lottie let out a long breath through her lips. It probably fogged up the air in front of her from the cold, but she couldn't tell in the dark. "I'm sorry."

"It's okay. You didn't know. Anyway, I'm sorry too. I know you worked your ass off for that phone. I'll find a way to pay you back."

Lottie nodded, even though she didn't think it was true. Something quiet inside her whispered that Messina really wasn't coming back to La Conchita this time.

Messina messed with the spot at her hairline she always picked at. "I didn't think finding this trail would be so hard. It's not like I need a neon sign or anything, but I think a part of me was expecting something that clear."

"I'd pictured a yellow-brick-road sort of deal."

"I know you think it's crazy," Messina said, tapping on the cover of the book, "but I thought she'd be leading us. She really has been talking to me. That day I left La Conchita and stole Fucker's van, she told me to go."

Lottie thought about the line she'd seen by her name, the way it conjured the memory—*I was ravenous for love*—how it spoke to her as if it knew her. "No, I don't think it's crazy."

Messina flipped through the pages of the book again, looking hopeless. "It's like I dropped her signal."

"No, you didn't. Look." Lottie pointed to the dog-eared page Messina had stopped at. It was a wall of unmarked text, something about the Oregon section of the trail. There, in its center, sat two words surrounded by quotation marks—*green tunnel.*

22

GABE

He was outside Lottie's place. He didn't know why—it was the middle of the night, and he knew he wasn't going to find her here sitting with Val's urn, regretting her decision. But he had to check anyway. He had to be sure.

No one was home. He couldn't even remember the last time he'd seen Maggie's car parked out front.

He shined his phone light into Lottie's open bedroom window. All these years knowing her, and he'd never stepped foot inside her room. A bed and desk were the only furniture. A bulletin board littered with pictures taken with Val's Polaroid camera. Rows of his sister's face smiled back at him, photos he'd never seen.

Lottie's cat leapt up onto the window's edge, scaring the shit out of him. Gabe exhaled hard and pressed his hand against his chest where his heart pounded.

"*Grimace.*"

The cat purred and rubbed his face against Gabe's shirtsleeve. A huge bowl of cat food sat in the window with lines of ants leading from its sides down the trailer wall. Gabe took a little handful of food, dusted off the ants, and held it out to Grimace. The cat ate from his hand, eyes closed in bliss as he chewed, dropping little spit-covered bits back into Gabe's palm.

When Gabe left Lottie's, Grimace followed him into the street. The smell of smoke drifted in on the breeze. Someone at the party had said there was a fire out in Simi. Gabe wondered if the smell was from that one or if a new one had sparked somewhere. A yowling made him turn around. Grimace sat in the middle of the intersection, like he knew he wasn't supposed to wander any farther from his home. Gabe turned back and scooped the cat up by the belly.

"Come on." He tucked Grimace over his shoulder, giving his head a little rub. "We'll figure out how to find her tomorrow."

23

MESSINA

Their lights bounced off the corrugated steel rings surrounding them.

"Shit!" Lottie slipped and grabbed hold of Messina's arm, nearly bringing them both down as they navigated the hell tunnel, trying to avoid the center where a foul-smelling gunk grew.

When they emerged on the other side, Messina wanted to feel relieved. But there was nothing to greet them but more darkness and chaparral.

"What do we do now?" Lottie said.

"No idea. We're in the same place we started, just on the other side of the looking glass." They shined their lights around them. Messina's caught on a bare patch of ground, only about a foot wide. It looked different somehow. Intentional. "Is that the trail?"

Lottie's light joined Messina's. The bare patch wound its way into the chaparral. "Maybe?"

"Why the hell isn't it more obvious?"

The answer hung there silently between them. *Because maybe this isn't the PCT.*

The trail wasn't wide enough to walk side by side, so they went single file, Messina in front. Not because she was braver, because she didn't trust Lottie to steer them in the right direction. Sounds like screams erupted all around them. It took Messina's panic-flooded mind a beat to process them—coyotes.

"It's okay," Lottie said, like she could sense Messina's alarm. "They're just calling to each other, marking their territory. It doesn't mean we're in danger."

It didn't make her feel better. They were too close. It sounded like there were a hundred of them. "How do you know that?"

"Val."

It really was weird how they'd both hung on to such different pieces of her. Messina couldn't recall anything about coyotes. That was probably the kind of stuff she missed when she'd been grounded instead of out hiking with them or car camping with Val's family. Jeffucker had kept her so chained. A twinge of jealousy rang through her—Lottie had gotten so much more time with Val than she had.

The coyotes called again, their yips echoing through the night air. "Are you sure they're not killing something? That sounds really murder-y."

"Why would they invite everyone else to dinner and have to share?"

That made sense. Messina still couldn't convince her anxious mind of it though. She didn't want to be in front anymore and made Lottie switch with her.

"You remind me of a coyote a little bit," Messina said without thinking that maybe it was the kind of thought better kept on the inside.

"What do you mean?"

What she meant was that Lottie was built for survival more than for love and friendship, which was why the thought was an inside thought, not an outside one. Messina bit down on her tongue, frustrated at herself. "You're built for survival," she said, hoping it sounded complimentary, "just like they are."

More coyotes joined in the chorus, sounding closer than ever. Messina whispered to herself, *You're.okay.You're.okay*, but the fear in her blew like the Santa Anas, twisting around inside her, making her dizzy. She started singing—hoping to chase off the fear in her as much as the coyotes—the song from the car ride, humming in the spots where she couldn't find the words. She hated singing out loud. But she belted as loud as she could, trying to claim the territory as her own.

Lottie joined in too, her voice drowning out Messina's. *"He was gone, a father to a fawn on a Christmas sleigh . . ."*

Messina laughed. "What are you singing? A father to a fawn?"

"What about you? I'm pretty sure there's nothing in there about being 'tossed in your hat and stung today.' "

"I don't know, it's a weird song."

The repeating line of the chorus was the only place where they both seemed to know the words. *And this child better leave, uh-huh.* There was also the line about God dying, but Messina didn't sing that one out loud.

She felt braver as they hiked and sang at the tops of their lungs. Some tiny part of her started to believe this really was her territory, her space to belong.

24

MESSINA

"Just a little farther," she said again.

She'd said it at least five times already, hoping each time that she'd feel a sense of calm once they passed the next stretch, but it never came. They'd been hiking forever.

She was something past exhausted now. And she was hearing things, her sleep-deprived mind making up sounds like the bending whoosh of a passing car. She shook her head, trying to detach the crazies, when her light caught on a rounded white triangle on a metal post. Clean and white, clearly emblazoned with the words **PACIFIC CREST TRAIL.**

Just beyond it was a two-lane paved road. A car zoomed past, and Messina backed reflexively toward the brush. She knocked into Lottie and brought them both down.

"Shit. Sorry." Messina sat up, brushing dust from her butt.

"Is that a marker?" Lottie hoisted herself to her feet. She was already walking into the road, oblivious to its dangers. Where there were roads, there were cars and police and the Fucker and getting caught and dragged back. Her mind was spinning with it. She checked for headlights.

"We did it. We're actually on the right track," Lottie said. "We should camp here."

"On the side of the road? L, we already look like vandals, walking around with backpacks and flashlights in the middle of the night. You want to add a big-ass tent into the mix? If anyone calls the cops on us, I'm dead."

"Right. Fuck. We keep going then." She said it like she didn't want to, but like she understood they had no choice. She looked up and down the road. "Which way?"

Messina didn't know. The trail was gone, dead-ending into the road. The marker didn't point them in any direction. "Through town, probably," she said, trying to sound more confident than she felt. "I don't think it would bring us this way otherwise. Maybe it's a resupply point."

Everything was dark, aside from the staggered glow of streetlamps and the occasional set of headlights. Messina spooked every time a car passed. They made painfully slow progress, but finally, the buildings thinned, and the remnants of town were left behind them. Another marker at a dirt road directed them up the foothills looming in front of them, back into the wild. Lottie hung back, like she was hoping this meant they could stop now, but they were still on the edge of town. It wasn't safe. Messina pushed ahead, looking back to make sure Lottie was following.

"Just a little farther," she said, starting up an incline. She was sweating, even in the cold air. Her feet slipped on the loose dirt. Her mind was playing tricks on her. It was impossible to walk up something for this long without reaching the top. Was she awake now, or was this a dream?

"M, you've got to be kidding me." Lottie's words pulled Messina from her trance. "How far do we have to go for you to be okay?" All the kindness was gone from her voice. The tender moment they'd shared a few hours ago had disintegrated beneath however many miles they'd tread.

Messina didn't know the answer. She was still as scared as she'd been when they started—of Jeffucker, of animals, of everything. She was so tired of being scared. So tired of walking. "Let's just stop here."

Lottie swept her flashlight over their surroundings. It lit up unfriendly-looking plants and rocks covering the sharply sloped ground. "Lovely spot. We can either sleep standing or with our heads going down the side of the mountain." She dropped her pack in the middle of the trail and ripped open a candy bar, shoving half into her mouth in one bite.

"Can you help me get the tent up?" Messina had never set up a tent before and didn't have a clue how to do it, but she didn't want to say that.

Lottie was sitting in the dirt, leaned back against her pack. She took another bite of her candy bar, talking around the wet chunk of nougat in her mouth. "There's no room for it. We're going to have to sleep in the open."

That wasn't an option. The open was too . . . open. Messina dragged out the tent bag and emptied its contents onto the trail. It wasn't a tent, it was what was left after someone had skinned and deboned one. She wrestled with the pieces until she was breathless and spent. Even if she'd known what she was doing, there wasn't enough room, and the ground was too slanted and rocky. She ended up with a deflated tarp, propped up just enough to sit in its mouth and still have an airhole. She was strung out on fear. She thought she'd be rid of it by now, but it kept on thumping inside her chest, strong as her heart.

Lottie was already asleep. Messina hated that she could be so comfortable being completely exposed. She ate a few handfuls of peanuts and tried not to drink too much water, afraid of having to wander into the brush alone to pee. Just thinking about it started her bladder kicking with the urge to empty. Messina shut her eyes and willed it away. All of it—the urge in her bladder, the night, the fear in her belly, her envy and frustration at Lottie. She willed it all away, until there was nothing but the sound of wind blowing.

25

GABE

He spent the morning preparing. The key was to not focus on the problem—*fucking Lottie*—but instead, to focus on the steps of a solution.

Step one: Gather supplies.

He catalogued the items on his bedroom floor. He was still missing batteries and sunblock, but he loaded everything back into the backpack from the woman at Lu's. He found half a bottle of SPF 50 in the bathroom cabinet and knocked the batteries out of his electric razor.

Step two: Find Lottie.

That one was a little more complicated. He knew she was on the PCT—the missing map and ashes didn't leave much of a riddle to puzzle out—but not specifically where. It was a long-ass trail, spanning the whole western side of the country. And it wasn't like he could drive up and down it searching for her. Bikes weren't even allowed, let alone cars. He scanned the map he'd downloaded onto his phone, along with the navigation app he'd found in Val's notes. It would use his phone's GPS for navigating once he was out of cell range.

He needed to find a place to wait for Lottie—some point that she hadn't crossed yet but would be coming to soon. Another complication: He didn't know where she started. His best guess was the nearest entry point. Well, not the *actual* nearest—that one would have had her hopping off the middle of the freeway to get to it—she'd have to be crazy to do that. He traced his finger farther along the map. The most logical point of entry would be Agua Dulce, so he needed to find some place north of there. He was only guessing at how fast she could hike. The truth was, he had no idea, and this whole plan hinged on a lot of guesses all being right. There were a million points for it to all go wrong, but thinking about that wasn't doing him any good.

He went back to packing. He needed to figure out how to keep his phone charged out on the trail. He didn't know how anyone did that—solar, maybe? He swiped open his phone, sure that Google had the answer.

A pounding at the front door interrupted his search. Chicken went crazy barking. Gabe figured his dad would answer it, until he remembered he'd gone to the store to get eggs for Grimace. That cat was never going to want to leave now that he was getting spoiled by Gabe's dad and having the time of his life terrorizing poor Chicken with his zoomies. At least his dad seemed a little more cheerful.

The pounding continued. Gabe looked out his window, expecting to see one of his friends' cars, or even Merilee's, but he didn't see either. He bounded down the stairs two at a time as the knocking got louder, threatening to break in the door. Gabe pulled it open and found Messina's stepdad with a dark look hanging off his face like a five-o'clock shadow. Chicken pushed his nose through the door, panting and slobbering, trying to smell him. He'd never been a very discerning dog. Gabe tugged him back by his collar.

"I'm looking for my daughter."

It hadn't occurred to Gabe that Messina might have gone with Lottie—he should have put it together when he saw the minivan she'd taken to the party parked at the end of his street last night instead of in front of her house—but he suddenly knew that was what happened. It was a realization he kept to himself for the moment.

He looked at Messina's stepdad, the guy she called "Jeffucker," and quietly assessed the risks of the situation. The sweat along the man's brow, reddened knuckles along his fist from where he'd banged on the door. Eyes that were filled with anger, not worry.

"I don't know where she is," Gabe said. He'd never been great at lying—that was Lottie's talent.

Jeffucker looked at Gabe like he knew he was full of shit, but it didn't change anything. Gabe lifted his chin.

"She's underage, you know."

Gabe didn't know what he meant by that. *Underage for what?*

"Like I said, I haven't seen her." A police cruiser rolled down the street. They both watched it.

"I called them in," Jeffucker said. "If you know anything, you're going to be in it just as deep as she is. She stole my van. That's a felony."

"You mean that one?" Gabe pointed down toward the end of the street where the burgundy minivan was parked.

Jeffucker narrowed his eyes at it and stalked off toward the van without another word. Gabe shut the door. He was glad Messina was with Lottie—at least it kept her out of range of her stepdad's rage for the moment. And maybe she could keep Lottie from doing anything crazy.

26

LOTTIE

The asshole sun woke her again. She rubbed her eyes, sure she'd only just closed them. Her clothes were sweat-soaked and reeking, the heat of the sun already at full force. The sound of unzipping came from higher up the trail. She cracked an eye and saw Messina's head pop out of her deflated weather balloon, wet hair stuck all over her face.

The world looked different in the daylight. Bigger. And worse. Everything about it was harsh and unwelcoming—brown mountains so dry they looked ready to crack open, spindly low brush that rolled out like barbed wire in every direction. It looked back at Lottie asking, *Are you sure about this?*

Fuck off, she thought back.

Then she saw the food wrappers, shredded and gnawed-on and strewn all over the place.

"Shit." She reached behind her and checked her pack. It was wide open, half its contents dragged from its mouth. "Motherfuckers stole my food." It felt so personal, like the time someone graffitied dicks all over her locker.

She jumped up and nearly fell over from the tightness of her body, like her muscles and joints had all been superglued while she slept. She tried again, moving more slowly this time. Wrappers were everywhere—candy bars, ramen, chips—all of it was gone or shredded and chewed beyond saving. Whatever animals had gotten into her pack had taken nearly everything. The only thing left was a box of beef sticks that was probably too heavy for them.

How could she have been so stupid, falling asleep with her pack open? She cursed to herself as she picked up the pieces of wrappers, while the ghost of Val in her mind screamed at her about leaving no trace of trash or anything else behind. Her eyes burned with the threat of tears. She was already ruining things again. Shame and hate and every stupid feeling she'd ever felt bloomed in her gut like a giant mushroom cloud, toxic to everything it touched. Her mind zoomed out, watching herself dissolve in a black cloud of self-loathing. Some part of her was glad, feeling like it was what she deserved.

"I'll help," Messina said. "I just need to pee."

She let out the world's longest pee in the scrub—Lottie didn't even know a body could hold on to that much fluid—and helped her pick up the remaining shreds of wrappers, bending to catch bits of plastic before they blew off in the breeze. "We've still got my food at least. We can get more whenever we cross into the next town."

Lottie wasn't sure which of them she was trying to comfort. No one had just eaten fifty dollars of *her* money. Between the food and the phone, Lottie was starting to feel her losses carved right through her center. Of course they didn't get Messina's food. Her bag had been tucked safely in the tent, probably closed and cinched, unlike Lottie's that was left wide open all night like a fucking wildlife 7-Eleven. Messina made a sighing sound as she bent down to grab another wrapper. The parentheses were everywhere. They hung from the sky like giant streamers marking Lottie's idiocy.

She shoved the wrappers back into her pack while Messina dribbled water onto her hands and rubbed them over and over against her pants. Lottie knew she was trying to get off whatever animal germs might have been on the wrappers. She supposed she should have been glad that whatever got her food had been small, instead of a bear. She'd never seen one, but they were around. They'd occasionally get into someone's yard or pool and end up on the news.

The two of them ate dried fruit from Messina's supply in silence. Lottie ached for her phone, for the distraction of strangers talking in her feed. For something to make her laugh or smile or make her feel less like she'd just fucked everything up again.

She was in a rotten mood. The sun hammered at her skin. There were no trees here, just low scrub for as far as she could see. "Did you get any sunscreen?"

Messina shook her head. She opened her mouth to say something, then closed it again.

"What?" Lottie shot.

She shook her head again. Closed her eyes. Ground her teeth. It was Charades from hell.

"Oh my god, just fucking say it."

Her eyes flicked up to Lottie. Parentheses shot out of them like little moons. "It was on your half of the list. Back in the shed."

"No it wasn't."

"Yes, it was."

Lottie dropped her handful of cranberries back into the bag. She wasn't hungry anymore.

She dug through her pack for fresh clothes, pulled off her shirt and shorts, and scrubbed her skin with water she dumped into her hands. She'd been smelling her own stink all morning.

"You shouldn't waste it," Messina said. Her eyes were darting all over the place, trying not to look at Lottie's body. Nakedness made her uncomfortable.

Lottie took off her bra. "You used it for your hands. It's the same thing."

"I only used a little! You've already wasted half a bottle."

Lottie dumped more into her hands just to get a rise out of Messina. They had plenty of water. And that stupid map was littered with blue lines. Lottie stripped off her underwear.

"Dude!" Messina yelled, covering her eyes and turning around like she might be blinded by Lottie's skin. "Will you please stop? Half our food's already gone—if we run out of water we're going to fucking die out here."

Lottie dumped more onto her body than was necessary, out of spite. "We've got like eight hundred bottles, and we just crossed through a town. Do you want to turn around and re-up?" She put the bottle down on a rock and scrubbed her armpits again, wishing she had some soap to help kill the smell.

"No! I want to go forward and not run out of water." Messina pushed her hands through her hair like she wanted to pull it clean off her head. "And I want you to cover yourself up." The strain in her voice almost made Lottie feel guilty, but not quite.

"This bullshit is why we aren't friends anymore," Lottie said.

"Because you can't keep your clothes on?"

When she reached for the bottle again its mouth was on the ground, tipped, the entire liter completely emptied. The ground was already swallowing the shallow puddle it made.

"No," Lottie said, all the vengefulness gone from her voice now, replaced with shame. "Because you always treat me like I'm a fuckup who's going to ruin everything." A voice inside her said, *That's what you are.*

Messina didn't refute it. She kept her back turned until Lottie said, "I'm dressed."

Lottie silently wished she could abandon Messina and hike the rest of the way on her own, just so she wouldn't have to endure Messina's disappointment. But Val's ashes kept them glued together. Just like the living Val had done before.

27

LOTTIE

The world was stripped of everything but sun and heat and the weight of her pack. Even the anger she'd felt at Messina from the morning had mostly burned off in the heat of the day. The only thing left was her anger at herself. And her thirst. It was impossible to keep it in check. She'd never sweat so much—it ran down her arms and back and between her legs. The sun burned her skin everywhere it touched.

Lottie kept thinking about the stupid **LU'S ARTISAN ICE CREAM** caps Lu had made for the employees that Lottie refused to wear. She would have given a month's pay for one now. The eyes of Val's ghost watched her, staring through the metal urn and the fabric of Messina's backpack, relentless, condemning. They burned her skin just like the sun.

They'd passed under a clump of squatty oaks this morning, but since then, they'd been walking through nothing but rock and scrub and dying yucca. And a weird cactus that grew in phallic shapes. *Dick cactus*, Lottie called it in her mind.

She tried to keep her eyes on the trail—the landscape was too cluttered with pieces of Val. A yucca bloom decayed just ahead of her. *Chaparral yucca,* Val's memory said. Lottie pushed back against it, but it came anyway, along with Val's smiling face. *You know, it only blooms once, and then it dies.*

They were everywhere now, the dead yucca. They were probably beautiful just a few weeks ago, giant white blooms on towering stalks lighting up the mountainside like torches. Now they looked like something from a nightmare, dead and skeletal, with dried, ruptured seed pods hanging from their branches like hungry mouths. The ground was littered with their remains. Lottie swore they kept passing the same one, with a pinkened stalk leaning to the left.

She stopped mid-stride. Messina slammed into her back.

"Dude. Give me a warning before you just stop."

"We keep passing the same yucca."

"L, we're in the *land* of yuccas. It's the Where's fucking Waldo of yuccas out here. There's no way we're passing the same one." She reached back to grab her water and took the tiniest sip. It made Lottie's mouth go dry just watching her. "Remember last year when you ate gummies and swore we kept passing the same tree and that we were stuck on an invisible treadmill?"

"Yes, but I'm not high now," Lottie snapped.

"I'm just saying, I was right then, and I'm right now. We're not going in circles." She eyed Lottie. "You look thirsty." She pulled the bottle from the side pocket of Lottie's pack and handed it to her. "Drink. Dehydration is just as bad for your brain function as being high."

Lottie shook her head. "I'm good."

Truth: She was not. She was terrible and dying of thirst and becoming the raisin-y version of herself, but she'd already drunk so much water today and wasted even more this morning, and she was beginning to worry that she might have miscalculated how far away all those crisscross-y blue lines on the map were. Her own words came back to her. *Everything within a hundred-mile radius of us is a tiny black dot.* The blue lines could've been hundreds of miles away.

They resumed their march. The incline they'd been struggling up flipped and became a descent. "See, we're going down now," Messina said. "Definitely not going in a circle."

They came up on a lone manzanita tree. Memories of Val echoed inside Lottie. *You can always tell manzanitas by their smooth, red bark. Fun fact: Their berries are edible!* Lottie didn't feel like testing that—she'd fucked up enough for one day.

The tree was short and gnarled, like it had struggled against nature just to exist. They stopped and sat beneath it, hunched in its shade. Lottie guzzled water despite her efforts not to. Her thirst was too strong. Messina passed her a bag of nuts and a protein bar. Lottie offered Messina a beef stick, knowing she wouldn't take it, but she was trying to be nice all the same.

Messina shook her head. "I bet the racoons didn't take those because they don't smell like actual food."

Lottie peeled hers open and devoured it, licking the salt and grease from the wrapper. She tossed back a handful of nuts that tasted so bad she nearly spit them out on the ground. "Ew, why did you get the unsalted kind?"

"Accident. At least they won't be hard to ration—they're disgusting like this."

They were. It was worse because she didn't have any spit to wash them down. "How far do you think we've gone?"

"I don't know," Messina said. "I feel like time and distance have lost all meaning. It's like we're in a weird dimension where neither of them exists."

"Have we passed a marker today?"

"The last one I remember is the one after the town last night."

"That was like," Lottie looked up at the sun, attempting to gauge what time it was—it burned her eyes, but she did it anyway—"fifty quarcels ago." Green-blue spots erupted all over her vision now. She blinked, but they hung stubbornly in place.

"Is that distance or time?"

"Both."

Messina shook her head, like this was wrong. "You've got to include all the height we've gained too. We've definitely gone about ten thousand by now."

Lottie laughed. It wasn't that funny, but she kept on laughing, like it was the funniest thing ever, until it spread to Messina and the laughter morphed into something crazed and hysterical, born from exhaustion or sun-sickness or the absurdity of what they were doing. They both shook with it, eyes watering.

"I can't believe Val wanted to do this," Messina said, laugh-tears streaming down her cheeks. "Why the fuck would anyone want to do this?"

"I know, it's like voluntary torture!" Her words sent them both rolling again.

When the moment passed, it left a strange emptiness, like a dropped call in the middle of a conversation. Lottie wiped her cheeks with the back of her hand. "Maybe that's the point, right? This was the part of her that didn't make sense to us. Maybe we're supposed to let her show us."

Messina took a loud swallow of water, her eyes on Lottie. "Careful, you're starting to sound woo-woo."

Lottie stared at Messina's pack where the lump of Val's urn sat. Maybe she *was* sounding woo-woo. But if she was going to fix things, she had to believe it wasn't just her guilt that brought her here. She had to believe that Val wanted them to come.

28

GABE

He was outside a town called Lake Hughes on a road called Lake Hughes. But he hadn't seen a lake or any other signs of water. The light of day was almost gone now, but he could still make out stretches of endless foothills and mountains that his sister would have known the names of. She would have known their histories and compositions. *These places have so many stories to tell. How can you stand not knowing them all?* It wasn't that he didn't want to know—his brain just didn't have the capacity to absorb it all at the rate hers did.

His navigation told him he'd arrived at the spot he'd chosen to wait for Lottie and Messina. The trail cut directly across this road. He pulled his truck off next to a wooden sign announcing the fire restrictions. **EXTREME FIRE DANGER. NO CAMPFIRES. NO CHARCOAL FIRES. PORTABLE STOVES IN DESIGNATED CAMPGROUNDS ONLY.** A few feet away from the sign, his headlights lit up a post with a white rounded triangle on the top. **PACIFIC CREST TRAIL.** It was pocked with holes, like someone had used it for target practice. It gave him a bad feeling he couldn't quite name.

He took out his phone and tried to call Lottie again. No bars.

He'd tried both her and Messina at least a hundred times already. Always straight to voicemail.

He cut his truck's engine and got out to take a closer look at the Swiss-cheesed marker, like it might be able to tell him who did this to it and when. He shined his phone light over the holes. Rust had collected around their edges. At least they weren't recent. He googled "hunting season PCT" and stared at the blank screen until his brain caught up and realized nothing was going to pop up without service. *Right.*

He climbed back into his truck. He had a tent in his pack, but being out there on the ground didn't look much more inviting than the cab of his truck. He opened his windows to let in the chilly night air and unwrapped the drive-thru chicken sandwich he'd bought.

He chewed his food, trying to ignore the gnawing feeling that this was the wrong spot to wait in. No, he'd been over his options a thousand times yesterday. This was his best bet.

His phone dinged, pulling him from his thoughts. It had found a single bar of service in his passenger seat that disappeared the second he picked it up. A message from his dad hung on the screen: *Did you get there safe?* Gabe had told him he was going on a camping trip in Cambria with Marcus and his family. He didn't want him to worry or to know about Val's plans. He didn't think his dad's heart could stand it. He would have hated that Val kept it all secret from him, but he never would have let her go if she'd told him. Too much risk.

Gabe had spent half of yesterday getting a replacement urn in case his dad finally decided to go into Val's room. He still couldn't believe Lottie had actually stolen it. It stung a part of him that was still tender from the other night. Gabe didn't need to be Lottie's boyfriend, but she could have at least had the decency to include him in her plans to hijack Val's ashes and come out into the middle of nowhere with them.

Lottie's hair band still sat limply at the base of his gearshift, strands of her hair sticking out from it in different directions. He pulled it off the shifter because he didn't want it there. He didn't know what to do with it once it was in his hand. There wasn't a trash can, and he didn't want to litter, but he didn't want to see it anymore. He wadded it up in the wrapper of his chicken sandwich. It was only marginally better, not having to look at it, because he still knew it was there, plaguing him, just like the real Lottie.

29

LOTTIE

The asshole sun was going kill them. Lottie wasn't worried about running out of water anymore—they were going to cook to death long before that. She'd hoped yesterday's sunburn would improve while she slept. It hadn't. She stuck her arms into her T-shirt the way she used to as a kid when she was cold, leaving the sleeves empty and dangling. Everything that wasn't covered was sizzling.

Messina was in front wearing Lottie's sweatshirt, hood pulled up against the sun. And the shorts Lottie had on the day Tristan gave her a ride home. She hadn't realized they were in the clothes she'd given Messina to try on—she should've burned them. The memory of that day flew at her.

They'd hit gridlock on the 101. Tristan exhaled cinnamon smoke out the window. A slow smile slid across his mouth. Another dare. His hand slid between her legs. Slid down her zipper. Her body answered *yes.* A sharp thrill rose in her at the unknowing faces in cars next to them.

His voice whispered in her ear, "Do you like that?"

Her mouth answered *yes.*

Lottie slammed into Messina. They both stumbled forward. "Jesus-fuck-sorry." Lottie stared at the ground, terrified Messina could see the memory all over her face. "I didn't know you stopped."

"I said 'fork' twice." She pointed ahead to the unmarked split in the trail. "Did you go zombie again?"

Lottie didn't love this name for it. She'd heard Messina use the same term for her mom, but Lottie was nothing like that. Messina's mom was empty and vacant, like someone had scooped out her insides and replaced them with those beans they put in stuffies to give them an upright posture. She ignored the question, looking at the split in the trail. It wasn't marked. Dick cactus still littered the ground around them, covered now in bright orange strings so dense they netted together. Lottie remembered it was some kind of plant.

Dodder. Her mind coughed up the word in Val's voice. It coughed up other things too, but Lottie shoved them back down before she could hear them.

Messina had the look again, impatient, like she'd said something that Lottie hadn't heard. "Which way should we go?"

"Flip a coin?" Lottie said, but her lips were so dry they stuck together, and the words came out like *flikaoin*?

"No." Messina wiped the sweat from her forehead. "There's only one right way. If we choose wrong, we could be wandering around in the desert for a week."

"We're already wandering in the desert. We should just pick—it's got to lead somewhere. If we go the wrong way, we'll make our way back."

"How can you be so casual about it?"

Lottie shrugged. "What other choice do we have?"

"We can ask the book."

Lottie didn't want anything to do with that book right now. She was terrified they'd open it and see *Lottie fucked around with Tristan and drove me to my death* penned out in Val's manic writing.

"No," she said, trying to keep her thoughts off her face. "Don't you think Val brought us out here to learn to rely on ourselves?" The words felt acidic on her tongue, a lie made out of her own self-interest. "You should choose. You'll take us the right way."

Messina looked uncertain.

"Val was always telling you to trust your instincts more," Lottie said. This was the truth now, even though she wasn't saying it for the right reasons. Messina really did need to stop overthinking the hell out of everything and trust herself. But Lottie didn't think it mattered that it was the truth. Having something good come from it didn't make it less of a shitty thing to do.

Messina reached behind her, touching her pack, and Lottie knew she was feeling Val's urn beneath the material there. "I think we're supposed to go left," Messina said. "It looks like there's less of that creepy orange stuff this way."

"Dodder," Lottie said without thinking.

"Looks like silly string from hell." Messina took a drink from her water bottle, dumping just a little into her hand to rub over her face. "We're still good on water, right?"

Lottie nodded. She bent down and let her fingers scrape against the dodder, tangling in the net of tentacles. It felt synthetic—plasticky—like finely wound fishing wire or Barbie hair.

It's a parasite, Val's ghost whispered. *It survives by draining the life from those around it.*

Lottie knew she wasn't just talking about the dodder.

30

MESSINA

She thought hiking together would feel more . . . together. They walked in silence. Being with Lottie was worse than being alone. When Messina was alone, she could focus on herself. But Lottie was a giant vacuum, sucking up mental space. Even now, Messina couldn't not look at her, her arms tucked into her shirt to keep them from the sun, an extra T-shirt in a giant turban-style knot on top of her head, her red, sunburnt face making her look like a human flare. It put Messina on edge. They hadn't run into anyone, but she was sure it would only take one glance at Lottie to know that the two of them shouldn't be out here.

Messina adjusted her hood, trying to keep the sun off her face. Trying to hide. They started up a set of switchbacks—sections of trail that folded up the mountainside to make the steepest parts passable. Messina had learned that word from Val's book. She wished she hadn't given it to Lottie—she never looked at it or read it. It just stayed buried in her pack. It was like having Val taken from her again. Last night, Messina stole it from Lottie's backpack, just for a few minutes, to read Val's words.

She kept trying to appreciate all this the way Val would've

wanted her to, but she was afraid of too much here. The elements, the animals, afraid Lottie was going to do something crazy and get them killed. Afraid Jeffucker was going to find her. She looked back, scared that thinking of him might have accidentally conjured him. He wasn't there, but half the world was spread out before her. She never knew you could see so much of it at once. The trail they were on clung to the side of a mountain, layers of foothills overlapping one another spilling out below them for ages. In the distance, more mountains.

She heard Val's voice whisper that wherever Jeffucker was, he would have seemed small from this distance. She whispered that Messina was the big one now.

But her feet throbbed, ruining it, stealing her back to the present. She hated her boots and how they tore at her feet. Her skin hurt everywhere, not just from her stupid boots, but from the sun and the way her pack rubbed against her shoulders. And from the loneliness. Her skin held so many memories of Val. She didn't know it would grieve along with the rest of her. It made sense that her mind and heart did, but it caught her off-guard, the way she ached for Val's touch—not in a sexual way, just in a human one. Val communicated love through touch in a way Messina hadn't known since she was small, and even then, back when Messina's mom was still Mom, her hugs somehow took more than they gave. With Val, it wasn't like that at all.

Hugging Val was like standing under a waterfall. Sometimes Messina didn't want to let go—she just wanted to stay like that forever, drinking in Val's warmth. The hugs and hand-holding and knocking shoulders, the softness of her fingertips when she'd brush a stray eyelash away. Messina missed it with a deeper sadness than she'd known possible. Without Val, her life was completely devoid of touch—of the good kind, anyway.

She closed her eyes and rubbed her hand along her own arm now, trying to imagine it was Val's. She tripped on a rock and hit the ground.

Dirt and pebbles jammed into her palms and knees, her skin weeping red. She stood and dusted herself off. She let herself admit that she hated it out here. She couldn't understand why Val had loved it so much, why she would come here seeking comfort. Nature was the opposite of comfort. It was awful. Indifferent and unforgiving. To Messina, it was just like having another mom that didn't care enough to protect her or see her or comfort her. Nature was just another mombie.

A hot wind blew over her, like from an oven or hell, or maybe from Nature who didn't appreciate being thought of as a mombie. Messina whispered an apology to Nature and undid the mombie thought, whipping her hand through the air. *Undo.* They'd wound their way to the back side of the mountain now. A sprawl of flat, hot desert stretched out below them, looking harsher and more frightening than the kind of soft, brush-filled desert they were in now, like a reverse-mirage of dirt and sand instead of water. Was that where they were going? Messina hoped not.

31

LOTTIE

Memories exploded like landmines. Lottie rubbed against a plant jutting into the path and was catapulted by its scent to Val's couch, sick with a cold and fever, a steaming cup of tea being pressed into her hands. *Here, drink this. It's sagebrush tea. It'll help your throat. I made it myself.*

Everything here was tied to Val—the plants, the smells, even the bugs. Val nearly broke her ankle last year trying to avoid stepping on a fig beetle. *I'm a guest in his home. I wouldn't want someone to come into my home and step on me.*

A whitish succulent caught in Lottie's peripheral vision.

See that plant? Chalk dudleya—it grows straight out of the rocks. Don't you love how something so beautiful and strong could come out of such a hostile environment? Fun fact: It reminds me of you.

Those were the worst ones, the memories filled with Val's love. They gutted Lottie, leaving bits of her insides scattered along the trail. She tried to ignore it. She focused on the sound of her shoes, on the ceaseless rhythm of hiking.

Everything here was a rhythm. Her footfalls against the dirt.

The breath in her lungs. When they'd climb a steep ascent, it was her own heartbeat in her ears—*ga-gung, ga-gung, ga-gung.*

She was pretty sure it was their fourth day on the trail, though she was beginning to lose track. Here were the things she was sure of: They were critically low on water, they'd lost half their food, and they were on the edge of burning alive.

She was hallucinating from one of those things—either thirst or hunger or sun exposure. Or maybe all three of them. Creatures, little things that were dark and furry, kept catching in the edge of her vision, but when she turned her head there was nothing but brush and dirt. She rubbed at her dry eyes with dirt-covered fingers.

In her peripheral vision, she saw a fox scurry past.

Water always finds the lowest point.

Lottie's heart pounded with Val's words as the trail descended toward a shaded area. There were trees. *Trees know where the water is. Find the trees, you'll find the water.*

Lottie's knees ached. They'd become so used to climbing, they protested at the change in motion as she plodded down toward the tree line. The relief of the shade fell over her, but she didn't stop.

"Dude, slow down," Messina said, but Lottie kept on in search of the bottom. Finally, she came to it. A wooden bridge. It crossed over a dry, sandy ditch. There was nothing, not even mud. Only cracked, dead earth.

Lottie let her body sink down into the dust. Messina was thrilled at the cover of the trees—they stayed there for a quarcel,

Messina basking in the relief of it. But Lottie couldn't bask. She'd already fucked up this entire journey—she couldn't even do penance right.

The truth of it whispered to the rhythm of her steps as they hiked on. *Fuck-up-your-fault-fuck-up-your-fault-fuck-up-your-fault.*

32

GABE

He couldn't think about Val without thinking about Lottie. All his memories of his sister were twisted up with her, like they shared the same blood supply. Memories of Val turned to memories of Val and Lottie that turned to memories of the way he'd lie awake in his room whenever Lottie would stay over. How he'd wait, listening for that quiet creak of Val's door opening in the middle of the night. He'd go down to the kitchen, pretending he needed a glass of water, trying to time his steps just right so he could run into Lottie outside the bathroom.

"Are you going to sleep?" he'd say.

She'd shake her head and smile. Sometimes he could tell she was looking for him too.

They'd sit shoulder to shoulder in the hall on the threadbare rug, talking in whispers for hours while the rest of the house was asleep. Sometimes Gabe swore Val only slept on the nights when Lottie was there, like her presence brought her some kind of peace that Val couldn't find otherwise.

It was special, this secret time that was just theirs. Gabe never cared that he was exhausted and useless the next day. It was always worth it. He never felt so much like himself as he did on those nights with Lottie, doing nothing but sitting on the carpet.

A pair of coyotes popped out of the brush just past his windshield and trotted down the road ahead of him, bringing him back to the present and the baking interior of his truck. They were thin and scraggly, like they hadn't eaten enough. Droughts really screwed up wildlife—less food, less water, less cover. Animals started acting weird. The only times he'd heard of people getting attacked by wildlife, it was during droughts.

He let out a noisy sigh. He'd been here two days. He thought for sure Lottie and Messina would have passed this point by now.

He didn't know what to do. Moving was risky. Not moving was risky. There were too many possibilities. He'd picked this spot based on them choosing the most logical point of entry, but that might have been a horrible decision. Since when did Lottie and Messina adhere to any kind of logic?

His thoughts ping-ponged around in his head. He had no idea where they were on this hell-trail.

What does your gut tell you? That's what Val would have said. She was always talking about listening to your instincts. *Your gut is connected to nature. It knows what your mind doesn't. Listen to it.* But that wasn't something Gabe knew how to do. He knew how to think with his head, calculate risk. That was about it.

Out his window, a pair of hikers approached—two women, heavy packs on their shoulders. His heart skipped a beat in the second it took his mind to process their outlines, the way their shapes weren't those of either Lottie or Messina. But still, he was glad to run into them—he could ask them if they'd seen his friends. If not, he'd go farther up.

He opened his door. The women locked eyes with him and stopped dead in their tracks. He froze as well, startled by their response. The risk of him was being assessed. Gabe waved, trying to convey friendliness, but they were already turning around, going back up the trail in the other direction. *Assessment: High risk.*

"Hey, I'm okay," he called across the stretch of road, but they'd already gone. He was probably just making it worse. He hated the way they'd looked at him, like he was a threat. Not that he could blame them, he thought, looking back at his beat-up truck out here in the middle of nowhere, seeing through different eyes. It was completely blocking the trailhead. It made sense when he'd done it—he didn't want to miss Lottie and Messina. But those hikers couldn't have passed him without interacting. If he'd been a woman coming up on something like that, he would have turned around too.

He felt even worse when he realized he was shirtless, shiny with sweat—he'd stripped off his T-shirt when the day got hot. He shook his head at his own stupidity—he didn't just look like a threat, he looked like a predator.

He felt like he should go. He doubted there was another way around, and he was certain those hikers were around the bend, waiting for him to leave so they could cross. He could hear his instincts loud and clear now—or maybe that was stupidity and regret—saying *go.* Saying to look for Lottie and Messina farther up the trail.

He started his truck's engine and drove north.

33

MESSINA

"Where the hell's the lake?" Lottie said, looking at Messina like she might actually have the answer. Like she was Val. "Why would someone name a road Lake Hughes Road if there's not a big-ass lake on the other side of it?"

"Maybe it's down the road a ways," Messina said.

Lottie squinted her eyes like she was trying to see it, ready to march off in search of the mystery lake. But that wasn't going to happen. Roads were dangerous. They needed to get the hell away from here as quickly as possible.

"We should find it."

"L, we don't even know which way. We could walk miles in the wrong direction looking for it. And that's if it even exists. Maybe this road was named by an asshole who liked to confuse people. Or maybe the lake existed fifty years ago and has dried up now. We can't go looking for it." Lottie looked ready to argue, but Messina spoke again before she could. "We need to get away from here. It's giving me a bad feeling."

Lottie's face dropped, and Messina knew she understood her meaning. "Right. Okay," she said, and they moved on, crossing the road. The PCT marker they passed looked like it was shot full of holes. It made Messina even more anxious to get far away from this place.

Lottie was sullen the rest of the day. She was being dramatic, but Messina understood her disappointment. She couldn't stop thinking about the lake either. Jumping in, soaking her feet—they were killing her. As soon as she acknowledged the pain, she couldn't stop thinking about it.

Feet weren't supposed to feel like this. Like someone was peeling her skin off a piece at a time. Like they were being crucified. She wondered if this was how Jesus felt, but the thought felt blasphemous.terrible.punishable so she undid it with a motion of her hand, flicking the air to get it far away from her mind. But then she reminded herself that she didn't have to do that if she didn't believe in God or Jesus or any of them, so she redid it again and undid it again and again and again because being scared of God's punishment was almost worse than the pain in her feet, which was worse than everything in the world.

She stopped. "I can't go any farther."

Lottie kept walking, like she didn't hear her. Messina wondered if she was zombified again. She'd been doing that more since they came out here. "HEY!" Messina yelled—or maybe screamed—at her, which wasn't nice, but being alone here was terrifying. She needed Lottie to stay with her.

"I can't go any farther," Messina repeated to the living version of Lottie. "My feet are done."

Living Lottie squinted at the horizon. "Sun's sinking anyway."

The landscape had shifted strangely to trees now, some standing, others lying dead. The air was cooling too. She was glad they hadn't descended into the scarier-looking desert she'd glimpsed earlier.

They set up the tent on an almost-flat spot. Inside, Messina unlaced her shoes and peeled back her wet socks as gingerly as possible. Mountains of blisters covered her skin. Some had ruptured, leaving raw, pink patches with nothing but little flaps to protect them. Lottie de-shoed as well. She had a few pinkened bumps, barely even in the blister category.

"Why don't your feet look like mine?" Of course Lottie's didn't look like hers. Hiking was just another one of those things—like talking or flirting—that came easily to her. At least Lottie's sunburn was worse, she thought, and instantly felt terrible for it. She flicked the air.

"Maybe it's your boots." Lottie unclasped the safety pin that was acting as a button from the top of her shorts and held it out to Messina. "They'll feel better if you pop them."

Messina shook her head. Her eyes zoomed in on Lottie's dirty fingers holding the pin, the gunk beneath her nails that held unimaginable things like bits of her skin or even boy skin or below-the-waist things, and the pin that had rubbed against Lottie's sweaty body all day and she couldn't look at it anymore.

"I'm good," she said.

"They're going to burst and get infected if you don't drain them."

The world spun. She'd been getting dizzy spells all day, probably from the heat, or maybe because her feet were already getting infected and the bacteria was in her blood eating her from the inside out.

She needed to clean them. She stuck both feet outside the tent and poured the remaining water in her bottle over them. Just the touch of the liquid, hot from the day's sun, stung the blisters like fire, opening the little flaps that covered the ones that had burst. They were still nowhere near clean. The water had only cut a few flesh-colored streaks through the dirt.

"It hurts just to pour water on them. I'm not going to be able to stick that dull-ass pin into them."

Lottie sighed and held the pin over the flame of a lighter. "Lie back. Close your eyes."

"No."

"Are you going to do it then?"

"I can't!" Panic was rising from Messina's chest, pitching her voice up. She hated how scared she was, how small it made her feel. She wanted an option C, where she could just leave the blisters alone and let them heal. But that didn't exist.

"So, your plan is to leave them to get infected?"

"I don't have a plan. I just don't want you to touch me with that." She pointed at Lottie's hand and the pin it held. One was just as likely to injure her as the other.

"Why don't you trust me?"

There were a million reasons. Messina didn't answer right away. She hated confrontation—it was easier to pretend things were fine and move on—but she was more afraid of doing nothing and becoming frozen like her mom.zombie.mombie than she was of fighting with Lottie.

"You left me at the party," she said, surprised to hear the words come out of her, surprised to hear that they sounded so angry. She knew Lottie was surprised too. She could see it, the way her face dropped the moment the words landed against her ears.

"You said it was fine."

"You said you were going to get beer."

"So, you're going to fuck up your feet for that? To prove that I'm an asshole? Because I think that fact's been well established."

"I'm not trying to prove anything. You asked me why I don't trust you. I answered."

Lottie closed the safety pin and tossed it at Messina. "Fine. Pop them yourself."

34

LOTTIE

The cold and the bugs bit at her in equal measure. She sat alone outside the tent, barefoot in the dirt, her skin still stinging from the day's sun. A billion stars blinked at her, beautiful, like someone had thrown glitter over the sky. She hated that she was outside again, but there was no way to un-storm out, so she and her pride were banished until Messina fell asleep.

The tent had felt like a refuge after being exposed to the elements all day. She thought the night air might be refreshing, but being cold sucked nearly as much as being hot. She hadn't even eaten any dinner. She had one of Messina's protein bars in her pocket, but she couldn't stomach another one.

She shivered, wishing she'd thought to at least grab her jacket. All she had was the fresh water bottle she'd taken out to rinse Messina's blisters. It was their last full bottle. She knew it wasn't going to last them long. It was warm between her hands. She imagined herself shrinking and diving into its mouth and swimming around in it and gulping and gulping and gulping.

Thirst was messing with her head.

Truth: She was afraid they were going to run out of water. She wondered how close they'd been to that lake today. If there had even been a lake.

She tried not to think about it. If she caved and downed the bottle, she wouldn't be able to undo it. That was the messed-up thing about life, that rash decisions came with permanent consequences. Like existence was one giant test to gauge her impulse control, and spoiler—she didn't have any. That was why she was outside. It was why she'd fucked over Gabe. And Messina . . . and Val. She needed an Undo button. Her brain never seemed to understand the consequences of things until they'd already been cemented into reality.

Other truth: Even if they found water, she was afraid they might not get through this.

She cracked the lid on the bottle and drew the smallest sip into her mouth. It was hot and wet and the best thing she'd ever tasted, soaking into every cell of her body, giving her life. She twisted the cap back hard and set it down before her instincts could kick in and have her guzzling the rest of it.

Some kind of biological signal sprang to life at the taste of the water, and she suddenly had to pee like she'd been holding a gallon in her bladder all day. Now that she thought of it, she couldn't remember the last time she'd peed.

She took as many steps into the brush in her bare feet as she dared, which was five. She squatted in that way that women have to when peeing outdoors—deeply, so it didn't run down her legs, but not so deep she'd get a branch of chaparral in her ass, trying her best to face the downhill slope so it wouldn't run back over her bare feet, tugging the crotch of her shorts absurdly far from her body so any spray wouldn't get them, all while keeping a lookout for things that might slither or crawl too near and attack her while she was exposed. The universe had played a fucked-up joke on women when it formed their bodies.

She regretted not having the foresight to bring toilet paper. Truth: She regretted not having the foresight for anything.

Something rustled in the brush ahead of her. She bolted up, hiking up her shorts before the stream had completely ended. *Great.* She squinted into the darkness. Nothing. She exhaled a foggy breath into the night air and cursed the dampness between her legs. She made her way back toward the tent, dirt and sharp things sticking into the tender skin between her toes. She wished now that she'd at least stuck her feet into her shoes before she'd stormed out of the tent. Damn lack of foresight.

Exhaustion fuzzed her mind as it crept higher and higher—it wouldn't be long before it swallowed her whole. Messina had to be passed out by now. Lottie grabbed hold of the tent zipper and heard the rustling again. She looked and saw a dog—coyote—fox—*something*—staring her down. It stood just feet from her. She stared back, half-convinced it was another dehydration-exhaustion-induced hallucination, only this one was in front of her, instead of haunting the edges of her vision.

Neither of them moved.

The creature blinked like it recognized her. She recognized it too.

It was Val.

35

MESSINA

Everything was wet when she woke, just like every morning in the tent. The same condensation dripping down the tent walls, the same rank smell. But this morning was different. She'd woken unafraid, not thinking about where Jeffucker was or what he was capable of. It was a feeling she hadn't thought possible.

Lottie was still in a heap beside her—she must've snuck back in after Messina fell asleep. Messina had taken *Wild* from Lottie's pack again after she'd stormed out of the tent. She'd found it buried in the bottom with a fresh crease in its cover.

She'd flipped through its pages by flashlight, scanning Val's cryptic messages—notes about plants and rocks and other bits that seemed nonsensical to her—until she found a page where Val had written *STRENGTH* in all caps along the top margin. A thin blue line trailed down from the word to a single line of circled text from the book: *That I could bear the unbearable.*

She'd stared at the words, knowing Val had marked them for her, reminding her of her own strength. Messina had spent so much of her life feeling small and weak. But that was the opposite of the truth. The truth was in everything she'd been through and the fact that she was still here despite all of it. She locked the message deep inside her and kept it there, a secret she shared with Val.

The book was still tucked beside her in her sleeping bag. She slipped it out and stuck it back into Lottie's pack. Lottie moaned, stretching her legs so they pressed against Messina's. She inched back to give Lottie more room. Lottie always needed more.

Messina didn't know where they stood now. Sleep had cooled most of her anger at Lottie. What was left felt like the heat in the toaster after the bread pops, still there, but not hot enough to do much damage. She wondered if Lottie would feel the same way.

Lottie sat up and wiped her damp face with her arm and immediately let out a groan of pain—her skin was peeling horribly now. She unzipped the flap on the tent, letting in the morning sun.

"Fuck you, sun!" she shouted.

Messina followed her as she crawled out of the tent, but when Lottie stood up to stretch, Messina stayed down. She'd hoped the night would heal her blisters. It hadn't. They were just as gnarly and painful as yesterday.

She planted her butt in the dirt, keeping her feet lifted, and wiped at the sweat and tent-water dripping from between her legs. Her hand came away smeared in blood. The crotch of her shorts was soaked with it. "Shit."

Lottie turned. "Shit," she echoed. "Did you bring anything?"

Messina shook her head.

"Me neither. We'll figure something out." Lottie climbed back into the tent. Messina scooted on her butt, trying her best to keep her blisters out of the dirt. Lottie was already digging through her pile of socks. "I think I've still got a clean pair down here somewhere."

A folded-up sock was Lottie's old trick for a makeshift pad. She'd taught it to Messina back in middle school when they'd both had to endure their periods without supplies or guidance and only had each other to lean on. Lottie's came first, so she already had things figured out when Messina came asking for help. She showed her tricks she'd devised, like how to use an extra pair of underwear and stuff the folded-up sock between the layers at the crotch, so it wouldn't fall out during gym.

"It works almost as well as a pad," she'd said. "You just have to change it out more. Try to use the same ones every month, or black ones if you have them, so all your socks don't get stained. I try to wear my stained ones with pants so no one sees."

Messina hadn't even been educated on her period or anything else about her body back then, because Jeffucker opted her out of the sex-ed days at school. *Blasted school thinks it can groom our children!* Messina had heard the other girls talk enough to half-understand what was coming, but it didn't take away the shame she felt when she didn't have any way of dealing with it. She'd been glad for Lottie's help, but she didn't want to walk around with socks in her underwear all the time. She couldn't tell her mom. Mombie didn't talk about those things. Mombie didn't talk at all since the Fucker. Mombie sat quietly. Cooked. Cleaned. Didn't love or protect or care didn't.didn't.didn't. She had tampons in her bathroom cupboard, but Messina was too afraid of TSS and the idea of putting something into her vagina, so she stole pads from other girls and strangers and stores and then even Val's house, until Val started using tampons too.

Val tried once to teach her to use them so they could swim together. Messina got one in, but her brain just screamed that she would die, and she pulled it out in the ocean and went home early and cried in shameshameshame because she wasn't normal and she'd never be normal. There was so much anger at her mom who was right there but not there at all.

Messina took the pair of socks Lottie handed her now, using one as a pad and the other to wipe the mess and double as an extra layer. She changed her clothes with some effort—the blisters still covering her feet were complicating everything more than her period was. She needed to pop them. *That I could bear the unbearable.*

"Can I borrow your safety pin?"

Anxiety swelled in Messina as she took the pin between her fingers. Its tip looked back at her like its only purpose was to inflict pain. She uncapped a bottle of water, pouring some out over her feet. They were nowhere near clean. She poured more. Again. Again.

"Is that your water from yesterday?" Lottie asked, mercifully interrupting Messina's loop.

Messina shook her head. "That one's gone. I think I grabbed yours. It's okay, right?"

Lottie got a strange look in her eyes. "Do you want to sterilize the pin?" She reached into her bag and passed Messina the lighter. Messina held the end of the pin over the flame until it was so hot it burned her fingers, and she dropped it onto her sleeping bag, dirtying its end again. Another anxiety loop was cresting inside her.

"Fuck. I need help."

"Okay." Lottie picked up the pin and held it over the flame for another second. She lifted Messina's heel from the tent floor with her other hand.

"Wait, can you just rinse them one more time? Please?" She held out the water.

Lottie reached for it but froze halfway. "M, we—"

"I know." Messina cut her off. She knew Lottie was still upset about what she'd said last night. "And I'm sorry. I know we can't do this if we don't trust each other. I shouldn't have said it." She pressed the bottle into Lottie's hand. "Are we okay?"

"Yeah." Lottie's eyes were strange and far away, but she uncapped the bottle and poured the tiniest trickle over Messina's feet.

Messina's mind conjured biblical metaphors about foot-washing and betrayal, and suddenly she was terrified Lottie would do something awful. She hated those stories, stuck in her brain like barbs. She wished she could unlearn them so they wouldn't remind her of the Fucker and angry gods and fear and all the things she didn't want to think about. She wanted to take that lighter and sterilize her mind like the head of the pin, burning off all the bad thoughts and memories until there was nothing left but being here, right now.

She closed her eyes as Lottie poked the pin into her skin. She barely felt anything except the hot liquid dribbling from her foot. Lottie repeated the motion, her fingers pressing softly against Messina's skin. She put ointment and Band-Aids from the first-aid kit over the blisters, then covered them in Gorilla Tape. It was nice, comforting. The sense of touch poured into a hole that had been carved out by Val's absence.

There was something else too, a bond she and Lottie used to have that she hadn't felt in a long time, the way they used to take care of each other back when it was just the two of them. She hadn't realized she'd missed it.

36

LOTTIE

Val's book kept trying to climb out of her pack at night. She was sure Val was getting pissed at her for burying it. For not reading it. For causing her death and fucking up this trip and for everything. Everything. Everything.

Lottie's nose was starting to blister from the sun. It felt like a suitable punishment. Maybe things would start popping up all over her body soon. Like boils. She hadn't had a drink in more than a day now, except for the sip she took last night. If she knocked into something, she'd shatter into dust like a piece of chalk. She was trying to stretch their supply, hoping they'd come up on some water before they ran out. Before she'd have to tell Messina she'd fucked up again.

The air buzzed with flies. Lottie hated them—she couldn't even swat at them without untucking her arms from her shirt, exposing more of her skin to the sun, so she did nothing as they swarmed around her. They felt like a bad omen, reminding her of death. Of how she and Messina were inching toward it, thanks to Lottie. Maybe that was why Val brought them here, so they could be together in death, like they'd always imagined.

Messina veered left at a fork. Lottie was sure Messina knew the way because Val was in her backpack, and Val wasn't going to let Messina die. She was going to lead them to water and shade and trees and something besides up up up and hot and—

"Snake!" Messina ground to a halt, but it took too long for Lottie's brain to tell her legs to stop, and she knocked into her, nearly pushing them both over onto the rattlesnake stretched in the middle of the trail. They kicked clouds of dust as they stumbled backward. The snake looked at them like it didn't give a shit they were there, its rattle-tail lying idle in the dirt while it sunned itself.

Lottie and Messina backed up farther down the path to give it some room.

It didn't move. They waited, hunched in the half-shade of a scrub bush. Messina took the water bottle from her pack. There was less than an inch left inside.

It was gone in a single swallow.

37

MESSINA

"Dude, is that snake ever going to move?" Messina stood up from the shade that wasn't actually shade.

The trees had vanished quarcels ago, the landscape morphed back to rock and chaparral. She leaned over Lottie's pack to get another water. She'd just gotten the top of the backpack open when Lottie whipped it shut.

"What are you doing?"

"Getting more water. Why are you freaking out?" The answer was there, all over her face, but Messina didn't believe it. She didn't believe Lottie would be that stupid and put them in mortal fucking peril and then lie about it right to her face. "Lottie, tell me that we still have water left."

She didn't answer.

"Tell me that I didn't just drink the last swallow of everything we had because you kept saying we had enough even though we didn't."

She didn't answer.

"Is all our water gone?"

Nothing. She was ZombieLottie.

"Fuck!" The wild air ate her scream so it sounded small. She screamed again, louder, "FUCK!" She wanted it to shake the earth and cause an avalanche of rocks and dirt and rage. She wanted to get the hell away from Lottie. She didn't want to be anywhere near her.

She picked up rocks and began hurling them at the snake still stretched across their path. They landed feet away from it, then inches, as something awful built up inside her.

ZombieLottie came to. She stood beside Messina as she hurled another rock at the snake, missing by a mile. It was taking all her self-control not to hurl one at Lottie.

"I promise it's going to be okay," Lottie said.

Messina hurled another rock.

"We just need to keep our heads on straight. We shouldn't panic. We'll probably just use up more of our bodies' water stores that way because it'll raise our heart rates."

Messina rounded on her, rock in hand. "Is that how it works, Lottie? Are you science-ing this out for me right now?" She could feel herself swelling up with feelings that threatened to overwhelm her, ready to pop like her blister mountains. A quiet voice inside her whispered *righteous anger*. It scared her, but that didn't do anything to quell it. She picked up another rock and hurled it into the bushes. "Fuck!" she screamed again, wanting it to vent some of the awfulness building inside her. It didn't. "Why do you have to lie about everything? What is *wrong* with you? We're in the shit-middle of nowhere with no water and we're probably going to die. Why didn't you just tell me before I drank the last of it?"

Lottie's face went far-off, like she was answering silently to herself. That one, the one in her head, Messina knew was the real answer. She would be given the bullshit answer.

"I thought I could fix it before you found out."

"Yeah, well it didn't fucking work out that way, did it?" Messina's voice came out like dragon-fire. Lottie's betrayal cut so deep—she'd put everything at risk. She wasn't a friend, she was a liar.

Messina threw another rock. Finally, she hit the snake, smack in the middle of its body. It hissed, its rattle shaking. Messina thought she'd feel satisfied as it darted into the bushes, but she felt sick. She hated the feeling in her gut, like a fire made of acid and rage. She turned it on Lottie. "You fuck up everything you touch." Messina felt the impact of her words crack against Lottie's skull. *Righteous anger.*

She stormed up the trail, not bothering to see if Lottie had followed.

38

LOTTIE

Neither of them ate dinner. They were too thirsty to be hungry. At least Lottie was. A rolling nausea washed through her body, coming in waves that made her wish she could vomit. She assumed that was why Messina wasn't eating either but couldn't be sure, because Messina was refusing to speak to her.

It was probably for the best, skipping a meal. They were running low on food—all they had left were jerky sticks, unsalted nuts, and those godawful protein bars—but they were certainly going to die of thirst before they starved to death. Lottie wondered which would hurt more, dying of thirst or dying of hunger. *Or falling off a mountain*, her mind whispered.

"Shh," she said to her brain because she didn't want to hear its whispers. She didn't realize she'd said it out loud until Messina shot her an ugly look. Lottie lay back and stared up at their blue nylon ceiling. It was nicer than the blue sky she'd been staring at all day because it didn't have a sun. The sun was still waiting in line to kill them too, she thought. But the thirst was definitely going to get them before the rest.

She felt delirious. It was probably the dehydration.

She licked her lips, stiff and cracked, and tasted blood there. She was surprised her body still had the ability to bleed when it was this dehydrated. She wondered if Messina was still having her period or if being dehydrated would stop it the way not eating enough did. Lottie had gone three solid months without hers back in eighth grade when Maggie disappeared to live with her boyfriend at the time, before Lottie worked at Lu's and started buying her own food. She shifted her thoughts away from food before the pukey feeling came back.

Her mind wandered back to periods—it had nothing else to occupy it since Messina was giving her the silent treatment. She half-recalled hearing a story of two menstruating women killed by a bear, probably a silly urban legend, but the thought rolled around in her exhausted, dehydrated brain.

"Do you think bears and mountain lions can smell blood?" she said, speaking out loud again before she remembered Messina wasn't talking to her. Sharks could smell blood, she thought, keeping the notion to herself now. Her own period was usually about a day behind Messina's. If predators could smell blood, she thought, they were about to be a walking all-you-can-eat buffet.

She curled herself into a ball and fell into a fitful and nauseous sleep. Her dreams were full of bears and mountain lions. And a fox that looked like Val.

39

GABE

ZombieTown was the worst place ever. Gabe called it Zombie-Town because it didn't seem to have a name, and if someone asked him to close his eyes and picture the place where he thought the zombie apocalypse would start, this was the exact image he would conjure. It was the actual middle of nowhere, only worse, because of the creepy chain-link fence up the way with a rusted sign that said **I E TOWN**—obviously, it used to say ZombieTown. Past that were a bunch of weird, metal outbuildings that Gabe didn't explore for fear of either being shot at or turned into part of the army of the dead.

He was somewhere between Lancaster and Gorman on the 138. He'd driven less than half an hour, but it was so much hotter here. *Fun Fact! Did you know California is the most climatically diverse state in the country? It has hundreds of microclimates. You can drive just a few miles and it feels like a whole new world.*

This microclimate sucked. Drier, hotter, flatter. Zombie-er. He thought about turning around and going back to Lake Hughes, but Lottie and Messina had probably already passed that by now. And there weren't any better-looking options ahead of him. Besides, the farther he got, the longer he'd have to wait for them.

At least he'd put more thought into how he looked to outsiders this time. He'd made it a point not to block the trail with his truck. And to keep his damn shirt on no matter how hot he got. He still probably looked like a creep, lurking at the trailhead, looking for two teenage girls. A pair of twentysomething guys had passed him this morning—they told him they hadn't seen his friends, but they'd definitely seemed weirded out by his asking.

At least he had cell signal here. The thought made him realize he'd never found a way to keep his phone charged on the trail. When Messina's stepdad had come banging on his door in the middle of packing, he'd lost track of what he was doing. Maybe he could borrow whatever Lottie and Messina were using for theirs. The thought of them, out there hiking along the PCT with Val's ashes while he was stuck in ZombieTown, nearly burned a hole through his chest.

His phone buzzed with a text from Merilee. He left it sitting in the seat.

Why didn't he like her? Why did he insist on torturing himself with Lottie instead? Even while his mind raged at the thought of her and the things she'd done, his heart still thumped a mutinous beat inside him—*Lott-ie. Lott-ie. Lott-ie.*

Val had once told him about a mechanical heart scientists were working on that moved the blood almost silently, with a quiet whirring sound rather than a heartbeat. He tried to imagine it inside of him, completely silent. Instead of the constant beating that whispered Lottie's name.

40

MESSINA

They'd gone a million quarcels without water.

Anger was making her ears ring. Or maybe that was the heat. Or her thirst. *Did you know even mild dehydration can inhibit your ability to think clearly?* Val whispered. Messina couldn't tell if she'd said it from the ashes, or if she'd somehow found a way to whisper to her from inside Lottie's pack.

She wished she had the book. She wished she had Val. It wasn't fair that Val had gone away instead of Lottie. She wished it had been Lottie instead.

She flicked at the air, undoing the thought.

The ringing in her ears was getting louder. It was definitely a sign that she was losing her mind to dehydration. They probably only had hours to live—what was that rule about air-water-food? Three minutes, three hours, three days? That didn't seem right. The ringing was coming in waves now, forming weird rhythms. *Tss-tss-chk-tss-tss-chk.*

She felt like she was going crazy from the sound. It was tinny, familiar. It reminded her of something from a lifetime ago, but she couldn't place it. She looked at Lottie to see if she'd heard it too, but she just kept walking, head down with her arms stuck inside her T-shirt, zombie-mode.

It grew, closing in on them. *Tss-tss-chk-tss-tss-chk. Tss-tss-chk-tss-tss-chk.*

Messina was sure now that it was music. She turned and looked back at the switchbacks zigzagging below them. Someone was coming, pedaling up fast on a bike. She watched them wind their way up the trail toward them, not knowing whether she should flag them down or hide behind a bush until they passed.

She blinked, and it was too late to make a choice. He rode up on them. He was twice as big as either of them, with long hair and a beard that touched his chest, sun-leathered arms with faded tattoos. The air changed with his presence, tightening like a pulled rubber band.

"Whoa, you snuck up on me." He stopped his music.

The world came into sharp focus. Messina tensed. Lottie was suddenly at her side, flanking her. She stood tall now, even beneath the weight of her pack, survival-mode kicking in for both of them. Lottie's arms were out of her T-shirt now, *so she can use them,* Messina thought. She and Messina had opposing tendencies—where Messina froze in place, Lottie became more unpredictable.

Messina was so keenly aware of her female-ness, of the fact that she was bleeding from between her legs, of the spots of dried blood on the back of her shorts where the sock-pads had leaked. Of the fact that even with the two of them, they wouldn't be able to stop this guy if he decided he wanted to hurt them. It felt so unfair that encounters like this were nothing to men. But for women the risk was a constant, endured their entire lives. Always wondering, always careful, always looking over their shoulders.

Sweat and sunblock dripped down the man's face into his beard. Messina could smell the stink from his skin.

"Sorry about the music. I lost my earbuds somewhere a ways back. I didn't expect to see anyone out here in the middle of nowhere." He squinted at them. "Are you lost?"

They must've looked it, horribly sunburned, with ill-suited shoes, Lottie with a T-shirt wrapped around her head. Embarrassment and shame flashed through Messina, but it paled next to the fear.

"No, we're hiking the PCT," Lottie said, and Messina wished she hadn't. Rule number one with strangers—don't tell them where you're going.

"Oh man." His mouth formed a concerned shape. "I hate to tell you, but this isn't the PCT. They don't allow bikes there."

Neither of them said anything. Messina shook her head in disbelief. Like *no, you're wrong, stupid rando biker dude.*

"You sure you're not lost?" he asked again, like it needed repeating. Like they were children. "Here," he said, opening the map on his phone and turning it so they could see. The blue dot throbbed in its center, miles off from the green line that was the PCT. "You're at least seven or eight miles west of that now. This is the middle of nowhere. It's a rough section of trail in this heat. No water. No help."

No help. The words sent a shiver down Messina's spine. The guy seemed friendly enough, but that meant nothing. Monsters wore disguises. The guy took his water bottle from its cradle on his bike and squirted it into his mouth. He squeezed it empty. Messina's mouth would have watered if she'd had any saliva.

"You guys navigating with a GPS or just phones?"

"Phones," Lottie lied. "We just ran out of charge."

The guy nodded. "Unlucky spot for that. You need a lift back to the trail?"

Messina imagined them trying to somehow get onto that bike with him. Even if they'd fit, which they wouldn't, she wasn't about to put her arms around this guy and his giant sweaty body.

Lottie was probably thinking the same, because instead of answering the question she said, "Do you have any extra water?"

"Oh shit." He looked at the bottle he'd just drained. "Are you guys out? Yeah, here."

He unclipped a nozzle from the vest he had on over his shirt, turning its end and passing it to Lottie. She leaned in and put it in her mouth, gulping from it. She didn't seem to care that her face was just inches from him, looking like she was suckling from this guy's weird blue alien teat. Seeing her drink like that, like she was in a place that was beyond desperate for water, Messina wondered how long she'd gone without it, trying to keep her secret that they'd been nearly out.

Finally, she pulled the nozzle from her mouth and held it out to Messina. The guy leaned forward toward her so it would reach. Messina's mind warred—it wasn't even the germs or Lottie's mouth or whatever nastiness was surely in this guy's mouth—she was too thirsty for that. But she couldn't get her body to move close enough to his to be able to drink from it.

“You don’t want any?” the guy said.

“I do, I just . . .”

The guy looked at her, lines around his eyes from either sun or age—she couldn’t tell. A fresh bead of sweat made its way down his brow and hung from the end of his nose.

“You want me to unclip it?” He’d already started by the time she answered with a nod. “You gotta say what you need.” He passed her the vest, wet from his sweat. Its insides sloshed as she took it and held it awkwardly, trying to put the tube to her mouth. It was clearly meant to be worn, not held. She still felt like she was suckling from it, even without it being attached to him. The water was so hot it hurt to drink, but she took it down all the same, her body’s instincts kicking in.

“Thank you,” Lottie said. Messina still drank, her throat burning, but she nodded her thanks too.

“We’re about two miles from my car. If y’all can get up there, there’s more water in my trunk I can give you. I can give you a ride back to the PCT too. It intersects the same road I stopped on.”

Messina realized now what he’d meant about giving them a lift back to the trail. Of course he wasn’t offering to take them on his bike. She pulled the blue tube from her mouth, the pack empty. She and Lottie looked at each other, questions in both their eyes, but neither responded.

“Tell you what,” the mountain man said. “When I get up there, I’ll wait around for a while. I’ve got to draw this bike route I’ve been scouting anyway. If you all come along and want some water or a ride, I’m happy to help.” Messina held out his pack to him, and he clipped it back around his chest. “Can’t get lost. It’s a straight shot from here, and you can follow my bike tracks," he said and rode off up the mountain.

"I don't even know how we got lost," Messina said. "We haven't hit a fork since that first one, and we saw a marker after that."

"There was another fork a while back, and you veered left. I thought you saw it."

"Why didn't you say something?" She was yelling again. The open space around them swallowed it up, taking its power. It sounded nothing like the booming echo she felt inside her.

"I. Thought. You. Saw. It."

Messina pressed her fingers against her temples. "You make it really fucking hard, you know."

Lottie dropped her head and swallowed, like she'd ingested the words. "I know." She kept staring at the ground. "We should go get that guy's water."

"You trust him?"

"I don't know. But what other choice do we have?"

41

LOTTIE

The guy's name, it turned out, was Craig. They rode along in his old, sticker-covered Subaru with the bike on the top. Messina sat silently in the back, Lottie up front.

He told them about how he used to work in finance doing something with data analysis, but then his life turned so stressful that he became an alcoholic and his wife divorced him. Now he was sober, and they shared custody of their ten-year-old daughter—he got her every other weekend—and he worked as a route director for a bikepacking publication, riding out into the middle of nowhere and mapping long-distance routes.

"It doesn't pay much, but it makes me happy and keeps me on my bike and off the booze." It sounded like the kind of thing Fox Girl from the ice cream shop was into. When Lottie told him about her, he said, "Oh yeah, that's an adventure-cyclist for sure. But bikepacking and racing are two different beasts. Racing is about proving something. About going fast, days with no sleep, and who can suffer the most to win it. Bikepacking will take you on those very same trails, but the purpose is different. It's not about winning, it's about communing with nature. About clearing your mind and getting back to where you came from."

Lottie smiled. "You sound like our friend, Val."

"Where's she? Sounds like she'd want to be on a trip like this."

Lottie swallowed the lump in her throat. "She's meeting us a little farther up."

He nodded like that was a normal thing, and like he didn't think for a second that her ashes were in the backseat with Messina.

"Do you have dogs?" Lottie asked, swatting at a ball of hair that floated up in front of her and letting it go out the open window. Her seat was covered in them.

"Oh, sorry about the fur. My mom volunteers at a shelter up in Lone Pine. I help her with some of the fosters."

He pulled the Subaru alongside a PCT marker on the right side of the dirt road. "Here, take my sunblock." He handed them a tube with a yellow lizard on the front. "It hurts me just looking at how red you all's skin is."

Lottie rubbed her thumb over a bunch of little holes in the tube, trying to figure out if it was going to leak.

"Don't mind the teeth marks," Craig said. "Racoon or something grabbed it out of my pack the other night, but it didn't get far. Probably realized it wasn't food. I think he was after the coconut smell." He hopped out of the car. "Extra water's in the trunk."

Messina and Lottie followed with their packs, their shoes crunching on the dirt and gravel. Craig opened it up, revealing a whole lot of In-N-Out wrappers, but only a single bottle of water.

"Shit, sorry. I thought I had more back here. I must've gotten really thirsty after my last ride. Anyway, take it, but you'll need to fill up soon." He took out his phone, with a map already pulled up. "Looks like there's a cistern just a couple miles up on the PCT. That should get you there. Then make sure you keep your reserves full—you're heading into the desert."

"Aren't we in the desert?"

"Nah, this is just backcountry. You're about to drop into the Mojave—that's where it's gonna get real." He looked at them, at the panicked look growing on Messina's face. Lottie wondered if hers reflected the same thing. *It's gonna get real* felt a little ominous, considering they'd just come within a day or two of actually dying of thirst.

Craig gave them a worried look. "I'm heading up near Kernville in a couple days. You could hang out at my place for a day or two, rest up, then I could give you a ride back out toward the trail, farther up if you want. It's been a dry year. The desert sections are going to be rough."

Lottie's heart skipped a beat. Trading the desert for a cooler, greener trail that was closer to their destination sounded like a dream. But even at the thought of it, Lottie could feel Val's disappointment in her again. Val wasn't planning to drive to a point on the PCT, she wanted to hike it. Taking a ride would just be another way that Lottie screwed up her journey. Plus, even though Craig seemed nice, she didn't like the idea of crashing at his place—it felt like the kind of thing a pair of girls would do at the start of a horror movie. She looked at Messina, trying to read her.

When they didn't answer right away, Craig picked back up where he left off, already talking himself out of the idea. "Nah, you guys have a reason you're on the trail, huh? You can see it in people's eyes. Some people are just out here for fun or adventure. Other people have a purpose, something they have to get through. I can see that's what you're doing. Can't skip the hard parts when you're on a soul journey.

"You'll be alright in the desert. I've seen people with a lot less gusto than you two take on that trail. Sure, maybe they had more experience, but you guys are scrappy. You'll do alright." He looked like he even doubted it himself now, like maybe the pep talk was as much for his benefit as it was for theirs. "Just make sure you keep those bottles filled from here on out. Heat and thirst are your biggest adversaries out there."

He stuck his hand out to shake theirs, like a formal *wish you well* kind of thing, first at Lottie, then Messina.

"Can you give us just a sec?" Messina said when it came her turn to shake. She pulled Lottie's arm and half-dragged her until they were standing in the scrub. "I can't do this," she said, still holding on to Lottie. Her grip was tight, like one of those blood pressure cuffs. Her eyes flashed with panic. "We're completely ill-equipped."

Lottie tried to steady herself, to bring calm to the situation like Val would have, in the hopes that Messina would pick up on her energy and it would calm her, too. She took a deep breath and blew it out through her nose before she spoke. It all felt fake, like she was playing pretend at something she didn't really believe in.

"I know this is hard, but—"

"No, L. Leaving home was hard. Being your friend is hard. But *this*," she motioned at the wilderness around them, "is crazy. We could literally die out here—we nearly did." She pressed her hands against the sides of her head again—she kept doing that, like she was trying to keep her brains from spilling out. Lottie felt like she was watching a tornado spin inside her friend, but she didn't know how to stop it. Even though she was certain she was the one who'd caused it. "I can't do this, Lot. You're . . ."

A fuckup, Lottie thought, guessing at the words Messina didn't say.

"So what are you going to do, hike back home?"

Messina's face turned to something painful. "There's no going back for me."

"Then what are you going to do?"

"I don't know!" Lottie could hear the panic in her voice. She looked behind them toward Craig. He stood by his Subaru, engine still running, while he looked at his phone. "I'll ask him to drop me off in whatever town he said he was going to."

"Then what?"

"Fuck, I don't know—I'll steal money, find a bus to Oregon. I don't have it all figured out yet, I just know I can't do it with you. I feel like I'm trying to swim across the ocean with sandbags strapped to me."

Truth: Lottie was the sandbags. Dead weight.

"If I stay, we're both going to drown." Messina dropped her pack into the dirt and lifted Val's urn from its innards. She held it out to Lottie.

Lottie didn't take it. She just stared at it, fear and anguish rising in her chest like fire.

Messina pushed it toward her, but Lottie backed up like it might burn her. "L, you have to deal with this. This is your journey—the whole thing was your idea. Why are you so scared of having her, anyway? You were going to put a scoop of her in a Ziploc, for fuck's sake."

Lottie didn't know how to answer. There was too much. She was scared of being on her own with Val, scared of the truth, of what she'd done and what she was about to do, scared that Gabe would never forgive her. Scared of another friend leaving and never coming back. Scared that everything in the world felt like her fault.

Messina held on to Val while Lottie wavered. She held her differently than she had back at the house when she'd held her like a baby. She had her in one arm now, tucked over her hip, like Val had grown tougher and sturdier on the hike, just like they had.

Messina tried again to pass Val's urn to her. "I'm not going to put her in the dirt, so either take her or I'm going to keep her."

Lottie's heart hammered inside her chest. She took Val's urn, half expecting her hands to catch fire the second she came into contact with it.

Messina turned back to Craig. "What's the town you said you're going to?"

"Kernville."

"Is there a bus station there?"

"Believe so."

"If you're still willing, I'd like a ride, actually."

Craig looked at her with a sadness on his face, like he was the one being abandoned. "But you can't do that. You've got to stick together out here," he said.

He looked like he was going to tell her no. Messina looked to Lottie for help. Lottie hesitated, thinking if she didn't intervene then Craig might say no, and Messina might not leave her. Messina's eyes pleaded. *Please, we'll both drown.*

Lottie reminded herself of how many times she'd wished Messina hadn't come with her, of how she'd have her phone and how she wouldn't feel like such an asshole all the time if she were doing this on her own. This was how she should pay her penance to Val—Messina was right. She deserved to be alone in this.

"Oh, I'm good," Lottie said. "Remember, I'm meeting our other friend, Val. And Messina's coming back. She's just got to take a little detour."

Criag looked unsure, but that seemed to satisfy him.

Dust flew up from their tires into the darkening sky as they drove away.

42

MESSINA

She hadn't been afraid when Lottie was in the car. Now her thoughts whirled, the winds inside her kicking up dust and rocks and fear and terror as she sat alone, next to this stranger of a man. He seemed harmless enough when it was the three of them, but now with the sun sinking low, in the quiet of the night with no small talk or cheerful chatter, things felt weirder.

Who was he anyway, stopping to help a couple of stranded teenage girls, offering to let them stay at his house—who did that? Psychopaths did that. Rapists. Serial killers.

"What's your errand?" Craig asked.

"What?" The question shocked her out of her thoughts.

"Your friend said you had to do something before you join her back on the trail, right?"

"Oh, yeah. I'm . . ." Messina was terrible at this. She didn't know how to come up with innocuous things that wouldn't prompt follow-up questions on the fly. "It's personal," she said. It came out cold. Covered in barbs like the cactus they kept seeing.

"Oh." Craig made a little frown, like she'd stung him. She wished she hadn't, suddenly afraid he might want to sting her back.

She wished Lottie were here to make conversation and smooth out the tension in the air. She wished Lottie were here to make her feel less frightened. She wished Lottie were here. She reached up to the scab on the back of her head. It was fully formed again, which meant she must not have touched it in days. She ripped it clean off in one big chunk, then wiped her finger on her hair to hide the blood. She held the scab pinched hard between her fingers, hidden.

It occurred to her that if something went wrong now, she'd be on her own. *No help.* She watched Craig out of the corner of her eye. She replayed their few words looking for clues, indications of danger. Messina refused to watch scary movies, but their trailers were unavoidable, burning themselves into her mind whenever they popped up as ads. They played on a loop now, women screaming, saws, zip ties. She wiped the sweat from her palms onto her shorts. She tried to think of things she could use as a weapon if he decided to attack her. The sturdiest thing she had without digging in her pack were the boots on her feet. No one now would even know if something happened to her. No one but Lottie would care.

This was a mistake. She should have stayed with Lottie. They were bound together. Neither of them might have mattered to the world, but they mattered to each other. It was a bond that should have kept them together, even through a day like today, but she'd just broken it. Val would've been so disappointed in her. She reached back to her pack, but she didn't have any pieces of Val left. The book, the urn—they were both with Lottie now.

The tires hummed along the road. *Go back*, Val's voice shouted at her. She thought about that chapter in *Wild* she'd glanced over because she'd been afraid of what was happening. The one with the hunters. Now she wished she'd read it. She wished she knew what Cheryl Strayed had done to keep herself safe.

Messina's Santa Ana winds whipped up thoughts inside her. She wondered if she could jump out at this speed. If she could open the door and roll away from the car, or if they were going so fast that all her bones would shatter on impact. She touched the door handle. She scooted forward on the seat, her shorts half-sticking to it.

Wetness, hot and tacky, collected between her legs. She'd bled completely through her socks into her shorts and the seat upholstery. Shame and fear rose in her cheeks, hotter than the blood between her legs. She knew what would happen if she were in Jeffucker's van. The violence of it filled her. She hated this. She wished she were a guy with muscles and a big build who didn't have to worry about bleeding from a vagina or about getting beaten or assaulted or killed. She wished Lottie were here. She couldn't breathe.

She adjusted herself in the seat. The stickiness was everywhere.

She wished Lottie were here.

She wished not to be scared.

She wished Lottie were here.

Go back.

The winds roared inside her.

They hit a bump in the road, and she let out a yelp.

"You okay?" Craig said. His hand was on her knee. Maybe it was kindness, a fatherly instinct. Maybe it was something else. *Go back go back go back.*

"No," she said. "I changed my mind. I need you to take me back to my friend." She was so aware of how powerless she was, trapped here. He could say no. He could do anything. She never should've gotten into this car alone with him.

She ground her teeth together. She waited to hear the click of the door lock, but it didn't come.

She watched the corners of Craig's mouth pull back into a smile. "I knew you'd do the right thing," he said, pulling the car to the side of the road. He turned it around, heading back toward the trail.

Messina shot out before the car fully stopped. She ran for the trail with her pack only half-on, not bothering to wave thanks or goodbye or to see how much blood she'd left on the seat. She hoped that under the dark sky Craig wouldn't see it.

The trail was empty. Lottie was long gone.

She was completely alone.

43

LOTTIE

When you're carrying the body of your dead best friend on your back, you can't hide from the truth of what you've done.

The truth was all of this: She'd screwed around with Tristan. She'd broken Val's heart. Lied to Messina. Crushed Gabe. She'd fucked up again and again. She was the one who deserved to be dead and riding piggy-back with all that was left of her stuffed into a metal jar.

It seeped into her skin like poison and acceptance. So, when she finally found the cistern full of water with a rotting animal corpse bobbing inside and realized she didn't even have the filter to attempt to make it drinkable, she was resigned to it.

This was what she deserved.

44

MESSINA

Blood ran down her legs in earnest now. She shined her flashlight over them. She looked like a stabbing victim. Why did Lottie have to say that thing about mountain lions smelling it? Now she was terrified. Some distant part of her mind laughed at this, knowing she would've been terrified of a hundred other things if Lottie hadn't said that.

Blood pooled at the tops of her socks, seeping into the fabric. Her fear told her to wait near the trailhead, that Lottie would come find her, but she knew that was stupid. It was wishful thinking, because she was alone in the dark and afraid of wandering in deeper and getting lost and killed. But dying out here was better than getting attacked in the car of some stranger. Only, he hadn't attacked her. He'd turned around and brought her back. Maybe she should've just stayed in the car.

"Stop it!" she screamed at herself. A sound skittered in the brush behind her, something small, like a lizard. Her ears had learned to hear the size of things. "You have to find Lottie." Her voice sounded commanding and sure of itself, just the way Val's did inside her head. Val's voice, which she'd somehow managed to hear inside the car, even though the book and the ashes weren't with her. It occurred to her for the first time that maybe it wasn't Val's voice she'd been hearing. Maybe it was her own.

The thought didn't take away the fear inside her, but it made her feel a little stronger. Like it was okay to be afraid.

She aimed her light down the trail and got her bearings. She tripped on a rock and half-ripped one of the soles of her boot off. It flopped with every step like a dying animal. The blood running down her legs itched. She heard the high-pitched whine of a mosquito. The smell of her blood was probably drawing it to her. She swatted it away and realized she had to be near water. She recalled Craig's words, about a cistern being ahead on the trail. That was probably where Lottie stopped for the night.

She moved down the trail, not knowing what she was looking for—what the hell did a cistern look like? Her light flashed against a dark shadow carved into a tree, an arrow pointing to her right. She turned the corner and found what must've been the cistern—it wasn't at all what she thought it would look like. A giant, browning plastic barrel in a clearing. It stank. Bad, like death.

She cast her light around. Lottie wasn't here. The smell of the cistern was so foul Messina pulled her shirt up over her nose.

What was she going to do now? She moved away from the cistern and its death-smell and dropped onto the ground, defeated. The dirt stuck to the blood along her legs and butt, making a blood-mud paste, but it didn't matter. Everything was lost. She felt her insides crack open, her winds spilling out of her. A sound poured out that was everything she'd held in, a moan and a scream and a cry all at once. She had no Lottie and no Val and no Craig—who might have truly wanted to help, but she'd just traded that help to die alone in the wild. She let the tears come, rolling freely down her face, just like the blood down her legs.

A hand on her shoulder made her jump and scream. She swung her flashlight like a weapon, making contact with what she could now see was Lottie's face.

"Ow! What the hell, M?"

"Fucksorrysorrysorry. Are you okay?"

"I'm fine."

"No, look," Messina reached toward the little gash below Lottie's eye that was puffing around the edges—her light must've made it—but Lottie waved her off.

"It's fine. I deserve it."

Messina shook her head at Lottie's words, taking in the rest of her face now. Her eyes were red. Tear tracks cut through the dirt on her cheeks. Whatever she'd endured in their time apart had been just as awful as what Messina had gone through. Maybe worse.

Messina grabbed her. She pulled Lottie toward her in a hug so violent and desperate, she thought they both might snap in two, but she didn't let go. "I shouldn't have left you," she whispered, and Lottie's body shook with tiny explosions. When they finally broke apart, they both dropped onto the dirt, drained of everything.

"There's a rat corpse in the cistern," Lottie said, wiping tears and snot from her face with her arm. "At least that's what I think it is. Whatever it was, it's definitely dead. I don't think we can drink it, even if we filter it."

Messina nodded. "That's the smell." It didn't surprise her, really. Life never took it easy on them.

"Why did you come back?"

So much had gone through Messina's mind in the car. She searched for the real reason, the one hidden under all the noise. "I wasn't supposed to leave you. It was a mistake." Regret washed through her—she'd almost lost Lottie. "I also flipped out and thought Craig was going to murder me." She laughed a little at how ridiculous it sounded now. She shined her light along her legs, dark veins of half-dry blood wending their way down her skin. "And then I bled all over his car. I think I might have gone a little crazy."

"I don't think you were crazy," Lottie said. "Not even a little bit. I think you're finally listening to yourself—leaving home, getting out of Craig's car. If your gut told you to get out, then that was the right thing to do. It told you that for a reason. You've spent your whole life arguing with yourself, but now you're letting your instincts take the wheel."

Messina pinched a spot of blood on the cuff of her sock. Her fingers came away sticky.

"But I don't want to let it take the wheel. What if it's wrong? Like what if Craig was just a genuinely nice person, and I misread him and ran screaming from his car and left a puddle of blood in his seat as a thank-you?"

"Then that's kind of a bummer for him, but that's also the price of being a dude in this world. Just like the price of being a woman is always wondering if every random guy you encounter alone in the street or on the trail is going to try to hurt you. And bleeding out your vagina once a month. But you only even have the luxury of making this argument right now because you're still alive, so I'm sticking with my original point—it's worth being wrong. And anyway, look at you."

Messina looked down at herself in the glow of their flashlights, covered in blood. "I look nutso." She scrubbed at a dried spot of blood with her palm. Fresh hairs stuck out of her legs like cactus spines. "What am I going to do about this? I can't use the water Craig gave us."

"You don't look nutso," Lottie said, wiping a fingertip along Messina's knee, through a sticky line of still-wet blood. "You look fucking terrifying."

She dotted the blood up Messina's forearm, painting her skin. Lottie's touch felt like water, quenching a dry well inside her.

"Messina of the wild," Lottie said.

Messina smiled at it. The power in the sound of it, the power in her blood. She felt connected to it for the first time, instead of embarrassed and ashamed. She slipped her fingers into the wetness, covering them in red, and painted her other arm to match. She felt like a warrior. Like she had a wind inside her that could knock down a hundred-foot palm tree.

Lottie's smile shone devilish in the moonlight. Messina smiled back, all teeth, while she painted herself more.

A lone coyote barked in the distance. Before its cousins could echo, Messina tipped her head back and yipped in response. Lottie joined her, both of them howling up at the moon, wild.

They set up the tent far away from the death smell and ate protein bars that tasted like papier mâché. Messina stayed awake long after Lottie's snores came. Her body was exhausted, but the power she still felt ramped her up like adrenaline, making sleep feel far away. She slipped *Wild* out of Lottie's pack and read by flashlight. She missed Val. She wished she were really here with them, that Val could see her wild and blood-smeared. She knew Val would be proud.

She flipped through the book, reading bits here and there, running her fingers over Val's scribbled words, until sleep wound its tendrils around her. The last thing she read was the author's words Val had highlighted in yellow. *I decided I was safe. I was strong. I was brave. Nothing could vanquish me.*

She felt Val smiling at her, just as sleep pulled her under.

45

LOTTIE

Lottie unzipped the tent and found Messina awake, rubbing the sleep from her eyes. It was so wet and hot inside she was surprised steam didn't pour out when she opened the flap.

"Did you steal my blood?" Messina said, staring at Lottie's blood-covered forehead.

"Dude, no. I told you, my cycle's right behind yours."

"Oh, yeah." Messina pushed her mess of hair back and tied it with the band on her wrist.

"What were you doing out there?"

Lottie raised her eyebrows. "Pooping. Period cramps make me go."

"What did you do with it?"

"With . . . my poop?"

Messina nodded. It felt like they were back in middle school and Messina was asking her period questions, wanting to know what it was like. Only, Messina had pooped before.

"Buried it," she said. Just like Val had taught her, using a rock to dig as deep a hole as she could—which wasn't very deep at all in this dry, compacted dirt—and covering it. "Why, what did you do with yours?"

Messina went a little wide-eyed. "I've been holding it."

"The whole time we've been out here? Even with all that dried fruit?"

"I've never pooped outside before! I didn't know how it worked."

Lottie couldn't have held her shit that long if her life depended on it. "As soon as we fix your boot," she said, pulling the roll of Gorilla Tape from her bag, "it's time to go find out."

Messina was taking quarcels—it was probably all lodged in there like bricks. Lottie's mind was on their lack of water. She kept thinking about that cistern with the dead thing, but no matter how much she thought about it, she still didn't think they should try to filter that water. They only had half the bottle left from what Craig gave them. They were going to be screwed again in a matter of hours.

She brushed her teeth without water and stared out at the ever-shifting landscape—it had begun sprouting oaks again. Several of them ran in an arched line in a low spot below the trail.

"Do you have another pair of shorts?" Messina said, stepping up behind Lottie. "These are pretty fucked." She held out the ones she'd been wearing, stiff with blood. Lottie found her a dirty pair of cutoffs. They hung low on Messina's barely-there hips, but at least she could walk in them.

"I think there's water down there," Lottie said. She pointed at the snaking line of trees.

Messina squinted at the spot. "It's way off the trail."

"What does your gut say?"

"That it's the middle of summer in a drought year and it might have dried up. That it might be dangerous. That we might not be able to find our way back."

"That's not your gut, that's your head. What does your spidey sense say?"

Messina drew a V in the dirt with the freshly taped toe of her boot. "That we're going to be screwed if we don't get more water soon."

"Great, it's settled then."

"No, it's not. What if we can't get back up?"

"Stop listening to your brain," Lottie said, frustrated.

"I don't want to stop listening to my brain! It's there for a reason. And operating without one isn't doing you any favors."

"What the hell does that mean?"

Messina shoved her hands into her pockets, making the shorts sag down even further. "It means you scare me sometimes. And that I don't know which one Val was listening to when she climbed up the ridge that night. Was that her brain or her gut? Would one of them have saved her?"

No, Lottie thought. *Having a better friend would have.* She wanted to tell Messina the truth of it, to let out the poison that was trapped in her veins, killing her. But she knew Messina would never forgive her. She'd abandon her on the trail all over again.

"So what do you want to do?"

"Let's balance it out. Having both of us being impulsive is a recipe for destruction. So if I start listening to my brain less, you have to listen to yours more."

"Fine."

"Good." She looked at Lottie. "What does your brain say?"

"That we're going to run out of water and die."

Messina sighed. "Same."

46

GABE

This heat had him blowing through his water supply.

Tell her to be careful—conditions are dicey out there. The words from the woman at Lu's echoed through his thoughts.

He wondered how Lottie and Messina were doing. He'd been able to pile as much water as he wanted into his truck. He was sure he'd have significantly less once he could only have as much as he could carry. He chugged from a hot bottle. It was almost noon, and the shade beside his truck was gone, so he was baking inside it with the windows down when the highway patrol cruiser pulled up.

Gabe's heart ga-gunged in his chest. Cops always made him nervous. He looked around for a no-parking sign again, even though he'd checked before he stopped here. Dirt and gravel crunched as the officer approached. Gabe's truck was a disaster after living in it for days—his open pack spilled out over the seat, clothes and food wrappers scattered—but there was nothing to do about it. Hastily throwing a bunch of stuff under the seat didn't seem like a great idea at the moment.

The officer appeared at Gabe's open window.

"Hello," Gabe said. He tried not to sound guilty of anything.

"It's going to be a hot one today."

Gabe had never had an interaction with the police start this way. It felt like a trap. He nodded and kept quiet. The cop eyed the inside of Gabe's truck.

"You planning to hike?" Sunlight bounced off the metal tag on the officer's shirt. Gabe squinted against it.

"Yes, sir. I'm just waiting on a couple of friends. We're planning to meet here and hike together."

"You'll need to find a parking area. You can stop here to change a flat or make an emergency call, but that's about it. This isn't a place to park, even if you're occupying the vehicle."

"Oh." His heart sank. He couldn't wait at a parking area—he needed a place directly on the trail. Otherwise, he risked missing them. "I understand. I'll get moving."

"I'll need to see your license and registration. Been getting reports of a vagrant out here."

"Oh, sure." Gabe opened his glove box for the registration. Lottie's sunglasses popped out and hit the floor, pricking at his heart.

"What are the names of these friends you're meeting?"

He hesitated. "Marcus and Merilee," he said, not knowing why he lied. Something in his gut, and the memory of Jeffucker's eyes, told him he should. The cop pulled down the reflective shades he was wearing and looked at Gabe. He was a horrible liar. His conscience vibrated inside him, urging him to confess the truth, but he gave the officer his best innocent smile instead, hoping he couldn't see his heart banging through his T-shirt.

The cop took the license and registration back to his cruiser.

Relax, Gabe thought. *You're not doing anything wrong.* He wiped his sweaty palms against his shorts.

The cop came back. "I noticed you live in La Conchita."

Gabe nodded.

"You know anything about Charlotte Mitchell and Messina Williams? They're about your age, recently listed as missing persons, possible runaways."

"No, sir." Gabe said. His conscience didn't vibrate this time. It hid beneath his other organs. "I don't know anything about that."

The cop looked at him. It felt like his eyes were boring into Gabe's chest, viewing his insides like an MRI. Lottie's face was probably all over the place in there, stitched into every layer. "You ever know anybody that's run away from home?"

Gabe shook his head.

"I always find those cases tricky to handle. Gotta think if they left home there must've been some reason for it." The cop handed Gabe's license and registration back to him. "Well, you and your friends—what were their names again?"

"Marcus and Merilee."

"That's right." He nodded. "You all be safe out on the trail. Desert's a rough place to start a hike, especially on a year like this."

"Thanks, we will."

"And make sure you move your truck. I'll have to ticket you if I see you here again. There's parking about thirty miles up, on Tehachapi Willow Springs, a little ways outside of town."

"Thirty miles?"

"Give or take," the officer said. "Let your friends know—change of plans."

47

LOTTIE

It turned out that blood didn't attract mountain lions—it attracted flies. Not the normal, noisy kind they'd encountered before. These ones were near-silent. Tiny things that came in droves once they'd left the trail in search of water, flocking to their blood-smeared bodies. Hordes of them swarmed around their faces, like they were trying to find a way into their bodies through their eyes or noses or mouths. Maybe it was the way the coconut scent of Craig's sunblock mixed with the blood that attracted them. They'd slathered it over themselves, the white mineral kind, smearing their blood paint.

"Get away from my eyeballs, little fuckers!" Messina yelled at them, waving her hands in front of her face. The blood had unleashed the wild in her.

"Almost there," Lottie said, trying to encourage herself as much as Messina. She swatted a fresh swarm of the flies.

They'd made a straight shot down, hoping for the least chance of getting lost. They left their tent up as a beacon to help them find their way back. They took the food in their packs though—Lottie wasn't going to make that mistake again.

Finally, the shade of low trees touched them. As they continued down, the scrub oaks morphed into actual trees. And a dried-up creek bed. There had been water here recently. The ground at the lowest point was still soft from it. But there was nothing to collect for filtering.

"Shit." Lottie exhaled the word.

"I've got to pee," Messina said, heading off to the right. Lottie did too. It occurred to her that until Craig had let them drink his entire pack, she hadn't peed in over a day—they'd been dangerously dehydrated.

"Lottie!" Messina's voice sounded panicked. Lottie ran toward her, following the path of the creek bed. When she found her, she was standing in mud. There was a small puddle of dirty water in front of her. "I found it."

She was also standing in a knee-high cluster of poison oak. Lottie looked down and found it around her own legs too. She hadn't been paying attention.

"Okay, don't freak out, but you're standing in poison oak."

Messina jumped and swatted at the plants like they were attacking her. "This is what happens when I try to follow my fucking instincts." She reached up toward her face, but Lottie caught her hand.

"Don't touch anything. Just hold on for a second while I think." One of Val's annoying facts scratched at the edge of her brain, something about how nature would kick your ass and then give you the medicine to heal your injuries.

She looked around, scanning a million plants she didn't recognize, looking for something that looked medicinal or protective somehow. It wasn't like any of them were going to be painted with a red cross. She was about to give up when she saw it, growing up like miniature trees from the mud, dark green, with sawtooth leaves. *Fun fact: The antidote grows right next to the poison.*

Lottie grabbed handfuls of it, stripping the leaves and smashing them up in her hands. Its sharp smell filled the air. Green juice ran down her arms, adding fresh color to the wild canvas she'd already made of her skin. She rubbed Messina's hands with it first, afraid she'd touch other parts of herself and spread the poison oak.

"What is this?"

"Mugwort," Lottie said, scrubbing her skin with it, just like Val had shown her years earlier. It was right after Val's mom died. They went hiking all day with no destination. Lottie wondered if they'd ever go back home. She would've been happy like that, staying in the wild with Val. Messina had been grounded, like always. Lottie and Val had walked down by a creek, and Lottie stepped into a thick patch of poison oak, not even knowing what it looked like back then. Val had scrubbed Lottie's skin with the mugwort, showing her how it grew right alongside the poison oak.

"Ow, gentle," Messina said.

Not gentle, Lottie thought, remembering Val's words again. Nature wasn't gentle. It was harsh. No apologies. Lottie remembered wondering why she would choose to come to such a harsh place to heal, but Val was always pulled to nature, like she was looking there for the mom she'd lost.

The memories flooded her, Val's words, everything she'd stored up and pushed aside. She let them come. Tears stung her eyes, but she didn't wipe them, for fear of putting the poison oak into them.

When she'd finished covering Messina, Lottie scrubbed her own arms and legs with the poultice.

"So much for the water," Messina said. "It's surrounded by that shit."

"It's okay. The mugwort stays on your skin, like a protectant. Even if you touch it now, it won't give you a rash."

"Why do you know all this stuff?"

"I'd go out with Val sometimes when you were grounded. I guess the memories stuck."

Messina frowned, like this was unfair. Lottie agreed, it was. If anyone deserved more time with Val, it was Messina. And Gabe. And Gabe's dad. Guilt struck her anew. She held it all back, but a single choke of tears and snot and spit shot out of her—she couldn't keep it in.

Messina put an arm around her. "I miss her too."

It took them half a quarcel to figure out how to use the filter, but they managed to get three bottles from the puddle before it became too thick with mud. They hiked back up toward the tent with their spoils. The water was a cloudy brown even after filtering, and it tasted like mold and dirt. But even so, it felt like liquid gold.

48

MESSINA

"That was amazing. You're amazing," Messina said. It felt like they were really hiking the PCT now, covered in their blood magic and plant poultice and coconut sunblock. It felt like they were unstoppable.

"That was Val," Lottie said over her shoulder.

"No, it was you."

"I only knew how to do it because of Val."

"Yeah, but I didn't know it, and you saved us from getting poison oak on top of everything else. It was pretty badass."

Lottie didn't respond, like she didn't want to accept the compliment.

"I don't get you, you know. You always think I'm calling you a fuckup when I'm not, and then I try to tell you how amazing you are, and you won't have it. It's like you're hell bent on thinking my opinion of you is shit."

Lottie stayed silent.

Messina grabbed the top of Lottie's pack, so she'd stop walking and listen to her. "And I know the sunblock wasn't on your half of the list." She held out the ripped piece of paper she'd found in the pocket of the shorts Lottie had lent her. Sunblock was nowhere on it. "Why didn't you just show me this and prove me wrong?"

"Because it wouldn't have changed anything. You were going to believe what you wanted to. You always do."

"But I don't think you're a fuckup."

"Yeah, you do."

Messina was about to argue when she realized Lottie was right. "Okay, maybe I do." Lottie looked surprised by the admission. Messina was surprised by it herself. "But not all the time. Sometimes you're a for-real fucking genius, but there's this Jekyll and Hyde thing you do where you turn all self-destructive sometimes, and I never know which side I'm going to get. Or if I'm going to get caught in the blast when you decide to blow yourself up. It scares me."

Lottie started walking again. She didn't say anything. There was only their footsteps and the creak of their packs and the constant hum of the air around them.

"I'm sorry for making you feel that way, though," Messina said. "You're not a fuckup."

Lottie still didn't respond. Messina wondered if she'd actually heard her.

49

LOTTIE

She looked out on the tri-blade wind turbines dotting the land far below them and remembered Craig's words, *You're about to go into the real desert.*

She felt like she was looking at the entire thing—all the desert in the world—because her mind couldn't imagine any more of it existing than the huge stretch that rolled out in front of them. It was terrifying.

But where they were now was suddenly pleasant, like a last respite before they entered hell. The plants had changed, unexpectedly becoming greener. They passed a campground that was flat and graded. It had signs and everything. And pines, though half of them were dead, littering the landscape like corpses, casualties of the climate war.

It felt strange, so much more civilized than the world they'd just been in. Clear markers were posted at regular intervals. "This is what I'd imagined it would look like when we started," Messina said.

"Yeah, me too."

They came up on a concrete trough filled with water. A clear trickle dribbled out of a metal pipe above it. It had only been a day since they'd found the mud puddle, and this water was so much cleaner than the brown, silty stuff they carried now. It felt like life was laughing at them. *You finally found your wild skills and learned to survive on your own? LOL you don't need them anymore!*

They dumped their dirt-water and filtered the water from the trough, filling up all their empties. They reclined in the nearby shade, resting and eating and drinking. Lottie poured water onto her protein bar. It still tasted like cardboard, but at least with it wet she could swallow it.

"How are your blisters?" Lottie said.

"Healing, I think. The tape's breaking the friction. My feet still feel like shit, but not like they did before."

Footsteps and voices came up behind them, and Lottie turned just in time to see a group of hikers rounding the corner.

Two men and a woman, probably in their twenties or early thirties. The woman and one of the men looked like a couple, with matching sun-protective shirts with hoods that Lottie felt envious of. They all carried hiking poles and professional-looking gear. The woman, who somehow looked clean and made-up, had her phone aimed at herself like she'd just been recording something. The other guy looked like he didn't quite belong, with a tie-dyed T-shirt and faded pink hair tucked under a cap, a wad of leather bands around one wrist.

At first, none of them seemed to notice Lottie and Messina. When the woman finally caught sight of them, she looked at them like they were the rat corpse that had floated in the cistern.

Lottie could feel Messina growing smaller beside her, looking down, tucking her head in self-consciousness. All the power she'd claimed over the last days vanished in a blink. Lottie felt suddenly protective. She glared back at the woman, probably looking feral with her tangled hair and her layers of blood paint and sunblock and mugwort juice. She was glad that for the first time they didn't need anyone's help.

The woman elbowed her partner. He turned, seeing them too. Shock registered across his face.

"Are you all lost?" he asked.

Lottie took offense, even though she probably would've made the same assumption. She hadn't seen herself, but Messina looked like a child of the woods from some documentary. It was safe to assume they were pretty much twinsies at this point. "No. We're fine, thanks."

"Are you PCT hikers?" the pink-haired guy asked. He seemed like the friendlier one of the bunch.

Lottie nodded, letting some part of that truth settle into her. *Yes, we're doing this. We're hiking the PCT.*

"We started at the Canadian border, so we're sobo," the guy said.

Lottie tried to look like she knew what that meant and like maybe she didn't care. She side-eyed them as they got water, hoping they'd leave soon. They'd changed everything with their arrival. Messina was still shrinking. Lottie heard the woman laugh and mutter something about *Lord of the Flies.* She wanted to launch at her, to show her just how savage she was right now, but Messina was furiously picking at a scab and trying to crawl inside herself. Lottie was afraid of making it worse, so she glued her butt to the ground and bit down on her tongue to keep quiet.

The couple-y pair started off again once they'd filled their waters, but the pink-haired guy hung back.

"Sorry about that," he said, turning to Lottie and Messina. "I'm not with them, so to speak. We just met on the trail. They can be pretty unfriendly at times. They're adventure influencers, so . . ." he trailed off, leaving them to fill in the blank for themselves.

Lottie had never heard of adventure influencers—it seemed like an oxymoron. "I didn't know adventure influencing was a thing."

The guy laughed. "I'm not sure it should be." He stuck out his hand. "I'm Mac."

Lottie reached out and shook it. "Lottie," she said, "and that's Messina." Messina stared at the ground, picking her scab. Mac frowned at her.

"You guys northbound?"

Lottie was pleased that she'd put together that sobo meant southbound. It hadn't crossed her mind that there were two directions to hike the trail. "Yeah, we're heading to the Three Sisters."

"Long trek ahead. Most of the water caches in the desert are empty, just a heads-up," he said, adjusting his pack. "Bet you're looking forward to those showers at Hikertown."

"What's Hikertown?" Lottie said. Mac laughed. It wasn't mean, like the woman's, but like Lottie had answered him with a joke. She laughed too, because she was exhausted from feeling stupid.

For a second, she thought it worked. But his face shifted. "You were serious?"

"Yeah. Our phones died, so we don't have a map right now."

"You've got a backup, right?"

"Of course," Lottie said, like it would be stupid not to.

"Great, I can mark it for you. It's about a tenth of a mile off-trail.

You're getting close, it's eight or ten miles from here." He waited for the map as Lottie reluctantly drew it from her bag. Their useless poster of the PCT.

He looked at them again, and his face shifted into something more condescending, like she and Messina were kids playing a game of make-believe they'd taken too far.

"Can I offer you some advice?"

"No thanks," Lottie said, but she could feel it coming anyway.

"You girls should go home. This isn't a place to mess around—it can kill you."

So can home, Lottie thought, pretty sure Messina was thinking the same thing. "Helpful tip. Thanks." She stood, like she was ready to get moving, and Mac waved to them and headed off in the opposite direction. Lottie dropped her pack. She wasn't ready to go anywhere.

"That was so humiliating. We looked like complete idiots," Messina said.

"When you curl up into a ball, it just makes it worse," Lottie said, but felt instantly bad for piling on. "Sorry." She nudged Messina with her elbow. It was as close as she could get to a reconciliatory hug. "Why do you care what they think anyway?"

"Because I care what everyone thinks."

"But they were assholes. They don't matter. That lady looked like she hadn't farted in five years."

Messina laughed, but her face turned serious again. "That's easy for you to say. People love you. I try with everything I have, and people still think I'm a freak."

"So stop trying. Let them think that."

"But I don't *want them to*. It makes me feel like shit. Val was the only person who ever thought I was cool."

"I think you're cool."

"You don't. You're just stuck with me." A bird flittered down from one of the trees to drink from the trough.

Lottie didn't bother arguing about it. Messina would believe what she wanted to. Proof or no. She watched the bird drink, not giving a shit about anything except its own survival. "No one knows you out here, M. You can be whoever you want to be."

They made camp by the trough, cleaning their skin with cupfuls of water they warmed on their tiny stove. It was the most luxury they'd known on the trail. There wasn't anything to wash clothes in, but they both used their cooking cups to wash out their used blood-socks, then hung them on the outsides of their packs to dry.

"What do you think he meant by water caches?" Lottie wrung out her last sock, watching the water run into the dirt.

Messina shrugged. "Places they stash water? Doesn't matter if they're empty, does it?"

Lottie didn't want to go into the desert where they wouldn't have water again. It felt like the most precious thing on earth now. She wanted to stay here, where they were rich with it.

"We've got seven protein bars left, plus some nuts," Messina said, counting their food.

"And my jerky." It was enough food to stretch for three days if they were careful.

"You think there will be a store in Hikertown?"

"No idea. I just keep wondering what the hell it is. All we know is that it has showers."

"I keep picturing ToonTown, but full of asshole hikers. I don't think I want to shower there."

Lottie dumped the remaining warm water from the pot over her hands and rubbed it along her arms and face. She'd have taken a shower anywhere right now.

"Which do you want for dinner?" Messina said, holding up the choice of remaining protein bars. "Chocolate, or peanut butter?"

"You pick."

Messina opened up the peanut butter bar and split it in two, handing half to Lottie. Lottie tapped her half against Messina's like *cheers* and choked it down.

50

MESSINA

Messina missed her period war-paint and the feeling it had given her, but she was glad not to be wearing it into whatever Hikertown was. She hated the way she'd felt around those influencer-hikers. It was like she'd found all this power and confidence, and it had vanished the second they showed up.

They were in a steady descent now, her pack heavy with water again. The last of the trees were behind them, except for the occasional Joshua tree now, as they headed down toward the desert. The *real* desert, as Craig had called it.

"So how do you do it?" Messina said.

"What?" Lottie looked like the question had pulled her from another universe.

"You said I can reinvent myself out here since no one knows me, right? So how do I talk to people? You can talk to anyone. How do you just fit in anywhere like that?"

"I don't."

"That's not helpful, Lot." Messina skidded a little on a wash, kicking up a cloud of dust.

"I'm serious—I don't fit. I fake it. It's like a survival skill I picked up somewhere along the way."

"So how do I learn?"

"I don't know. I think you're just a little . . . intense, sometimes."

"I'm not intense. I'm just saying what I mean." Their path shifted onto a road. They followed the sign toward Hikertown—*I E TOWN* actually, but Messina had guessed what it meant. "Why is there this whole other language of not saying the things you mean but still somehow communicating? I spend so much time trying to figure out what to say, and it always comes out wrong and rude-sounding, and you don't think at all and just say the perfect thing."

Lottie drank from her bottle. Messina already knew she was doing that thing where she didn't say anything because the answer was right there, the way a therapist on a sitcom would do. Lottie loved that shit. She swallowed her water and looked at Messina, eyebrows raised.

"I know, stop thinking," Messina said, annoyed. "You realize that's literally impossible, right?"

The low rumble of an engine turned their heads. A truck pulled up beside them. Everything about it set off alarm bells inside Messina. Big guy in the front, trucker hat, the stink of stale smoke.

They kept walking, heads down, Lottie in front. They didn't have to talk about it or even share a look—it was instinct.

"You want a ride?" the guy asked.

"No thanks," Lottie said without lifting her head. They kept walking. The truck inched along beside them.

"It's cool," said another voice. A woman. Messina looked up and saw that she rode in the back, along with three other people, two guys and another woman. She had been so focused on the driver that she hadn't even realized there were people packed into the bed of the truck. Not just people, hikers. "I promise it's safe," the woman said. "We're headed to Hikertown if you want a lift."

Messina looked at Lottie to see what she thought and found her already stepping up to the truck with one arm slung out of her pack. *So much for using your brain more . . .*

"You guys planning to stay in a trailer or camp?" one of the women asked.

Lottie looked to Messina, like an offer to be the one to answer. When she didn't speak up, Lottie said, "We might just have a shower and keep moving."

Messina could never have come up with something like that. It gave them an air of confidence and made them sound like they already knew everything about Hikertown. It even managed to make their dirtiness (even after cleaning themselves by the trough, they were still filthier-looking than any of these hikers) seem like no big deal—*we just came for the showers.* At least with the wind moving over them as they drove, Messina wasn't too worried about their smell.

Hikertown was a more bizarre place than she could've dreamt up. It was a sprawling dirt lot with a bunch of Western, saloony-looking trailers in its center, along with some old movie props and hand-painted signs saying things like **SHERIFF** and **POST OFFICE**. There wasn't a store, but someone in the truck said they were riding up to a nearby place in the morning. Others were hiking on to Tehachapi for resupply.

Lottie bought them both showers for five bucks apiece. When Messina was wiping herself dry with one of her dirty T-shirts, Lottie knocked on the metal door. “I’ve brought spoils!”

Messina already felt spoiled. She’d never known a few minutes of running water could feel so good. “Hang on,” she said, putting her dirty clothes back on over her still-damp body. She’d showered in her underwear—partly because they needed a cleaning just as bad as her body did, and partly because she didn’t trust the privacy of this stall made of corrugated steel with no ceiling and a door that wasn’t really a door. She’d brought in a few extra pairs to rinse, along with her blood-stained pair of shorts. She’d just hang them on the outside of her pack to dry. She was still bleeding, but at least it was starting to slow now.

She opened the door and found Lottie with her still-wet hair dripping onto the shoulders of her T-shirt, smiling hugely, holding out a handful of tampons. “Look what one of the other hikers gave me.” She fanned them out, an assortment of green, yellow, and purple wrappers.

“I can’t use tampons,” Messina said. She didn’t want to die of TSS.

“I know, I just thought maybe you could now, since it’s like this or a sock. I asked around for pads, but no one had any. Even these were hard to find—I guess most of the women are using cups.”

“Thanks,” Messina said, “but I can’t.” Her cheeks stung with shame as she fished a sock from the pile she’d made of dry ones she’d rinsed yesterday.

She wanted to go back to the wild.

The thought surprised her. She hated that they were in this public place now, around people, where she was nervous and overwhelmed and couldn't bleed down her legs and paint her skin in stripes with her own blood. She hated that she was ashamed again. She wanted so badly not to care. At least the sun had gone down and it was dark now, better for hiding.

51

GABE

Let your friends know—change of plans. He wished he could let them know anything. That he hoped they were okay. That he wasn't sure if they'd ever come. That he was so angry at them for doing this without him. That he was lost and lonely and desperate to find them.

He'd been stuck in windmill hell for two days now. A few days seemed the longest amount of time he could stay anywhere before something pushed him out, forcing him farther up the trail. He made a promise to himself not to move again. No matter what. Things got worse every time he did, and he didn't think he could stand anything worse than this.

He was in the middle of a wind farm now, turbines surrounding him on every side. White, three-pronged giants towering over his head. At night they flashed in sync, a sea of red eyes blinking through the darkness while the wind battered his truck, an invisible monster. It played tricks with his mind. He hated it here. He didn't have any cell signal. He missed home and the ocean and his dad and Chicken. And Val.

He missed Lottie.

A knock on his window made him jump. A light shined in at him through the dark, illuminating the inside of his truck. He couldn't see whoever it was. His imagination suggested the windmill monster, then defaulted to cop. Unsure, he smashed down the lock out of instinct and groped around the passenger seat for his phone.

"Hello?" said a woman's voice, followed by the knocking again.

Gabe shined his phone light out the window and saw an exhausted-looking woman standing in the wind, pack on her shoulders. He cranked his window down. Cool wind slammed against him.

"Sorry, I couldn't see you in the dark."

"Do you have any water?" she said, like she hadn't even heard him.

"Yeah, of course." He reached into his backseat and handed her a still-warm bottle. "Sorry it's hot."

She took it and chugged for a long time. She was probably five years older than him, with short, wind-whipped red hair. Her face was streaked with salt and sunblock. When she was done, she stared at him, still out of breath from the chugging or hiking or both. "Which way are you going?"

"What?"

"Are you driving north or south?"

"Oh, neither," he said. "I'm just waiting for my friends."

"PCT hikers?"

"Yeah." It was strange to hear it like that—*PCT hikers.* Val had always talked about it with such awe. He hadn't really thought of Lottie and Messina as actual PCT hikers, but they were. It stirred up a swell of feelings inside him that he couldn't name, both good and bad.

"Could I come in and take shelter for a minute?" She was getting clobbered by the wind standing outside, but he was still stunned by the request. Just days ago, hikers ran from him, and now one was asking to be invited inside his truck. He wondered what made the difference. *Desperation,* he thought, looking at her. The elements here were so much worse than at Lake Hughes.

"Of course, yeah." Before he could even feel bad for not offering, her pack thudded into the bed of his truck, and she'd climbed into the shotgun seat beside him.

He rolled up his window, cutting out the howl of the wind and making a sudden quiet inside the cab. The woman was covered in dirt from head to toe, and she stank. It made him conscious of his own smell. He'd baked in the heat for a week now with no shower.

He offered her a bag of chips, and she tore into them with dirty fingers. She picked up a half-drunk bottle of Gatorade from the floor and held it up like *Can I*? He nodded, and she downed the remaining half of it in a few swallows. "Thanks. I'm Eva, by the way."

"Gabe," he said.

"They're weird, right?" she said, motioning to the blinking red lights. "They go on forever. Feels like I can't get away from them."

Gabe nodded. He knew the feeling.

"Are you hiking?"

"No," he said. "I mean, I will be once my friends show up. Have you passed a couple of girls?"

She took another drink from the bottle and wiped her mouth with her arm. "Yeah I did, actually, just a little ways back. They seemed pretty angry at each other."

Gabe's heart leapt. "Were they my age?"

She looked at him and shook her head. "Older."

"Oh."

"Do you know when they're supposed to come through?"

"No." Having to answer the question deflated him. Like all the stuff he'd avoided thinking about was suddenly inescapable. "Honestly, I'm not even sure I'm waiting for them in the right spot. I keep getting pushed farther and farther up the road."

"It's a pretty insane year to hike this trail. A lot of people are bailing out. Most who are staying are skipping the worst of the desert sections, at least up to Walker Pass." She shoved three chips into her mouth and crunched on them, speaking around the food. "I'm trying to get to Kennedy Meadows, if you want to give me a ride. You might have better luck finding your friends there."

"No." He said the word out loud to himself, not her, just in disbelief that he might have guessed entirely wrong. That he might have been in the wrong section of trail completely. He didn't feel good. He leaned back against his seat and closed his eyes.

"Are you okay? How many days have you been sitting out here in the heat?"

He shook his head. "I don't know anymore. I'm okay," he said, taking in a deep breath and opening his eyes again. The red-eyed monster blinked at him. "I just don't know what I'm doing out here."

She smiled at him in the dark of the truck. "None of us do."

He drove Eva twenty minutes up the road to Tehachapi so she could try to hitch a ride from there, and returned right back to his spot by the blinking, red-eyed monster. She'd chatted with him all the way into town, reminding him a little of Val with her animated hands and inability to sit through a quiet moment. She told him about how she and her boyfriend in Washington were hiking the trail in opposite directions to meet up in the middle, but how the desert had just about killed her, so she was bailing out and going up higher.

"I hope your friends survive it," she'd said when she got out and waved bye to him. He knew she'd meant it lightly, as a joke. But he couldn't get rid of the sick feeling it gave him.

52

MESSINA

There was something very wrong about the feeling of nasty clothes against freshly cleaned skin. Her underwear was still damp from the shower. Even clean, she was starting to smell like roadkill.

They dropped their packs in a community area and followed the sounds of laughter to a picnic table where some hikers were gathered beneath a string of lights—two from the truck, and a few others they hadn't seen before. Lottie towed Messina to a spot, giving her a look that said, *Now's your chance.* Messina felt like everyone was staring at her taped boot. She couldn't stop thinking about how silly and amateur it made her look.

The group already had an easiness to it, the kind of camaraderie that didn't exist in the group they'd met earlier with the influencers. This group felt more like a band of outcasts—mismatched and sunburned and scruffy. But she and Lottie were misfits among the misfits. At least she was. Lottie was already settling in, being passed snacks, while Messina faced away from the others, picking at the peeling skin from her sunburn.

Lottie nudged her, and she turned to face the group. The

others introduced themselves—Gerdy, Snakefoot, Mountain Goat, Molasses, and Toots. They were all older, mid-twenties to forty or so. Toots looked like a misfit among the misfits too, sitting a little ways off from the others. He waved at the mention of his name and took a pull from a flask in his shirt pocket.

"I'm Lottie, and this is Messina," Lottie said.

"Are those your trail names?" the woman called Gerdy asked.

"What's a trail name?"

"It's a name you get out here, a nickname that says something about who you are out on the PCT." She held out a bag of pickle-flavored potato chips to Lottie and Messina, offering them some. They were salty and sharp and the best thing Messina had ever tasted after days of protein bars and nuts. She only took two, afraid of taking too much and seeming greedy. She licked her fingers after and hoped that wasn't gross. It was all she could do not to rip the bag from Gerdy's hands and dump its contents into her mouth.

"I thought Lottie might be a nickname. Like you're a whole Lott-ie or something," Gerdy said, laughing now. "And this one's a mess." She motioned to Messina, who picked at her skin more furiously. *This.one's.a.mess.this.one's.a.mess.* She tried desperately not to take it personally and retreat inside her head, but she was failing miserably.

"We were just talking about GPS," the one called Molasses said. "What kind are you guys using?"

"We're not using any," Lottie said, matter-of-factly.

Eyes went wide around the table. Several of them laughed, and

Snakefoot said, "Man, I miss being that young. Naive enough to think you'll be okay just by virtue of existing."

Lottie shot Messina a look that she instantly understood. Neither of them had ever been that naive. Messina tried to smile at Snakefoot, like the joke was funny, afraid the snack-offerings would stop if she came off as rude. She always seemed rude, so she tried extra hard now to be nice. And then she remembered Lottie's advice and tried not to try and her brain twisted itself into a knot.

Someone else passed her a bag of gummi bears. They were soft and warm and tasted like whatever actual heaven was. The others' snacks were so much better than the bars and nuts they'd been eating. But taking tiny samples of delicious food was torture. She was suddenly starving. She felt overwhelmed by the hunger and by trying not to try and by the noise of the laughter and conversation and the sheer number of people.

She stood and left the table. She found herself in the quiet of the common area where the packs all lay in a heap. Her old instincts and anxiety told her to start rifling through them and take what she could, but she remembered she could be who she wanted to be out here. She didn't think she wanted her new self to steal, especially from the kind of people who shared pickle chips and gummi bears.

It occurred to her then that she and Lottie were the only ones not sharing food. It wasn't in Lottie's nature to share. She never had enough. Messina dug the bag of nuts from her pack. It was a sad offering—they weren't even salted. *Don't overthink it,* Lottie's voice said inside her head. Right, maybe it wasn't gummi bears, but at least it was something.

She took her offering to the table, setting it in the center, like *help yourself.*

Minutes passed. No one touched it.

Gerdy finally picked it up and passed it back to Messina. “Mountain Goat has an allergy. We’re trying to keep the area free of them.”

“Oh.” She took the bag back and walked away from the table. “Stupid.stupid.stupid,” she told herself again and again, pressing her nails into her fingertips one at a time. She threw the nuts into a trash bin and wished she could crawl in right behind them and hide there forever.

She stayed close but out of sight of the picnic table, still hearing them all laughing and talking, while she waited for Lottie. Messina thought she’d come find her to make sure she was okay.

But she didn’t.

53

LOTTIE

The attention went to her head like booze. She'd been starved of it out on the trail. She got the feeling again of being a kid surrounded by adults, but it didn't feel condescending this time—it felt like respect.

"Is it rude if I ask how old you are?" Gerdy said.

"Seventeen. And Messina will be eighteen next month. She just graduated, but I've got another year to go."

"Damn. That's pretty badass. Nothing this cool was even on my radar at that age."

Lottie's insides glowed at the compliment, but she only half-believed it. The person she was, here at this table, was a lie. If they saw the real Lottie, they wouldn't say things like that.

"Is your friend starting college after the summer, or is this the start of travels in a gap year?"

"She's going to community," Lottie said, realizing then that Messina's plans were all likely to change after this. She really wasn't coming back this time.

She'd been gone for a while now. "Did any of you happen to see where she went?"

Gerdy shook her head, but the others didn't even hear her question, all deep in another conversation already.

54

MESSINA

She walked out into the night, away from the picnic area. Hikertown was even creepier in the dark, but she preferred being creeped out to the gut-punch of listening to her friend not give a shit about her, still talking and laughing with the others. She sat down on a railroad tie.

She heard footsteps and was relieved that Lottie had finally come to find her. Only it wasn't Lottie. It was Toots. He was already a little wobbly from whatever was in his flask. He sat down on the railroad tie by Messina and held it out, offering her a drink. She took it, reminding herself that alcohol killed germs, and drank, chugging faster than she should've. The flask *glug-glug-glugged*. Messina coughed, spitting up a little in her lap.

"Easy," Toots said.

Messina shook her head in disagreement. Whatever the hell was in that flask was already running into her veins, warming them. "No. Nothing is easy for me." She could feel Toots's eyes on her skin.

"I'll cheers to that." He lifted the flask from her fingers and drank. He passed it back to her and she drank again, slower. It tasted like acid, singeing her insides. Messina liked it, the way it burned things away, how she felt lighter with each swallow.

"Fuck 'em," Toots said.

Messina nodded in response, like *yeah, fuck 'em,* and took another drink. She wondered how old Toots was. Twenty-eight, thirty, maybe. She tried not to think about how he got his trail name. It was easy to not think about things now because any thought she didn't want just floated away like a balloon.

Toots stood up and walked away, which was fine, because Messina liked sitting alone better. She heard a zip sound behind her and a stream of liquid hitting the dirt, saturating it with piss until the sound turned splashy like a puddle. The sound of guy piss was disgusting. It always sounded overly aggressive—why did they all wait so long to go, until it shot out of them like a super-soaker gun?

The water-gun thought reminded Messina that Toots had a penis, which was even grosser than the piss sound. He zipped up and sat back down beside her again. She wobbled a little on the railroad tie, and Toots put his arm around her.

"You know who things are easy for?" she said. Her whole body felt warm from the inside out, like it was glowing. "Lottie. Everything's easy for her, like talking and being cool and flirting."

"You might be better at flirting than you think," Toots said, but Messina didn't care because she didn't like Toots or his super-soaker dick, and she was still thinking about Lottie. But she didn't say so because she still wanted to drink from his flask. But then he was looking at her funny, so she thought maybe she'd said what she was thinking by accident.

"Sorry," she said, and he passed her the flask again, so she knew he wasn't mad. She tipped it to her lips. It was almost empty now, even though it was full just a quarcel ago.

"That should be her trail name," Messina said. "Easy. Because things are easy for her. . . . and because she's easy," she said, laughing to herself at the joke.

Toots kissed her. His tongue tasted like booze and onions and things she couldn't name. Messina hated kissing. She hated the feeling of his tastebuds against hers and the slick bumps of the veins under his tongue and how it felt like she couldn't breathe. She pulled away just in time to vomit on the ground in front of them. She wiped her chin with her arm. "Don't do that," she said. "You made me puke."

Toots laughed, and Messina laughed too. He tipped the last of the flask into her mouth.

"Her trail name really *could* be Lottie." Her thoughts were back on her friend. "Because if you want her to, she'll do a whole Lott-ie. And she is a Lott-ie." Messina tipped the flask against her mouth, remembering now that it was empty. "She'll sleep with a Lott-ie guys," she said, laughing some more. Laughing felt good, like vomiting.

She looked up and found Lottie staring at her.

There was something in her eyes like sadness—or disappointment, maybe. Messina couldn't tell. Her thoughts were all being swept up in a tide. But Lottie's face reminded her of the time that woman in church saw her stealing from the collection plate.

"It's time to go," Lottie said.

Messina thought she was right because she didn't want to sit so close to Toots anymore. She tried to get up, but his arm was still around her shoulders. His other hand was on her thigh.

"You need to take your hands off her," Lottie said.

Toots raised his hands up like it was a stickup in an old movie. "Hey, I'm not looking for trouble."

Lottie tugged on Messina's hand until she was standing-wobblingfalling. Lottie caught her and put her arm underneath Messina's. It felt better than Toots's. Except Lottie was shaped all wrong and lumpy. Messina realized she was wearing both their packs and they were walking even though Messina didn't want to walk.

She threw up again.

Lottie yanked her arm so she was walking again even though she really didn't want to because it made everything spin and she just wanted to lie down forever.

"It's not safe here," Lottie said, tugging again.

Messina was mad at her. Or she was mad at Messina. She couldn't remember. One of them was always mad at the other so they wobblewalked until forever and Messina's legs were dead and broken and she slept.

55

LOTTIE

This was the desert Craig was talking about—*That's where it's gonna get real.* He wasn't kidding. It was windy, with air so dry it sucked the moisture from their skin as soon as it touched it, leaving it cracked and chapped. Lottie had gotten two nosebleeds already. Her sinuses burned.

Messina dry-heaved into the dirt beside them. She hadn't had anything to eat or drink since the morning, when she'd chugged half a bottle of water and immediately puked it all out. They were already running out again. They hadn't filled their bottles in Hikertown, and Lottie kept wiping what they had over Messina's skin every time they stopped just to keep her cool. She was pale, her lips the wrong color.

"Are you sure you want to keep going?" Lottie said. They'd been following the mostly buried pipe of the LA aqueduct through the middle of the Mojave and stopped to rest, crouched in the shade of a foot-tall bush. The temperature had to be in the hundreds. It was maddening to know that enough water for all of Los Angeles was right beneath their feet, but they had no access to it.

"How were there so many hikers in Hikertown but there are

none here?" Messina said, wiping her mouth and standing up again. It was painful to watch her move, like the Tin Man when he ran out of oil.

Lottie had listened as the others spoke about it the night before. Most of them were planning to skip this stretch of trail, others planned to hike it at night because of the heat and lack of water. The two of them had hiked a small section of it last night, when Lottie wasn't about to stay around that place with a fucker like Toots. Her insides raged just thinking about him. About what could've happened if she hadn't come looking for Messina when she did. She knew it was her fault—she should've gone after Messina sooner.

"Let's just go," Messina said. "Being stuck here is worse than walking in it."

"We could go back. You don't look good."

"I'm fine," Messina said, straightening her body to something more upright. "Let's go."

Lottie nodded. She couldn't tell if it even mattered—there was no relief in this place whether they were moving or stopped. The sun and the heat were relentless.

Their pace was a crawl. They found a plastic crate full of water jugs chained to a Joshua tree—probably one of the caches Mac was talking about—but they were empty, just like he said. They walked on, stopping again just a few minutes later for Messina to heave again. Sweat dripped from her face.

"No more," Lottie said. "We're stopping." Messina didn't argue. Lottie helped her into a spot of warped shade beneath a clump of scrub and poured sips of water into a bottle cap that she tipped over Messina's lips. The asshole sun didn't move. It flamed above them like a giant *fuck you* in the sky.

Lottie set up the tent for better shade, but within minutes it was hotter inside than out, an instant oven. The sun still didn't move. She was convinced it was never going to go down. It was going to burn them alive.

She drank only the smallest sips of water for herself, trying to conserve what they had.

She tipped more into Messina's mouth.

The world sizzled.

Messina's eyes were rolling back in her head by the time it cooled enough for Lottie to pull her into the tent. Her sweat had the sharp tang of old alcohol—her body was still wringing it out through her pores. "I'm going to get help," Lottie told her.

Messina said nothing. Her breathing was slow.

Lottie argued with herself, the way Messina would've argued with her, trying to think this through. *Who are you going to find? We're in the middle of nowhere, and we haven't seen a single hiker since Hikertown.*

You're right. It's probably useless, she thought, *but I have to try.*

"Messina." Lottie gently smacked her cheek, trying to keep her awake.

"Mmm?" Her eyes cracked open. She was soaked in sweat.

"I'm going to get water and help. Stay here. Stay alive."

She crawled out of the tent and into the night. She ran, following the narrow beam of her flashlight. Movement was so much easier without her pack, the sun finally gone. Until the wind picked up, blowing against her, another force of nature to battle.

Truth: She was terrified that she was about to lose her other best friend.

Her body was completely drained of energy, but she pushed through more and more steps, telling herself each time *just a few more, just a few more*, hoping for the possibility of seeing someone that could help—in the middle of the desert. Her pace slowed as she realized it was hopeless. There was no one out here. She was on a desert road that went for miles in the middle of the night.

The wind picked up even more, howling and raging against her. It blew dirt and dust at her so hard it stung her skin. It pummeled her, an invisible force working against her, the same as she'd felt all her life, only more tangible. She walked on. She didn't know what else to do. If she returned empty-handed, her only other option would be to go back to Hikertown. It occurred to her now that she could've gone in that direction for help. At least she knew she'd eventually reach a water spigot. If she turned around now, the sun would be well up by the time she got there. *Another fuckup*, the voice inside her said. Red eyes blinked at her in the distance.

For a moment, she thought she was hallucinating again. But they were real. Her heart skipped a beat as she thought they must be brake lights from passing cars . . . that were floating. Maybe she was near a freeway overpass. Or maybe she was going crazy.

But they weren't cars. They all blinked at the same time. The wind had turned, pushing her toward the blinking lights now. They looked alien. The wind beat against her body, a whooshing sound filling the air around her. Her senses were overwhelmed by the noise and the lights and the wind and her mind wondering what the hell this was, when she realized she was passing through a wind farm. Turbines were whirring above her head, their red lights blinking like Morse code.

Finally, she dropped onto the road, unable to go another step. There was no help here. Only the wind.

The ground was still hot from the day. She lay down, letting her body melt against it. She couldn't help Messina or Val or herself. Her friends would both die because she was a fuckup. The sky was full of stars. She thought there would be more of them in the desert. She closed her eyes.

Something breathed on her. She bolted upright, and whatever it was darted off. Lottie looked after it, watching its shadow as it disappeared into the darkness. She swore it was the fox.

"Val?" She squinted her eyes, searching for it. But it was gone.

In the distance, she saw the faint glow of something blue. Another hallucination probably, or some kind of malfunctioning light on one of the turbines. But it wasn't either.

It was the blue glow of a camp stove.

56

LOTTIE

She ran so hard she thought her legs might shatter. The closer she got, the more certain she was that the light was a camp stove. She ran against the wind. It filled her eyes and nose and mouth with dirt.

When she finally reached the campers, she was so relieved, not just that they actually existed, but that they were women. Two of them. Looking up at Lottie like they were unsure of her intentions, like she was a stray coyote that stumbled onto their camp. She remembered Messina's words about how she was built like a coyote, made for survival.

"Do you have water?" She panted the words, her heart and lungs still trying to recover from the run. "My friend is sick. She's in trouble."

One of them looked at her with sympathy. The other with coldness.

"I don't mean to be rude, but we can't help you," the cold one said. Lottie's heart crumbled. She sank into the dirt.

"That's not true," the other one said. "Don't do that, Kat."

"No. I'm sick of this shit." The cold one threw something she was holding into the dirt at their feet. "We can't keep helping every lost puppy who comes around here looking for scraps and help and our supplies. This isn't a charity hike. If you can't hack it, call for help and go home."

"I don't have a home. And I am calling for help. Please. That's why I'm here."

"Don't listen to her," the nice one said. "You're not a lost puppy—you're a fucking warrior. This is one of the hardest stretches, and nobody gets through it without help." She shot a look at the cold one and then turned back to Lottie. "What do you need?"

"My friend's puking. Her lips are pale. She can't keep anything down. I've been trying to keep her sipping water, but we're running low on that now too."

The nice one looked concerned. Even the mean one's face softened a little. "Has she been taking any salt? Sports drinks, electrolytes?"

Lottie shook her head. She remembered now Fox Girl talking about nearly dying because she'd run out of electrolytes. The only salt they had were the jerky sticks, and Messina wasn't eating them. All the puking after Hikertown and the heat of the desert must've made it worse.

The nice one turned to the other one. The mean one spoke. "You know you're going to go anyway." The friendly one went into the tent behind them and emerged with a bag slung over her shoulder.

Lottie led the way back to Messina. Getting back to her felt so much faster than looking for help. The woman—Lottie still didn't know her name—dumped a stick of electrolyte powder into a fresh bottle of water and tipped it to Messina's lips. She opened her eyes, taking a huge swallow.

"Slow slow slow," their savior said, taking it away from her. "Or you'll puke it all up." She handed the bottle to Lottie. "Give her a sip every few minutes."

"Thank you," Lottie said.

"I'll hang around outside to see how she's doing in a bit."

Messina took half the bottle without incident before she fell asleep. Lottie emerged from the tent to find their savior still waiting there, sitting in the dirt, the wind whipping strands of hair that had escaped her short ponytail.

"How's she doing?" She took a drag from the joint she was smoking.

"Good, I think. Sleeping."

The woman nodded. "Electrolyte imbalance in this heat will fuck you up properly." She blew smoke out of her nose, like a dragon. It reminded Lottie of Tristan. *Cinnamon vape, crooked smile, Do you like that?*

Yes. She liked everything.

Lottie pulled herself back to the present. "She's probably been running low our whole hike. Our food's not salty, except for jerky, and Messina doesn't eat meat."

"She needs to learn to."

They were both quiet for a minute, nothing but the sound of the wind between them. It had slowed a bit, and the tent blocked enough of it so they didn't get battered. "I'm Ash," the woman said, breaking the silence. "Trail name and real name—short for Ashley."

"I'm Lottie. Thanks for saving our butts, Ash."

Ash nodded, like it was no big deal.

Truth: It was a very big deal.

"Sorry if I caused you trouble with your friend."

Ash waved this off and passed the joint. Lottie didn't want any, but she felt obligated since Ash was being so nice and had literally just saved Messina's life.

"She's my partner. Probably soon to be ex." She took the joint back and flicked the ashes. "I think a part of me knew our relationship wouldn't survive this, but I wanted to come anyway. Honestly, that might be the reason *why* I wanted to come. I kind of make a habit of setting things on fire, hence the nickname."

"Same," Lottie said. "Except I never get to the relationship point—I usually start setting things on fire straightaway the morning after."

"Wow, a seductress and a warrior."

Lottie snorted, smoke coming out of her nose. It burned. She never knew why people blew it out that way on purpose. She could feel the weed going to her head. "I don't know if I'd call myself either of those things." She laughed, but she didn't know why.

Ash nodded, like this was good logic. She pulled her legs up to her chest, a huge dragon tattoo inked onto one of them. "To being serial fuckups, then," she said, holding out her fist.

Lottie reluctantly bumped it. It was funny Ash used that word, Lottie thought, in the way things weren't really funny at all. She didn't remember saying anything about being a fuckup.

"My last breakup was the worst," Ash said. "I slept with a coworker, who ended up quitting after things got weird, just to avoid me."

"I can top that."

"Bullshit. Spill it."

Lottie shook her head. She didn't want to relive it. She didn't know why she mentioned it. This was why she hated getting high—too much was out of her control, but she never really felt any kind of peacefulness—everything just got foggy and confusing.

"Does anyone know?"

"No," Lottie said. She didn't know why, but saying so made the corners of her eyes prick.

Ash leaned in and put her arm around Lottie's shoulders, offering her the joint again. Lottie took a long drag and blew it out, blinking to hold back the tears.

"Secrets are the only thing heavier than water."

Maybe it was just the weed, but it felt like Ash was reaching into her mind and soul.

"You can let it out if you want," Ash said. "I've got zero room to judge anyone. And you'll probably never see me again. It could be like confession." Ash took her finger and drew a little smiley face in the dirt. It winked at Lottie. "You religious?"

Lottie shook her head.

"My parents are Catholic, but they weren't really keen on the whole gay thing, so I split from it ages ago. I always liked confession, though—not the hail Marys and stuff, but being able to tell someone all my secrets. It helps. Like popping a zit, and all the nasty shit that's inside spills out and you feel way better. You should try it sometime."

"I think I'm good for now."

Ash nodded and passed the joint again. She had a nice nose, big. Lottie liked big noses, even though they were a thing you weren't supposed to like. Gabe had a big nose, Adrien-Brody-big, huge bone in the middle. Or was it cartilage? Big noses got her every time. *Gabe.* She took another drag.

"So what did you do?" Ash asked.

Lottie couldn't remember anymore why she hadn't wanted to tell her. "I screwed around with my best friend's boyfriend." Ash got a look on her face, like she was about to tell Lottie how it wasn't that bad, when Lottie said the rest. "And when she found out he cheated, she was so upset that she went off alone and drunk in the night, high up on a trail, and fell thirty feet and died."

That wiped the look right off her face. Her mouth was still hanging open in the shape of *That's not that bad.* But now she couldn't say it. Because it was. It was the worst thing that could have happened. The worst thing a friend could have done.

"Shit," Ash said, finally. "No wonder you're out here wandering around in the desert."

Lottie didn't say anything back. She was starting to feel sick, like the weed was bad. Ash was wrong about the feeling of relief. It didn't come, not even a little bit. Lottie just felt more exposed and scared than she had before. It all felt more real, like talking about it had encased it in concrete. And now she couldn't take it back.

She didn't want to be around Ash anymore, but she didn't know how to ask her to leave—she'd saved Messina's life and given Lottie half her pot. It wasn't like she could say *Thanks for the help. Could you go away now?*

“That’s your trail name,” Ash said.

An even worse feeling came over Lottie at the words. “What?” She blinked, waiting for it. When nothing came, Lottie hoped Ash was just as high as she was. Maybe she wouldn’t even remember this conversation tomorrow. Lottie hoped she wouldn’t.

“Brutus,” Ash said finally. “The ultimate betrayer.” Then she smiled at Lottie, like it was the best thing ever.

57

MESSINA

Her head felt like it had been cracked open, but at least she wasn't puking anymore. She sat up slowly, waiting for a fresh wave of nausea that didn't come.

She'd woken in the night and found the remaining half-bottle of sports drink beside her and taken it down in what felt like a single swallow. She wanted more now. She found Lottie sitting across from her, awake.

"How are you feeling?"

"Better." Messina rubbed her head and her eyes. Her clothes clung to her with wetness. "Is there any more of that drink?"

Lottie shook her head. "No, that was it."

"We should have stocked up on that stuff at the gas station."

"I don't think either of us expected you to lose all your electrolytes in the world's worst desert hangover vomit sesh."

Just the mention of it made Messina's head throb. She felt embarrassed and ashamed. "I didn't think I'd get that wasted. I was trying not to listen to my brain."

"How'd that work out for you?"

Messina looked down at herself, soaked in sweat, vomit stains on her shirt. "I don't think I did it right."

Lottie gave her a tight-lipped smile, pained. It stirred something in Messina, bringing a swell of hazy and warped memories. *Walking away from the group. Stupid.stupid.stupid. Drinking. Laughing. She'll do a whole Lott-ie.* Her nausea flooded back with the shame of her memories. She was dizzy with it. "Shit, I'm so sorry, L." She covered her face with her hands. "I was awful. I don't even know where that came from."

"It's cool."

"No, it's not. I never—"

"Can we just move on, please?"

Messina didn't want to move on. She wanted to properly apologize for saying horrible things, but she could see Lottie meant it. "Okay, yeah." She laid her head back down and another wave of memories and nausea crested over her. *Toots. Hand on her thigh. Tongue in her mouth.*

"Lot."

"What, M? This isn't moving on."

Messina held her eyes. "Thank you."

The annoyance on Lottie's face dissolved into understanding. She nodded. "That guy was a Fucker."

The heat of the day was already pummeling them. Messina didn't know the total extent of the damage she'd done to Lottie or recall everything she'd said, but it was clear the wounds were still raw. She started putting things into her pack, just to have something to do to cut the awkwardness.

"Do you feel like you can hike today?" Lottie said.

"I think so." She picked up the sports mix bottle. A few remaining drops of the blue liquid rolled inside it. Messina uncapped it and upended it over her mouth, thumping the bottle to get the last drip into her mouth. "Who was that person last night?"

Lottie looked startled by the question.

"No one. I mean, just another hiker. She helped and gave us the sports mix and some extra water. And she said you need to be getting more salt."

Everything Messina knew about salt, from the way it felt to swallow ocean water to what she was taught in health class, told her it was bad for you. It never occurred to her that more salt in one's body might be a good thing, or even a necessity. "But we don't have anything salty."

"We have these." Lottie held out her few remaining beef sticks. They made Messina frown. *Poor dead cow.* "It's better than dying, right?"

Messina stared at the jerky sticks. Brown, perfectly rounded. They didn't look like food—they looked like something to clean a pipe with. "I don't like this."

"You don't have to like it. But we're about to walk through the desert in the middle of the day, and you're barely recovered and we're going to sweat a fuckton."

She looked at them again. Her stomach did a somersault.

"You scared the shit out of me last night," Lottie said, pressing one of the sticks toward her, "so will you please just eat the jerky? We can get you some salted nuts or something as soon as we get to Tehachapi. Please."

She tried to think about how bad she'd felt just a few hours ago, not wanting to end up in the same state again. Brains were strange the way they tried not to remember pain.

She took the stick from Lottie and unpeeled it. It didn't smell like food either. She closed her eyes and tried to imagine it was tofu. Her stomach went tight. But the second the salt hit her tongue, something shifted. It awoke something animalistic in her, and she tore into the jerky, her body swept up in the urgency of consuming it. She made an *mmmm* sound. When it was gone, she licked her lips and fingers and the inside of the plastic wrapping, hungry for more.

Lottie stared at her, wide-eyed. "I've never watched anyone make love to a beef stick before . . . at least not that kind," she said, cracking herself up.

Messina scowled at her. "Don't make it gross. My body obviously wants salt."

Lottie belly-laughed again. "Oh my god, stop," she said between cackles. Messina rolled her eyes. She didn't say anything else for fear of making another accidental euphemism. Lottie could make anything into a sex joke.

They packed up the rest of their camp. The sun bit at their skin even through Craig's sunblock.

"I wonder how much longer we're going to be in the desert."

"Ash said Tehachapi is only about thirty miles away," Lottie said.

"Who's Ash?"

"Oh." Lottie's posture went suddenly stiff. "Just that hiker lady who helped us. Her name was Ash." She turned away, but not before Messina glimpsed the fear in her eyes.

58

LOTTIE

If two girls in the desert are walking thirty miles to Tehachapi, and they're walking at a pace of thirty-two miles a day, how long will it take them to get there?

Lottie was shit at math, but this was a problem she could do.

The head-scratcher was this: *If two girls are walking thirty miles to Tehachapi, and they're walking at a pace of thirty-two miles a day, how the hell are they still walking after two days?*

A) Ash was wrong about the mileage.

B) The desert had killed them, and this was actually hell.

C) They weren't walking anywhere near thirty-two miles a day.

59

MESSINA

The sun and heat and exhaustion made her loopy. Time folded in on itself like origami.

She dreamt of the sports drink.

And beef. Salty delicious wondrous beef.

But it was hurting her stomach, like her conscience was rejecting it. Like the cow body had come to life inside her and was chewing her stomach from the inside, trying to eat its way out.

The air was so hot and dry that she was cracking open and the sun was sizzling her brain through the top of her head. The windmill skeletons whispered *shhhhhhhh*.

She counted her steps to stay sane.

1 2 3 4 5 6 7 8 9 10 9 8 7 6 5 4 3 2 1 2 3 4 5 6 7 8 9 10

But she was losing her mind from the heat and the *shhhhh* and the sun and the thirst and the chewing in her stomach. Like her brain was detaching from her body, *shhhhhhh*.

She kept counting.

60

LOTTIE

The sun was an asshole. A giant hellball in the sky.

Fuck you, sun.

They walked and burned alive because they were walking on the actual surface of the sun.

The fox hallucination skittered in the corner of her vision. *Fuck you, fox.*

It wasn't Val. It was a figment of her imagination brought forth from her subconscious to torture her.

Fuck you, asshole sun.

Fuck you, fox.

It became an anthem, matching the pace of her steps, each one excruciating and slow. The life was draining from her.

Fuck you, asshole sun.

Fuck you, fox.

Fuckyousunfuckyoufoxfuckyousunfuckyoufoxfuckyousunfuckyoufox.

61

MESSINA

1

2

3

4

5

6

7

8

9

10

62

GABE

They weren't coming. Maybe they'd passed by him at night while he slept. Or maybe they really had skipped this section altogether.

A third option buzzed around his head like one of those tiny flies that lived out here, the kind that went straight for the eyes. But Gabe shooed it away. He couldn't even entertain the idea that something might have happened to them. His soul couldn't handle any more.

The wind turbines sat silent and still above his head. He was outside his truck hunched in the shrinking spot of shade again, sweating through his T-shirt. His weather app didn't work without signal, but the temperature had to be over a hundred. He reeked, like sweat and onions and something he could only identify as desert-rank.

His mind spun, trying to assess. Trying to make a new plan. *North, south, stay, go, Kennedy Meadows, Walker Pass . . .* He was so tired of it.

He tipped his head back against the hot metal of his truck. "I'm not going to find them," he said out loud. The wind turbines laughed in agreement. He'd been stupid to think he could sit along a 2,600-mile trail and just bump into them.

He stood up, bones creaking. He'd probably lost five pounds of muscle mass just sitting here for days on end, barely moving. He was done. He was going home.

He climbed into his truck and cranked the engine. He checked his mirrors.

Coming up behind him was one more pair of hikers. He sighed to himself. He'd ask if they'd seen Lottie and Messina, and then he'd go.

63

LOTTIE

She was hallucinating again. Seeing Gabe's truck parked roadside.

"Is that Gabe's truck?" Messina pointed at the figment of Lottie's imagination. Their visions were syncing up just like their periods had.

"No, it's a hallucination. I keep having them too."

"No, that's Gabe's truck. Look."

A not-real Gabe was getting out of the not-real truck and coming toward them.

Lottie blinked at him. It didn't make sense for him to be here. Something terrible must've happened. Panic shot up inside her like a rocket, and she ran to him as fast as her desert-worn body would allow.

"What's wrong?" she panted. "Why are you here?"

His face was strange—anger hung where she expected sadness or grief. "You stole my sister's ashes," he said in a voice that matched the look on his face.

She let go of his arms. She hadn't even realized she'd grabbed them. She backed up a step. The distance between them was suddenly a chasm. "Oh."

"Oh? That's what you have to say for yourself? Not 'I'm sorry' or 'I really fucked up this time'?"

It was all too much for her sun-sick mind to make sense of. Gabe wasn't supposed to get mad at her for taking the ashes. That was why Messina took them. It wasn't supposed to be Lottie's fault.

Messina finally caught up to them. She was hunched beneath the weight of her pack and the sun. She waved limply at Gabe.

He waved back. "Hey, Messina."

"Do you have any water in your truck?" she asked.

"Yeah, there's water and Gatorade in the back. It's hot, but . . ." She was gone before he could even finish, and his eyes snapped back to Lottie.

"So, are you here to take Val back?" she asked.

"No. I'm here to come with you."

"Gabe, we don't need rescuing."

He scrubbed a hand over his dirty face. "God, you really can't exist for a single second without making everything about you." The words clocked her across the chin. She'd heard them from Messina before, too many times, but it was different coming from Gabe. "This journey wasn't yours to take, Lot." The look in his eyes was frightening, like everything he was holding in might explode out of him any second, like a landmine was buried deep inside his organs. "How dare you do this without me? Val's my sister."

He was right. It never even crossed her mind that Gabe might have needed to be a part of this just as much as she and Messina did.

"I'm so sorry."

"Do you know how destroyed my dad would have been if he walked into that room and saw those ashes missing? I had to call the funeral home to get another urn. I had to *go there*, Lottie." His voice was jagged with whatever he was holding back. She could hear it trying to claw its way out of him. "I had to be in that place again and see it and smell it and relive everything." Tear tracks cut lines along his cheeks. He was nearly as dirty as they were. How long had he been out here?

"But you didn't stop to think about any of that because you're fucking *Lottie*. And you do whatever the hell you want without a second thought for anyone else." His shoulders dropped, like he was spent from the energy of dealing with her.

"Anything else?" She deserved so much worse. She deserved all the shards in his throat that wanted out that he kept swallowing down.

"Yeah." He let out a big breath, like he'd been holding it in this whole time. "I'm glad you're okay." He looked at his truck, where Messina was leaned back against the tire with an empty Gatorade bottle in her hand, a blissed-out grin stuck on her face. "I was worried about both of you." And for a second, Lottie thought he might hug her, but he didn't.

The truth was this: She didn't deserve it, but she was desperate for it.

64

LOTTIE

Val's ashes rested in Gabe's pack now. He drove them to the superstore in Tehachapi, one of those places that has everything from camo gear and hunting knives to diapers and fresh berry bowls. It felt so strange to be in a place where anything she could dream up was right at her fingertips, all in one enormous, climate-controlled box. She was surprised to find herself bothered by it.

The floor felt too hard and smooth as she walked the aisles. She grabbed two hats, sunblock, electrolyte powder, ramen, and three bags of gummi bears. She dropped her haul into the cart and passed the remaining wad of her cash to Messina, who was wide-eyed in the snack aisle.

"I'm going to fill our waters in the bathroom," she said, hoping Messina heard her. She looked like she was in a trance staring at all the shiny chip bags. "Make sure you get plenty of salty stuff," Lottie said over her shoulder. "You should see if there's a cheap pair of running shoes around here, too."

The truth was this: She was going to the bathroom to be alone as much as she was going for water.

She thought she'd feel relief once the door shut behind her, but it didn't come. *Probably because the person you're trying to get away from is you*, said the girl in the mirror.

Music played from speakers above her head while she filled the bottles, taking her time. That old song about manic Mondays. It felt like something from a world she didn't belong to anymore. She stripped off her shirt and washed her skin with soap and water from the sink. She looked more muscular now, with weird tan lines. Her sunburn was finally fading. Her skin was darker everywhere that was sun-exposed. New hair covered her legs and armpits. She wished she felt as changed as she appeared. Maybe she had, before Gabe showed up. She was starting to settle into the PCT, into her own wild. But his presence here felt like it erased all that. It made her remember she was stuck being Lottie, with parentheses.

She dried off under the hand dryer. Someone had graffitied the words **THIS BLOWS** onto its side in purple Sharpie. She swiped a roll of toilet paper from one of the stalls and walked out, half the water in her pack, the other half in her arms. She was still surprised by its weight every time. The cashier side-eyed her as she passed.

"These are old," Lottie said about the bottles in her arms. "I just filled them in your bathroom. My friends paid for our stuff already."

The lady looked like she didn't believe her but was too tired to give a shit.

The doors slid open on the air-conditioned box, letting her pass. The heat was a living, breathing thing outside, ugly and hostile, but it was real. It welcomed her back, enveloping her. Messina and Gabe were at the truck loading food and sports drinks into their packs. Messina was wearing a hideous pair of trail runners the color of tennis balls. Across the lot, Lottie saw two women, one with a green dragon tattoo winding up her leg.

Lottie turned her back to them, ducking, like there was incoming fire, and dropped one of the waters.

Gabe stopped it from rolling away with his shoe. "What are you doing?" He looked at her, standing in a half-crouch.

"Nothing. I just dropped a water."

He didn't even bother calling her out on her lies anymore. She was glad of it.

She'd avoided thinking about Ash and the things she admitted that night, like maybe if she didn't think about her, Ash would disappear, maybe it all would, but it didn't. She was afraid Ash would say something, the same way Val had accidentally spilled Lottie's secret about liking Brian West to their entire English class in eighth grade. Except Val actually cared about Lottie—Lottie didn't get the feeling Ash cared about anyone. *Who names somebody Brutus after they confess the worst thing they've ever done? And then laughs about it?* The thought gave her a rotten feeling in her gut.

Lottie kept her back to the other side of the parking lot. "Nice shoes," she said to Messina.

She smiled wide, like she didn't care how ridiculous she looked. "Clearance. They feel like cloud pillows."

She traded Messina the bottles in her arms for the ramen and gummi bears she was holding, along with Lottie's change—a twenty and a pile of coins. It was all the money she had left to her name.

"I promise I'll pay you back."

Lottie nodded. Her skin was burning with the feeling of Ash's eyes on her from across the lot. She pulled her hair down in front of her face, making sure she stayed behind the truck. She wanted to get out of there, but Gabe and Messina had already cracked open some of the snacks and were eating and chatting while they got their packs situated.

"What happened to your phones?" Gabe asked. "No signal or did they run out of charge?"

Messina told him she'd ditched hers with as few details as possible. Lottie could tell she was struggling with what to say about the other one—Lottie's that had been frisbeed out the window.

"Mine had a mishap on the trail," Lottie said, stepping in to save Messina. She was still wishing they could get the hell out of this parking lot when Gabe told them that a highway patrol officer had stopped him and asked about them. It flipped a switch in Messina, and she was suddenly just as motivated to get back to the trail as Lottie was.

"We're losing light," she said, though Lottie knew it had nothing to do with the light and everything to do with that highway patrol officer.

"Let me ask inside if I can park here, then we can hike up to Tehachapi Pass." Gabe ran off into the store.

"Tehachapi Pass," Messina said. Her face went dark as she repeated Gabe's words. "I knew Tehachapi sounded familiar."

"How do you know it?"

"It's where Cheryl Strayed started her hike." She blew out a long sigh. "We're not out of the desert yet."

Lottie tried to process that as Gabe returned, saying he could park his truck in the back of the lot. Facing more of the desert was a thought frightening enough to make her forget about Ash for a moment, until Gabe backed up, leaving her fully exposed standing next to Messina. She pivoted to face the store.

"You want to talk about what's going on in that mind of yours?"

Lottie just shook her head. *Nope.*

It took Gabe a hundred quarcels to park. Lottie chanced a look at the other end of the lot and saw Ash and her partner still there. They looked like they were arguing. *Good,* Lottie thought. *At least she's distracted.*

Relief washed over her when Gabe finally made it back to them, ready to go. They shouldered their packs and started back toward the road.

"Brutus!" The name brought a wave of acid up into Lottie's throat. At first, she didn't turn. She ignored it, pretending like she hadn't heard, like it wasn't her. But it came again. "Brutus!" Gabe and Messina were looking back now. Lottie looked back too, afraid it would be worse if she didn't, that Ash might run up to try to catch her.

Ash was waving at her from the back of the parking lot. She'd somehow spotted Lottie from where she stood with her partner. Lottie gave a sheepish wave back and turned away, continuing to walk.

"Who's that?" Gabe said.

"No idea." No one bothered to question the lie.

65

MESSINA

Gabe's story clawed through her mind. The highway patrol had been looking for her. She knew Jeffucker wouldn't stop. Police, missing persons—as long as he had ways to pursue her, he would use them.

But she was so tired of being scared. She liked feeling strong instead, the way she felt when she hiked now, with electrolytes pumping through her veins. They made her bionic. Super-Messina. She decided not to be afraid anymore, just like Cheryl Strayed. She remembered the words—*I decided I was safe. I was strong. I was brave. Nothing could vanquish me.*

She chanted them in her mind as they ascended back into the mountains. The salt hummed in her blood, giving her strength. Electrolytes were magic. And running shoes. Messina was starting to think she was a little bit magic too, her winds blowing strong inside her. She'd traded the weight of her fear for the weight of her pack. She understood now why Val talked about nature the way she did, like it was a god. The way it was vast and endless and showed you your strength if you were brave enough to look. If Messina did ever find a god she believed in, she was sure it would be in a place like this.

She was safe. She was strong. She was brave. Nothing could vanquish her.

Maybe Lottie was feeling the magic of the electrolytes and nature-power too, because she was hiking really fast. Or maybe she was doing that to punish Gabe.

Messina could tell Lottie was unhappy about him being with them now. But she was glad to have him on the trail. At first, it felt like his presence stifled their sense of wild, the way it had done back when they used to sleep over at Val's house and he'd come home from wherever, changing the entire vibe just by walking through the door and going to his room. But Messina liked her wild too much now to let anyone mess with it.

And she liked that it felt different with Gabe whenever they bumped into men now, how those encounters didn't come with the same sense of fear and vulnerability as they had before. They'd passed a guy coming down right out of Tehachapi Pass, a lone hiker. Messina hadn't even bothered looking over her shoulder after he passed, because with Gabe around, she knew the luxury of what it was to be a man, to not sense a potential threat at every encounter.

They'd been ascending for hours now, long enough for her thighs to burn and then go numb and start burning all over again. When she took her eyes off the trail, she was glad to be up high again. She looked out and knew she was taller than Jeffucker and anything else that had ever scared her before.

Gabe borrowed the solar charger that she and Lottie had never needed, and used the navigation on his phone to find a flat-ish spot to camp in—another thing about his presence that Messina liked. Even though she missed how they used to count things in quarcels. Everything was in miles and minutes and hours now, rigid and standardized, with no accounting for the heat or the incline. Quarcels were better suited for the wild.

"There's supposed to be a water cache about a half mile up," Gabe said while Lottie and Messina set up their tent. Messina remembered how hard it had been for her to do the first night. She could do it blindfolded now. "I'll go check and see if there's anything in it."

"How do you know about those?" Lottie said it like an accusation.

"I read some PCT blogs when I was waiting for you."

Lottie frowned and looked at his back like it had wronged her as he walked up the trail.

"Why are you being mean?" Messina said, once he was out of earshot. "He's just trying to help."

"I'm annoyed. It's like he got to study the SparksNotes version of the trail while we've been out here suffering through everything."

"Yeah, but we've only been suffering through it without him because we stole his sister's ashes and didn't bother inviting him to come along."

Lottie's face fell. "I know."

Gabe returned with his bottle half-filled and poured some into Lottie's and Messina's before setting up his own tent.

"Where did you get all the gear?" Messina asked him, taking a beef stick from the new pack and cracking open the plastic.

"A woman—I don't know her name—came into Lu's looking for

Val and left a backpack full of gear for her. It had almost everything I needed." He sat down outside his tent and held a lighter to his mini camp stove. "What about you guys?"

Lottie grabbed another beef stick away from Messina before she could open it and passed her a bag of chips instead. Messina had been getting the farts pretty bad since she'd started eating beef. Her body craved it now, but it was stuck in some kind of war with itself. "We borrowed ours too," Lottie said.

"Oh, good," he said, peeling back the top on his cup of noodles. "I heard the Petersons had their shed broken into after the party. There was a bunch of outdoor stuff taken, and something about rearranged garden gnomes. That must've been someone else."

Gabe watched Messina as she slipped another beef stick from the stash and pulled down its wrapper. A puzzled look stuck on his face. "Aren't you vegetarian?"

Lottie caught her too late. She already had half the stick in her mouth. "Come on, man. You're gassing me out in that tent every night."

"Sorry," Messina said around a mouthful of beef. She couldn't help it. Her body had taken on a mind of its own out here. "I'm still vegetarian," she said, answering Gabe's question. "But as long as I'm out here, hiking around, trying to exist in the wild, my body wants me to eat like the wild."

He gave her a look like what she'd said didn't make sense, but Messina didn't care. It made sense to her.

She finished her jerky and licked the salt and grease from her fingers, but it wasn't enough. Her body wanted more salt. She poured a pack of blue electrolytes into her bottle of water. A hint of a memory skirted the edge of her mind at the taste of it, making her think of the woman they'd seen at the superstore, the one who'd called Lottie Brutus. She felt familiar. Messina just couldn't remember from where. Or why Lottie was trying to hide it.

66

LOTTIE

Messina was right—the desert wasn't done with them. It stretched well beyond Tehachapi, teasing them again and again as it hinted at disappearing for stretches where they'd find pine trees and high mountain views with frigid nights, only to return a few quarcels later with its sagebrush and scrub. The elements were no less hellish than before—the wind and heat and the asshole sun—but at least with hats for sun protection now, and their new ability to find off-trail water sources and caches with Gabe's phone, a few parts of their hell were more tolerable. But there were new hells to endure with the presence of the phone too.

It dinged again. Yesterday when it somehow picked up a random bar of service, it blew up with a frenzy of texts from Merilee. Lottie didn't know how it managed to find a signal—solar flares, or maybe Gabe had a giant ball of tinfoil in his pack—but she hadn't thought phones would work in the actual middle of nowhere.

She watched from the back of their hiking line as Gabe checked the phone and tucked it back in his pocket. It was probably Merilee again. Lottie was irked by it. Not just that Merilee was texting him, but that texting even existed out here.

She hadn't realized how much she'd grown to love not being tethered to the outside world, relieved of all the internal noise and thoughts that came with it. She didn't want it out here on their trail in the peace they'd made.

"Why does Gabe get to keep his phone?" Lottie shouted up at Messina. She'd made her the unofficial peacekeeper of the group.

"Because Jeffucker saw him after we left—he doesn't have any reason to think he's with us. And we need his navigation."

"We needed mine too," Lottie shot. The phone dinged again. "Can you at least silence that thing? It's like Merilee is on this hike with us."

"It was my dad, actually. He was checking in about your cat."

Lottie's heart dropped. "What's wrong with Grimace?"

Gabe stopped and turned back to her. "Nothing, he's fine. He's just staying at our house. See?" He held out his phone, showing her the picture from his dad. His smiling face, framed in the beard he'd let grow since Val died, was next to Grimace, who lapped at a plate of scrambled eggs. They both looked happy, so Lottie wasn't sure why it upset her so much to see it. But it felt like she'd swallowed cactus spines.

"Why is he there?"

"The food you left him had ants all over it. I saw it when I went looking for you."

"So, you could have just replaced it." Her voice was harsh. It felt unfair, like she was being accused of being a shitty parent to Grimace because the best she could do was buy him crappy, off-brand dry food that sometimes got ants. "You can't just take my cat away like some vigilante feline social services."

"I didn't take him. He's just staying with my dad while we're gone. They both seemed lonely."

But he did take him. And Grimace wasn't going to want to live with Lottie again after eating scrambled eggs in an actual house every day.

He was the only friend in her life that loved her unconditionally and didn't care if she lied or who she slept with. Now he was gone.

"I just thought maybe they could use each other's company. Does that upset you?" That was what Gabe's words said. But his eyes said *Are you seriously being that selfish?*

"They both look really happy," Lottie said, trying to hide the hurt in her voice.

67

LOTTIE

They were hiking fast. She'd pushed their pace for days now, though she couldn't remember how many—three, maybe four since they'd met up with Gabe. The thought of Ash behind them had been rubbing against the edges of her mind, swelling like a blister since they left Tehachapi. She wanted to put some distance between them. Messina, alive with animal protein and electrolytes, was able to keep up, but she could tell Gabe was struggling, keeping pace with them out of sheer grit. His body hadn't adjusted to the miles and elements like theirs had.

The landscape still couldn't make up its mind. She could feel it trying to shake off the remaining dregs of the desert. More often now it was dotted with trees. Sometimes they were scraggly things that Lottie couldn't name, sometimes tall pines with wind whispering through their tops. The weather felt just as indecisive. Yesterday the wind blew so hard it threatened to push them from the trail—today, stillness. The more she hiked, the more nature felt like a singular, living being. Like someone she did not want to fuck with.

She could hear Gabe huffing behind her. "Do you need us to

slow down?" she asked again. She knew she'd just asked, but she also knew he was being stoic. Being *Gabe.*

He wiped the sweat off his face. "I'm fine. I'll let you know if I need to slow down." He looked like he was going to puke.

"Let's take a break," Messina said when they came to a shaded spot beneath a pine. Apparently, she'd noticed the pukey look too. "You doing okay?" Messina asked him.

He was leaned back against a rock, eyes closed, face up to the sky. He nodded. "I think I just need some calories. I can't stop thinking about In-N-Out."

"It's because that bird keeps saying 'cheeseburger,'" Lottie said. She'd been hearing its call as they climbed—*cheese-burger, cheese-burger*. Now, as they sat below the pine, she could see it, perched on a high branch above their heads. A little black and white bird, shaped like the lamp by Val's bed.

"I think it's a chickadee," Gabe said. His eyes were still closed, and Lottie felt a pang of guilt at how hard she'd been pushing him, knowing he'd try to keep up. She remembered how brutal Messina's and her first days on the trail were. "Val always said their song sounds like 'cheeseburger.'"

It was funny, Lottie thought, she didn't remember Val ever saying that. She thought about what she'd said before to Messina, about how they'd both held on to such different pieces of Val. Gabe probably had thousands of pieces that were just his.

She ripped open a smashed-up bag of potato chips and passed it to Gabe. "Eat," she said. "You'll feel better." Her feelings toward him were all so complicated now. She used to look at him and just feel happy. Now she felt a whole soup of things. He flashed her a smile of thanks, and the soup turned thicker.

The little bird kept singing its cheeseburger song. It felt special and sad at the same time. More emotional soup. She wondered if anything could ever just feel simple and happy again.

68

LOTTIE

She was drifting off to sleep when something slapped against her chest. She opened her eyes and saw Cheryl Strayed's face staring up at her from the back cover of *Wild* in the dim of the lamplight.

"Why is that always buried in the bottom of your bag?"

Lottie frowned at it. "So it doesn't wake me up when I'm trying to sleep."

"I'm serious.

"Why do you care?" she said. "You gave it to me."

"That's why I care. You haven't even looked at it."

She tossed the book at Messina. "So take it back."

Messina picked it up and smoothed out its cover, carefully. Like it had feelings and didn't like being jostled around or tossed. "I don't want to take it back. I want to know why you haven't read it. What are you scared of?"

Lottie made a face, like it was a stupid question.

Truth: It wasn't.

"Whatever it is, it can't be worse than what we've already been through," Messina said. Lottie knew she didn't just mean on the trail. She meant all of it. The things that connected the three of them—Messina, Lottie, and Val. Their shared understanding of pain. "Read it. Just a little."

"Why?"

"Because she'd want you to."

Lottie took the book. She rolled over and faced the other side of the tent. She didn't read it. But she didn't bury it in her pack either.

69

GABE

There was so much sky. It was everywhere. Cloudless, blue, *enormous*. How had he never realized there was so much of it before? It felt like he was standing on the very tip top of the world, other mountain peaks spreading out in front of him. *Let's go up on a mountain.* He could hear Val's voice everywhere.

She would have loved it here.

Gabe would have loved it too, if he weren't in so much pain. He was only able to appreciate it in scattered bursts, a quick second before it dissolved back into the misery of his body. Everything hurt. He loved seeing the world from on top of a mountain, but it didn't ever end. It felt like they never stopped climbing, even though they went down sometimes, they just went right back up another incline a moment later. He supposed he should've known—it was called the Pacific Crest Trail, not the Pacific Flat Trail.

He was perpetually thirsty. They had to ration their water so much more tightly than he'd had to when he had a truck full of it. Lottie and Messina seemed well adapted to sweating gallons and only replenishing themselves with sips, but he hadn't gotten used to it yet. Or the heat. Or the miles that just kept coming.

He thought he'd be better equipped for this from constant swim practice, but miles in a pool weren't like these—these were hot and dry and upright. He was barely keeping pace with Lottie and Messina, but he was determined not to slow them down. If he was going to crash their pilgrimage, the least he could do was keep up. He felt envious of how easy they made it look. The two of them moved out here like it was natural to them, like they'd somehow become a part of this new world.

He kept thinking of Val doing this all alone, without anyone to keep her company or encourage her on the rough stretches or share their water. It filled him with heartache and affection and admiration for her. She was the toughest person he knew, while at the same time the most fragile. No one was going to tell her she couldn't do something. Gabe, on the other hand, was hardly coping, even with friends, and it had only been a few days. According to his tracker, they were hiking close to twenty miles a day. Lottie and Messina had already gone over a hundred miles before meeting up with him.

He looked out at the view again, trying to ignore how his feet throbbed and how his pack rubbed against his shoulders, making sores. He had seen the same spots on Lottie's lower back whenever she bent over, where her own pack must've been rubbing. Hers were rough and calloused now. He kept waiting for his to toughen up, but they just grew more raw every day, weeping pink-tinged fluid onto his T-shirt.

He thought hiking the trail would make him feel rugged and

strong, but so far, it was doing the opposite. If Val were here, she would have shoved him hard in the shoulder, telling him *You've got this Gabey.* He smiled at the thought. He'd hated the nickname she made for him as kids that stuck, even as they grew—always sounding too close to baby. Now, he missed hearing it.

70

LOTTIE

The bathroom situation was massively improved, now that they had toilet paper, but it had become a lot less convenient with Gabe around. Lottie was free with her body, but that didn't include pooping around boys. She walked up the trail a ways after dinner, once Gabe had gone into his tent. Messina was still up, reading *Wild* by flashlight.

It was freezing out but beautiful. She knew for sure they were moving away from the desert now. She kept her jacket on at night, and there were tall trees now, the biggest they'd seen so far on their journey. They were so high up that she could see the stars straight ahead of her, without even looking up. Millions of them twinkled at her. Far off below, a few lights from a town she didn't know shined. They looked like stars too, only clumped together in a pile that hadn't been stuck up in the sky yet, patiently waiting for their turn.

The sounds of the night whispered around her, wind whooshing through the tops of the pines. She used to hate the quiet of night, always sleeping with the TV on to feel less alone. But the quiet had become something sacred to her now. She understood why Val wanted to do this—even if it did mean pooping outside at night in a hole you had to dig.

Lottie shivered as she banged at the hard ground with her rock, trying to carve out a decent-sized hole. Her hands were going numb in the cold while the rest of her worked up a sweat. The fox scurried at the fringes of her vision. Lottie was getting used to it now, the figment of her imagination. She waved hello to it.

She returned and unzipped the tent, its walls still lit up in pale blue by the light of Messina's flashlight. The smell that rolled out was so caustic it nearly knocked Lottie on her ass.

"Fuck, M. I can taste that." Lottie covered her nose and mouth. "It's a fart box in here. Aren't you freaking out about poo particles?"

Messina shrugged and grinned at the same time. A bit of jerky was stuck in her teeth. "It doesn't bother me when they're my own particles."

Lottie tugged her sleeping bag out from beneath Messina's feet and backed out of the tent. "I can't sleep in here."

"Zip it up—it's cold out there."

Lottie shook her head, zipping Messina in. "You're going to asphyxiate yourself."

She tossed her sleeping bag aside and kicked at the rocks and twigs on the ground, clearing a spot smooth enough to sleep on. Little dust clouds rose up into the night, catching in the blue glow of the tent.

"You can come in mine if you want," Gabe said, crawling out of his tent.

"I'm okay. Thanks though." She kicked at another stick that turned out to be a bit of tree root tethered to the ground.

"Lottie, come on. My clothes had frost on them this morning—it's freezing out here."

"I've slept in the cold before, Gabe. You don't have to be chivalrous."

"I'm not being chivalrous. I'm being your friend." He stood beside his open tent. It looked warm. "You don't always have to tough everything out all on your own, you know."

The words poked at something inside her. She nodded, and Gabe picked up her sleeping bag, following her into the tent. It was smaller than the one she shared with Messina, made for only one person instead of two, so they lay straight-legged and smashed side-by-side. Warmth radiated from Gabe where his body pressed against hers.

Val haunted her dreams as a gray fox weeping tears of blood who followed Lottie as she hiked. Lottie tried to outpace her, but the fox kept up. She followed her down the trail through hazy air to a two-lane road and darted across, just as a truck came barreling down. Lottie jumped out, trying to save her, just as it smashed into them.

She jolted herself awake.

Gabe's arms wrapped around her. "Shhh, you're okay." She breathed him in, the salt and sweat of his skin and whatever was in his DNA that made him smell like Gabe and no one else. "You're okay."

She leaned into him, letting him hold her tight. Letting him tell her she was okay. She wanted so badly to believe him.

71

MESSINA

The cows were taking their revenge. They came for her in the twilight just before sunrise, galloping through her insides. She'd consumed an entire herd of them, and now they stampeded inside her, wanting out. She darted up and ran into the bushes—no time to dig a hole. Everything came out of her at once, forceful and violent and painful. It stank of beef.

When she stood, her legs were stiff from the effort of squatting, and the sun was cresting over the horizon. She was done with beef. She was going back to being a vegetarian. Being a carnivore wasn't for her, wild or not.

She made her way back to the tent—gently. That was when she noticed Lottie was gone. She looked out into the brush, thinking maybe the beef had gotten her too, but she was nowhere. Her sleeping bag was gone. A terrible feeling swept over Messina. She unzipped Gabe's tent to tell him Lottie was missing and saw her lying there, Gabe's arms wrapped around her, just like after the party. At least their clothes were on this time.

But it stirred up a nameless dread in Messina, something that felt like being abandoned at that party. Something that felt like being forgotten.

72

LOTTIE

They ate ramen for breakfast. Messina had sworn off the beef sticks for good—thank God. Lottie stirred her noodles with her plastic spork, sending clouds of steam billowing up into the chilly morning air. She liked eating noodles for breakfast. It was so much better than eggs or cereal. She decided to keep having noodle-breakfasts, even after all this.

She didn't like the thoughts that came then, the *after* part spinning around inside her, the realization that this would end. When it did, Messina would leave. And Lottie would go back to La Conchita and her trailer and Maggie and everything she'd somehow managed to escape out here. The idea of it carved a giant hole straight through her center. She wasn't hungry for her noodles anymore.

The day turned hot as they hiked. Lottie had left her thoughts from the morning at their camp on the mountainside, deciding they weren't real. Only this, right now, was real.

"You know what I can't wait for?" Messina said as they descended into another valley. "Laundry."

They were only a day or two out from Kennedy Meadows now, the official end of the desert, and a stopping point with campgrounds and showers and a store that, according to Gabe's phone, had a washing machine. Lottie had been dreaming about it too, ever since they'd read the description of the camp. Every item of clothing she had was stiff with dirt and sweat.

As much as she hated having Gabe's phone with them, she liked how they knew what was coming now. Knowing what was coming was better than having it sneak up on you.

Their trail through the valley brought them to another big incline. They spent half their day trekking up its path, only to descend again right after. Even after more than two weeks of doing this, Lottie disliked how pointless it felt. *Why am I walking up a mountain if I'm just going to go back down it again?* She'd have preferred a steadier path that went around.

Gabe was hiking faster now, with less effort. She could tell his body was adjusting. But she tried not to think about his body, even though she kept staring at it as he hiked up in front of her. It was like her hormones were all fired up after being so close to him last night. And now all her cells vibrated every time she looked at him. The way the back of his neck sank down into his shirt collar in the perfect little slope, and how the veins stuck out along his forearms, and how swimming had made his butt and shoulders look like they'd been sculpted out of marble. She tripped over a rock and landed in the dirt.

Gabe must have been lost in his own thoughts too, because he didn't stop to turn around or even seem to notice. She wondered if he was thinking about her the way she'd been thinking about him.

She tossed around in the tent, unable to get to sleep. Gabe's arms had made it so easy last night. She sat up, frustrated, Messina soundlessly asleep beside her. Lottie climbed over her and unzipped the tent as quietly as possible.

She found Gabe sitting outside his tent on a rock, staring up at the sky. His eyes found hers in the dark.

"Hi," she said. It reminded her of the times they used to find each other in the hallway outside Val's room in the middle of the night.

Gabe's smile lit up the night around them. "Hi."

"Is there room on your rock for two?"

He slid over, making a space. They sat in the quiet of the night, neither of them talking. Finally, Gabe knocked his shoulder against hers and said, "Did you know you and Messina have hiked over two hundred miles together?"

"Really?"

He nodded. "Almost two-fifty."

Pride swelled in Lottie's chest. It wasn't something she would have thought herself capable of.

"Do you think she's happy that we're doing this?" she said. "Val?"

"All she ever wanted was for all of us to care about this stuff as much as she did. And now we're all out here together, accomplishing this huge feat in her honor. I don't think anything could make her happier."

It wasn't the question Lottie really wanted the answer to—*Do you think she forgives me?*—but it felt close.

"Does your dad know you're out here?"

Gabe picked at something invisible on the rock. "No, he would have worried. I told him I was going camping with Marcus. I just have to be back by Val's birthday."

Val's birthday. Lottie had lost track of time out here so much she'd forgotten it was nearing. It scraped against the wounds inside her that were just beginning to heal, reopening them.

Something scurried nearby. Gabe stared into the darkness. "Is that a fox?"

Lottie looked out and could just make out the shine of her eyes against the moonlight, her fox friend. "You can see that?"

"Yeah," he said, looking at her like that was a strange question. She guessed it was.

"I think she's been following us for a while. I was starting to think she was a hallucination."

"How do you know it's the same one? And how do you know it's a she?"

"Just a feeling," Lottie said. She already sounded crazy enough without the *I think it's your dead sister* part.

"Maybe she's hungry." Gabe leaned back toward his pack, but Lottie caught his arm.

"You can't feed them. It messes with their instincts."

"But what if she's starving? Maybe she can't find food in the drought."

"She's going to have to figure it out on her own." Lottie chewed at a rough spot on the end of her nail. "Did you always do that, even as a little kid?"

"What?"

"Try to help everyone."

"I don't know. I guess, maybe." His eyes were far off, like he was recalling part of his past. "But I'm not trying to be chivalrous or whatever. I just want to be a good person."

"You are a good person."

"Has your instinct always been to never ask for help?"

Lottie nodded. She pressed her lips together. The question was kicking up dust inside her.

"Why?"

"I don't know," she said. But inside her, the truth stirred, so big and monstrous that she shut her eyes against it. Splintered memories cut through, of being hungry, of being alone in the dark when the power was cut off, of the smell in the air when she caught fire. Of *needing* help, knowing none would come. The pain of it ripped straight through her center.

The truth was this: She didn't ask for help because it only made it hurt more when it didn't come. Messina's words about Jeffucker and camp echoed through her, *I'd rather keep it in than feel like that again.* They knew what it was like when the world turned its back, how it was worse than being alone. How it felt like being less than nothing.

The feelings rose up inside her like a tide of glass shards, shredding her insides. The pain of it threatened to pull her under. She numbed it the way she knew how. She kissed Gabe.

He kissed her back. It was like morphine. She could feel all the wanting inside him, the heat in his touch. It had her insides humming so loud it blocked out everything else. But a whisper of a thought snuck past it all—Gabe wasn't trying to numb anything.

Lottie pulled back. Her belly full of broken-glass memories and feelings screamed at her.

"Stay with me tonight," he said.

She didn't answer.

Truth: Everything inside her wanted to say yes.

She leaned in and kissed him on the cheek, giving his hand a squeeze. "Goodnight, Gabe."

She tried not to wake Messina as she made her way back into the tent.

"You're back."

"I thought you were asleep," Lottie said, tucking herself into her sleeping bag.

"I thought you were spending the night with Gabe again."

"No." She leaned up on her elbows. "I'd rather be here. Will it keep you up if I read for a while?"

Messina passed her the book in answer. "Thanks," she told Lottie.

"For what?"

"For coming back."

Lottie cracked open *Wild* and read by the glow of her flashlight, not Val's words, but Cheryl Strayed's. She read a hundred pages. About how Cheryl Strayed had lied and cheated. How she used heroin. Got an abortion. How she screwed three different men in five days, all while she was still married to a man who was good and kind and loved her. Lottie didn't dislike her because of any of it. She understood her. She felt understood *by her*. She read about how she had a friend named Val, who officiated her divorce. How she walked this trail, starting at Tehachapi Pass. How she changed her last name to Strayed.

Lottie ran her finger over the words that spelled out its meaning—*to be lost, to become wild, to be without a mother or father, to be without a home, to move about aimlessly in search of something . . .*

She wondered what Cheryl Strayed had really been in search of when she set out on the PCT. And if she ever ended up finding it.

PART III
ASHES

73

LOTTIE

Kennedy Meadows was nothing like Hikertown. It was beautiful. There were trees, big ones—pines that stretched up forever—and there was shade and water, and best of all, a man in a camper with a grill who offered them cheeseburgers and giant wedges of watermelon. He even had a veggie patty for Messina. His name was Bryce, and he called himself a trail angel. That definitely seemed like the right term for it, Lottie thought, gorging herself on watermelon. Nothing in her entire life had ever been so good, not just the food, but the random kindness of it—it felt like magic.

The three of them sat in the shade, giddy with the taste of real food, and laughed and ate with watermelon juice running down their chins. If Lottie could have frozen time, she would have stayed here in this moment forever.

"There are a few other hikers around," Bryce said, while he used some kind of brush against the grill. A patch of sunlight shining down through the trees caught on the little bald spot on his head, giving him a kind of halo. "Most of them are resting. Been a pretty slow day for passers-through. Y'all staying the night?"

Before they could answer, a woman with red hair tackled Gabe in a hug. "Gabe!"

Lottie watched, stunned that he somehow managed to have friends up here. Pretty ones. With red hair.

"Hey Eva," Gabe said, hugging her back. "I thought you'd be long past here by now."

The woman shook her head. "Boyfriend sent me a breakup text the night before I got here—he met someone on the trail. I've been hanging around since then, trying to figure out how to get home. I'm heading out tomorrow."

Lottie was doing a shit job of being inconspicuous while she eavesdropped, pretending to study the bark of a nearby tree. But she didn't care. Jealousy flowed wild through her veins.

She caught enough of their conversation to understand that Gabe had given her a ride to Tehachapi and that she'd been hiking up to meet a boyfriend at the halfway point. And now she was boyfriendless and flirting with Gabe.

Lottie knew he wasn't hers to get jealous over, but her cheeks were hot with the feeling anyway.

They set up their tents in the camp area close to Eva's. There was a wooden picnic table in the center with a bunch of cell phones spread in a circle on its right side, like some kind of sacrificial offering.

"What's that?" Lottie asked.

"Phone table," Eva said. "Somebody figured out there's a bar of service in that exact spot, so everyone's been leaving their phones on it to pick up messages."

Their plan was to stay the night and get moving again first thing in the morning. She and Messina would share a load of laundry for five bucks, which was only going to leave Lottie with five more after their showers. She wasn't sure what she'd do once she and Messina ran out of food again—either starve the rest of the way or ask Gabe if she could borrow some money. Starvation seemed like the least painful of the two.

Lottie sorted her clothes for the laundry. She'd have to leave one set dirty to wear while she washed the others. She decided to leave out the ones she'd worn in the desert—it was getting cooler as they trekked closer to that wall of mountains to their north.

Dirty water pooled around her feet as she washed herself, tiny bits of all the places she'd been that had hitched a ride on her skin—Hikertown, the Mojave, every valley and mountain they'd crossed. It was strange to think she'd really hiked all this way. She soaped her hair for a second time, avoiding the thought that kept skirting the edge of her mind—that it was all going to end eventually. She put her nasty desert clothes over her freshly cleaned skin, hating their smell and their desert dirt and the memories of the night with Ash they conjured. She was anxious for her laundry to finish so she could be rid of them. She stuck her wet feet into her shoes and walked back to their camp, her hair dripping onto the shoulders of her T-shirt.

Messina and Gabe were at a wooden picnic table with another camper. Her back was turned, but Lottie recognized her voice instantly.

"Brutus!" Ash stood and embraced Lottie in a hug. Panic paralyzed her. *Brutus.* She could feel Gabe's and Messina's eyes on her. She could feel them seeing right through to everything she was trying to hide. *The ultimate betrayer.* "I was just telling your friends I must've been right on your tail this whole time. They said you just got here a couple hours ago." Ash's face was dirty and sunburned, her chin sticky with watermelon juice.

"She was just telling us about how you met in the desert the night she helped Messina," Gabe said. He had on the same disappointed face he wore back in Tehachapi.

"I'm going to go grab a shower, now that it's empty, and catch a nap before dinner," Ash said, taking another piece of watermelon from the plate. "See you guys in a bit." She stuck the watermelon wedge into her mouth and headed off to the tent area.

Gabe tugged at Lottie's arm, pulling her aside, like he didn't want to make a scene in front of Bryce or Messina. "Why did you lie about knowing her back at the store?"

Lottie was silent. There wasn't any answer she could give that would make this okay. She hated the way Gabe looked at her now, like he was searching for the girl from last night.

"You won't tell me, will you?" he said, letting go of her arm. "You know, every time I think I've finally cracked through the shell and found the real you, there's always another layer. It's like an onion of bullshit."

The night couldn't come fast enough for Lottie—at least there was darkness to hide in and sleep to look forward to. Tomorrow, they would get moving again. Hiking was hard and painful, but not more than this.

She sat outside her tent making a cup of ramen while Messina stayed inside and buried her face in the book. They hadn't talked since Ash turned up.

Gabe sat down next to Lottie on the downed tree she was using as a seat, but far enough for there to be some distance between them. He'd spent the last quarcel with that Eva girl, chatting and laughing like they were great friends. Or more.

"I'm sorry for what I said earlier," he said. "You didn't deserve that."

Lottie felt a fresh shame at the memory of it. She hoped this was as bad as it would get, that she could get out of there before any more of her lies came to light.

"You don't owe me anything," Gabe said. "I should stop acting like you do."

A rough breath escaped Lottie. It felt like sandpaper. She didn't want them to not owe each other anything.

"We need to figure out the rest of the hike," Gabe said, "so we know how many more days of food we need."

They had to be getting close now. She and Messina had been hiking for almost three weeks. But even as she thought about how far they must've come, the miles Gabe mentioned the other night weren't adding up right in her head. She knew they'd been going too slow.

"What's the endpoint we're trying to get to?"

"The Three Sisters."

Gabe's fingers moved across his phone screen, tapping it out. He froze. "Three Sisters in Oregon?"

"Yeah."

She didn't like what his face turned into. It looked like disappointment or frustration, but it felt like *How could you be so stupid?* "That's over twelve hundred miles from here."

"No, it's not." That couldn't be right. Even running behind couldn't have *added* miles to their total. They'd checked at the start—it was six hundred miles and change from La Conchita. "Messina and I checked."

He turned his phone around to face her. It was right there on the screen. 1,248 miles.

"But that's wrong."

"Lot, it's another thousand just to get to the Oregon border."

"We checked it."

"How did you check?"

A sick feeling swelled in her belly. She didn't want to answer. She didn't want to feel stupid and know that she'd fucked everything up all over again. She could see the swooping red arc in her mind that her phone had drawn from La Conchita to the Three Sisters back at her trailer. No directions to a place had that direct of a route. The phone must've given her the miles as the crow flies. She just hadn't been thinking enough to realize it then. It was like Messina said. She never used her brain enough.

"I'm going to go talk to Eva," Gabe said.

"Why?"

"A friend is picking her up and taking her back down south tomorrow. Maybe we can ride with her back to Tehachapi."

"But we can't do that." Lottie caught his arm. The panic flooding her veins had her heart beating so hard she could feel it in her eyes.

She couldn't go back. Not before she fixed this and made things better for Val, and for herself. They had to keep going. "We have to take Val. We have to finish."

"Lottie, that's insane. We don't have the gear or the time or the skills we need to go anywhere near that far. We'd have to go through the High Sierras to get to Oregon—there's still snow. And we wouldn't even be back before school starts, much less Val's birthday. I can't leave my dad on his own for that."

"But what about Messina? She can't go back home," Lottie said. But she didn't feel like she was speaking. Her face was going numb as her brain tried to walk out of her body. She felt far away, even as she heard herself pleading with Gabe.

"I can take Messina wherever she needs to go once we get back to my truck."

"But we have to keep going." Desperation broke her voice into little pieces that scattered over the dirt.

"No, Lot, we don't. That urn's gone three hundred miles on the backs of her brother and two best friends. Val's memory and her dream have been honored. Whatever you're doing now, it's not about her." His unspoken words hung there in the air between them, *It's about you.*

The truth of it cut her deep enough that she felt it, even through the numbness. She couldn't look at him. She was too scared her reasons for wanting to keep going were all over her face. *I haven't made it right yet. She hasn't forgiven me.*

"It's over, Lot."

Lottie stared at the ground, wishing she could sink down below it, down into the dirt and keep going. Tears rolled down her cheeks. She wasn't here anymore. She was below the earth's crust, deep down, where it was warm.

Gabe let out a sigh. The war inside him was all over his face. "It wasn't a waste, you know. She'd be proud of you," he said. "You brought her out here. You hiked nearly three hundred miles."

His words found Lottie beneath the crust. He was trying to be kind, she knew, trying not to feel guilty about taking this all away from her. And maybe Val would have been proud of her, except no one is proud of the person who killed them.

74

MESSINA

Dried pine needles whispered and twisted over the ground as the breeze kicked up. The air was turning arid again. Messina could feel it every time she blinked, her eyelids so dry they moved like rusty hinges.

The world felt ready to go up in flames. Not just the air and the trees, but Lottie too. Ever since they realized they weren't going to make it to the Three Sisters, she'd had that look in her, like the tip of a match. Messina understood, at least some of it. She knew the pain Lottie was in, having to go back to La Conchita. Messina had faced it more times than she could count. Abandoning what they'd set out to do didn't feel much better. Messina agreed with Gabe—twelve hundred miles was an impossibly long distance. Still, she hated the way the disappointment jabbed at her insides, now that the hope of what they'd set out to do was gone. The Three Sisters felt like the place where they were supposed to take Val. It felt like it was where she belonged.

But Messina had other things to worry about, like what the hell she was going to do, come tomorrow. When Gabe asked her where she needed to go once they got back to his truck, she'd said,

"I don't know yet. I'm making a plan." And Gabe had nodded, like this was reasonable.

But Messina knew plans were shit. She'd made thousands of them. Plans to run away. Plans to get back at Jeffucker. Plans to go to college. They'd all turned to dust. Even this one with Lottie, to hike with Val to the Three Sisters. It had been the closest she'd ever come to making a plan that turned into something real, and now it was dead just like the others.

Messina didn't need a new plan. What she needed was something real. But all she had was a shred of out-of-date information—*there is a woman named Anna Collins who works at a community college in Brookings, Oregon*—that felt like an expired coupon.

Messina had tried to cash one of those in once, a years-old newspaper clipping for free French fries. The cashier had just laughed at her. She didn't think this time was going to be any different.

75

LOTTIE

"Knock knock," she said outside the tent. She didn't know why—before now she'd have just gone in—it was her tent too. But it didn't feel like her tent right now, not since she'd been caught in the lie about Ash. And not since Gabe had decided their trip was done.

His words banged against the inside of Lottie's head. *It's over. It's over. It's over.*

Messina unzipped the flap. "Why are you knock-knocking?"

Lottie shrugged, the words all stuck in her throat like a traffic jam. She climbed through the hole.

"Did you talk to Gabe?" she asked.

"Yeah." Messina's eyes looked tired, but worse. Like the hope had gone out of them.

"We're supposed to leave just after sunup to meet Eva's friend. I guess they'll take us back to Tehachapi." *It's over. It's over. It's over.* "Will you have him take you up to Brookings?"

Messina pressed her lips together, like there were words trying to escape her mouth that she didn't want to let out. "Yeah, I think so. What about you?"

Lottie couldn't bring herself to answer. That she hadn't accomplished anything. That she'd done it all for nothing. That even when she tried her hardest, it all turned out just as fucked as ever.

She didn't want to accept it. She watched Messina's eyes, how the lamplight reflected against them. "What if we keep going without him?"

Messina looked at her like she didn't understand.

"What if we take Val tonight and keep going? All the way to the Three Sisters—just the three of us—the way it was supposed to be."

"I want to keep going as much as you do. But we're out of money, we're nearly out of food, and Val's going home with Gabe because her ashes belong with their dad on her birthday. There's nothing to do about it, Lot. It's over."

It's over. It's over. It's over.

The camp buzzed with life as it got late. The campers who'd all been out or hidden away in their tents earlier were up now, stirring around, chattering, and eating like a horde of nocturnal creatures. The smell of cooked meat was in the air. Bryce had fired up his grill again.

Eva invited them all to the makeshift potluck happening at the center of camp. Lottie didn't feel like hanging out—she wanted to stand on a yellow line in the middle of the road and forget the world existed. She put on her clean clothes. She pulled her hair back into something close to a ponytail, only more tangled.

A little crowd of about a dozen people congregated in the picnic area, Ash among them. Her partner wasn't around. Lottie wondered if they'd broken up, recalling their argument in the parking lot and Ash's words *I make a habit of setting things on fire*.

This was the most people they'd been around in weeks. Lottie watched them, Eva especially, how she tipped her head and smiled at Gabe. Eva talked about longing for home, which Lottie thought was funny. Lottie felt more at home out here in the wild than she ever had back in La Conchita. Home was the last place she wanted to go. *It's over. It's over. It's over.*

Music hummed out of someone's portable speaker. Food and bottles were passed around. The bottles kept skipping her, along with Gabe and Messina, like they were the kids at Thanksgiving. But as the night went on, watchful eyes glazed over. Lottie dropped herself down in the mush pot and took a drink and a hit of everything that came her way. She watched Ash on the other side of the circle, wary. Lottie wanted to keep as far away from her as possible.

Lottie took another drink off a bottle. It tasted hot and bitter. Messina sat down beside her. "You should take it easy," she said. "We have to get up early tomorrow."

But Lottie didn't want to hear it. The hum of alcohol sang in her head. It was covering the banging drum of the words everyone kept repeating. *It's over. It's over. It's over.*

76

MESSINA

The music drove her crazy. It wasn't anything obnoxious—some kind of folk station with acoustic guitars. But after so many weeks of quiet, she was too aware of how much that sound didn't belong out here. It hummed and twanged out into the night air, probably making the animals just as nuts as it was making her. It was funny how protective she felt now about this place and everything in it, how much she'd grown to like existing here in nature—it was harsh and unforgiving, but at least it was always honest about it. No trickery, no lies.

She could feel parts of the wild running through her now, in the dirt stuck beneath her nails and in the sharpness of her senses. In the way the scab at the back of her head was finally healing. And the way she could reach down into herself and find the same power and strength she had when she'd painted herself in her blood. How it still ran through her veins, even though it no longer covered her skin. This place had changed her, and she liked it.

She half-chewed, half-sucked on the pickle spear from Bryce, trying to savor it while the girl in the speaker sang about kissing someone goodbye. Messina didn't know why she was out here, other than for the food. She still didn't know what she was going to do in the morning. She still had no plan, other than a city—Brookings. She'd spent the entire day poring over *Wild* for advice from Val or Cheryl Strayed and had exactly squat. All she knew was that she wouldn't go back to La Conchita, no matter what. She'd stay in the wild if she had to.

Lottie held out a bottle to her, but Messina waved it off. She didn't want any of the booze—she could still taste the memory of puking her guts up and nearly dying after Hikertown. She watched the people, most of them split into smaller groups. Ash was talking to a woman who looked uncomfortable. Messina got a weird vibe from her, even though she'd saved her ass and probably her life. Something about her felt like a loose cannon, like Lottie on a bad day.

It was all a shitty goodbye, Messina thought—to the PCT and to her friends. She wasn't sure what she'd hoped for on her last night with them, but it wasn't this. Gabe was avoiding Lottie, Lottie was avoiding herself, and Messina was stuck between both of them, but without either one.

Lottie handed her the bottle again. Messina took it this time, but she didn't drink.

"You're good," Messina said, setting the bottle down on her other side, away from Lottie. She was already half trashed. Messina could feel her teetering on the edge of something, she just didn't know what. "Let's go back to the tent and hang out."

Lottie leaned across her and took the bottle back. She drank from it. "I think I'll stay here."

"L, come on. I know you don't want to go home. But let's just have one last night together out here, you and me . . . I'm leaving tomorrow."

"You're always leaving tomorrow. You've been saying that for nine years."

The truth of it hurt. "But I'm not turning around this time."

Lottie held the bottle up to her like *cheers.*

"Fine," Messina told her. "Have fun cleaning up whatever mess you make this time."

She left Lottie and headed toward the tent, wishing it were farther off from the noise. A voice caught her ear, cutting through the din. "Bullshit, spill it." It was Ash, talking to someone from the party. Messina recognized it without looking, something in the inflection, the cadence of the words. It let loose something hidden inside her.

A memory, like water, flowed over her—voices through the tent wall in the desert, her head spinning while she sipped on blue liquid. Ash and Lottie outside. *I screwed around with my best friend's boyfriend.*

It was Lottie, talking about Tristan. Talking about Val.

Messina froze there, halfway to the tent, wishing she could unknow it. She wanted to go back in time, just thirty seconds, to before.

It felt like when she'd accidentally caught a bee in her hand, running her fingers along the mustard flowers that grew along their street in the spring. She hadn't meant to catch it and tried to let it go. But it stung her all the same.

77

LOTTIE

Her head spun, but not in the bad way—in the way that meant she was close to being able to stand on the yellow line and forget about *It's over.*

Gabe's phone buzzed against the wooden slat of the picnic table. Merilee's smiling face flashed on the screen. Gabe was too busy talking to Eva to notice, pretending he didn't know she was flirting with him. Lottie silenced the phone, but Merilee's face kept lighting it up, smiling with her pretty, white teeth. She flipped it over, so Merilee smiled at the table instead.

She felt herself getting sloppy and doubled down, taking a shot of something that tasted like cinnamon and fire. It reminded her of Tristan and things inside herself that she hated. She wanted to burn them out with more of the fire liquor.

"Easy." Gabe's arm slipped around her shoulder. She felt herself moving back toward the tent. Toward tomorrow. Toward La Conchita and failure and being a fuckup-nothing forever.

She kissed Gabe. He was drunk too, she could tell, but not like she was. He kissed her back like he liked it, leaning into her like his body had been starving for her touch. She lit up with the feeling of it. She kissed his neck. Her senses filled up with the smell of his skin, and how it was soft and rough all at the same time. His hands were in her hair and then on her hips, her skin buzzing. She slipped her hand under his shirt, the ridges and valleys of his torso beneath her fingers. She pressed him back against a tree and put her hand down his pants.

"Lottie, stop." He pushed back against her, putting a gap between them, redoing the button on his pants. "What are you doing?"

"I thought it was obvious," she said, leaning in, kissing him again.

"Stop." He backed up, making another gap. "I can't be this for you. I can't only have you when you're trying to avoid things." He put his hand on her shoulder.

Lottie smacked it away. "You're such a fucking girl, Gabe. You're not even good for a fuck."

"You're right, I'm not," he said, shoving a hand through his hair like it had been the one to wrong him, instead of Lottie. "I care about you."

"Yeah, well, you shouldn't."

His eyes reflected the moonlight. She could see the anger and hurt in them. She should have felt bad for it, but her own anger and shame burned too hot inside her to make room for Gabe's feelings.

"I'm starting to think you're right, Lot." He took another step back, putting even more distance between them. "Stop using me when you don't want to deal with your shit."

Someone laughed behind them, and they both turned to look. Ash and another woman were linked, arm in arm, stumbling together toward the other side of camp. Ash gave Lottie a booze-soaked grin as she passed. "Take it easy, Brutus."

Gabe rounded on her. "And why does she keep calling you Brutus?"

Cinnamon vape, crooked smile, Do you like that? Yes. The memory crashed over her. She was sick with it. She turned her back on Gabe and sped away so fast she nearly collided with Messina outside their tent.

"I was just coming to find you." Lottie was relieved by the words, glad their fight from earlier had blown over already. Her head was spinning with memories and Gabe and liquor. She just needed to sleep, to turn off her mind. "I need to talk to you," Messina said.

Lottie unzipped the flap to their tent. "Can we do it in the morning? I'm wrecked."

Messina caught hold of her arm before she could climb inside. Her face was too close. The sun had darkened the freckles across her nose. "This can't wait, Lot. I know what happened."

Lottie heaved out a breath. "What does that even mean?"

"I heard you talking outside the tent with Ash that night. I just didn't remember until now."

Lottie froze. Everything stopped except the sound of her own heartbeat booming in her ears.

"Lottie—"

It's not real it's not real it's not real. "You don't know what you're talking about." She tried to laugh, like Messina was being ridiculous, but the sound that came out of her was mangled, barely human. "You were bonked out of your mind. You probably hallucinated."

"I didn't hallucinate."

It's not real it's not real. She twisted against Messina's grip. She needed to get away. She needed to zoom out so far that everything became a dot, like on that stupid map.

She wrenched her arm free.

"I know you screwed around with Tristan," Messina said to her back.

Gabe stood right in front of her, eyes wide. There was no undoing it.

No one said a word. They knew what she'd done.

She ran.

Gabe and Messina called after her, but she didn't stop. She kept going into the woods until she couldn't hear them anymore and the flood of tears and shame consumed her.

They knew what she'd done.

She sank down onto the ground, pressing her face against the dirt. Everything came out of her, tears and snot and the liquor and wails from so deep down it felt like they came from inside the earth and up through her body.

They knew what she'd done.

She pounded the ground with her fists and screamed at it. She wished she could undo everything. But it was already cemented into reality.

When there was nothing left inside her, all her screams and rage and shame gone, and she was nothing but empty skin and bones, she didn't get up. She stayed there and pressed herself as hard against the ground as she could until she sank beneath it, down past the roots of the trees where no one would ever find her again.

78

LOTTIE

It was still dark when she woke. She didn't know what time it was, but they'd been up late. It probably wasn't long until sunup. She didn't feel drunk anymore. She'd puked up half the alcohol, and the rest had evaporated the second she was outed as a friend-murderer. It didn't take Lottie long to make her way back to camp, though she felt like she'd run miles into the woods last night.

She walked as silently as any of the animals as she snuck back through the crowd of tents to the light blue one that had come to feel like home these past weeks. She pressed her fingers along the zipper as she opened it, muffling its sound. Messina slept inside. Lottie was careful not to wake her as she slid out her pack and the book. She repeated the same motions at Gabe's tent, taking Val's ashes. Gabe was shirtless, locks of curly black hair hanging in front of his face.

Lottie knew he'd hate her for this, but it didn't matter anymore. She'd already done the worst thing, and now he knew it. He couldn't hate her any more than he already did.

She left camp and followed the beam of her flashlight on the trail out of Kennedy Meadows and into the darkness. She wasn't scared. It didn't matter what was waiting out there for her. It couldn't be any worse than what was inside her.

Lottie saw the glow of the sunrise as she hiked, how odd it was, too intense, with a strange and alien hue. She saw it, but she didn't notice. Because Lottie wasn't there. She was watching the movie of a girl who'd lost everything and was wandering alone in the mountains with her dead friend's ashes, somehow trying to fix what she'd broken.

79

GABE

His head throbbed. He stumbled, half-dizzy, out of his tent and saw that half the other campers were gone already. The smell of burning wood hung in the air. He didn't see Eva, but her tent was still there. He found his phone on the table and checked the time—six a.m., just after sunrise. He had nine missed calls from Merilee. He dropped the phone back onto the table. It buzzed.

He answered, leaning toward the magic spot on the right side of the table. "Hey, Merilee." He heard her start to talk through the other end, but he cut her off. His head was killing him. "Hang on, is it okay if I just talk for a second? I think you're really cool, but I'm just not in a place right now where I'm ready for this much attention. Nine calls in a night is a little overwhelming for me. I hope I'm not hurting your feelings—I just want to be honest." There was a beat of silence on the other end. "Merilee?"

"I was just trying to get a hold of you because there's a massive wildfire near Kennedy Meadows. You said you were headed there the last time you texted. It burned something like fifty-thousand acres overnight. They're evacuating everything nearby."

The call ended.

He found Messina outside her tent. Her face was ashen. "Eva said there's a fire. Everyone's leaving," she said.

"I just heard. We need to get Lottie and get out of here."

Messina shook her head. "She's gone."

"She's probably just passed out in the woods." He cupped his hands around his mouth and called her name. "Lottie! *Lottie!*"

Messina grabbed hold of his arm. "She's *gone,* Gabe. Her pack, the book—and I'm guessing Val's ashes—are all missing too."

Gabe's brain didn't want to accept it. It wanted him to verify, check the facts, assess. But he knew in that weird gut way that was sometimes tethered to the world deeper than any facts—the way Val always talked about—that she was right. Lottie was gone.

80

MESSINA

They were wasting time while Gabe weighed the risks. They needed to be out looking for Lottie. She couldn't have had that much of a head start. But all of Gabe's questioning had messed with Messina's head. *What if she didn't go north? What if she hitched a ride with someone instead of hiking? She might not even be on the PCT—she left drunk in the middle of the night. What if we leave and hike right into the path of the fire?*

Now he was pinned to the phone table, busy getting updates on the fire and trying to reach his dad while she sat here spinning circles and doing nothing. Nearly everyone had left from camp already, including Eva, all following the evacuation orders. They'd blown hours already while Lottie kept getting farther away from them. The only person left was one of the shop owners, hosing down the roof of his store.

"The fire's northwest of us, but new spot fires are popping up everywhere," Gabe said, as Messina paced back over to him, unable to sit still. "There's no containment with this wind. I called the fire department to let them know there's a hiker out there."

Messina knew that meant nothing. "They'll be too stretched

fighting the fire and trying to help people evacuate from known locations. They won't be able to do anything." Even she knew in fires like this, they didn't send anyone out looking for missing people. It was too risky.

Gabe's phone rang again. He answered, turning away from Messina.

The winds inside her howled, screaming at her to go. She made up her mind and got her pack. She emptied it of everything except a day's worth of food and water so she could move faster.

Gabe ended the call just as Messina came back to the table to tell him she was leaving. "That was my dad," he said. "He's still trying to get up here, but he says they've shut off access to the main roads because of the fire. He's trying to find a way around." He wiped his palm across his eyes, and Messina realized they were wet.

"He's worried about you, huh?" she said.

"He's panicked. I can't believe how selfish I was coming out here. If he loses me . . ." He dropped off.

"He's not going to lose you," Messina said. "Go up to the store. Help keep it doused with water."

"What are you going to do?"

"I'm going after Lottie."

His eyes took in the pack on her back. "A million things could go wrong."

"I know."

"What if she comes back? If she realizes it's not her fault and—"

She put a hand up, stopping him. "Lottie will never think that. Gabe, I have to go. I can't leave her."

He nodded. “And I can’t come with you.”

“I know.”

“Take my phone at least.” He held it out to her, but she waved it off.

“You’ll need it if your dad calls.”

He leaned in and gave her a hug, squeezing her tight. She didn’t know how much she’d needed it.

“Be careful,” Gabe said.

Messina nodded. Then she ran.

81

LOTTIE

She should have taken Gabe's phone. And food. And water. She never thought things through.

"Don't worry," she said to Val, reaching back to touch the urn through her pack. "There'll be other hikers to help, just like last time. We'll be okay."

The air was going dry again. She could feel it leaching the moisture from her, inside and out.

She stumbled down the loose dirt of a pass and landed on her butt. It was so steep that she stayed down and descended the rest of it like that, doing an ass-drag crab-walk kind of maneuver. The world was once again a foot-wide path that went up and down in an endless wave of climbing and descending. Simplified. It was better this way, she thought. Here, all she had to do was keep moving beneath the trees. There weren't lies to hide from or people to kiss. There was only climbing and descending.

She liked how things were greener away from the desert. She came to a road and waited for a speeding car to pass before crossing. She could just make out a kid in the backseat, normal people doing normal things. It was one of those strange spots along the trail where the wild world butted up against the other one.

She kept moving. Her body was empty of food and water. And of Lottie. It didn't make sense that it could still move, but it did. Up and down. After a down, she found a river and dropped to its edge, scooping handfuls of water straight from its side and drinking so frantically she choked, still lapping up handfuls of water between coughs. Finally, when she'd had enough, she lay there, by the river's edge, no energy left to move.

She wiped her nose, and her hand came away red. It was bleeding again. She didn't have any tissues to wipe it, so she leaned over and bled into the wet dirt of the riverbed, the drops spidering out into the mud. It felt like the water here in this place was the only moisture left on earth. The air was so dry her knuckles and lips had cracked open. It felt like the whole world might go up in flames if someone were to strike a match. It smelled like a campfire too, even though they weren't allowed out here. A hot gust of wind blew, the breeze lifting her hair.

She stayed there like that, lying in the mud, exhausted and hungry, too tired to move, until the sun was setting. It lit up the sky in shades of red and orange so brilliant it looked like someone had used a filter on it. She remembered Val's fact about how dirty air, the kind filled with particulate matter from smoke and pollution, made the prettiest sunsets.

She took Val out and set her in her lap. She wanted to talk with her like she used to, but now all she could do was talk to a pretty, flowered urn, which felt a lot like talking to herself. She looked down into the disconnected bits of her reflection in the tiny puddles that had formed at the river's edge from the imprints of her hands and boots. Her face stared back at her from the mess where the water and blood pooled. Broken, bloody, dirty. She knew she wasn't going to make it to the Three Sisters or anywhere else like this.

"This is stupid," she said.

She looked at Val. Val agreed.

Nothing had changed. She was still on her own, doing selfish stuff, hurting people she cared about, and making a mess of things. She was still being a fuckup. Only now, she didn't want to be. She wanted to be with her friends. She wanted to go back to that moment in Kennedy Meadows when they'd all had watermelon juice dripping down their chins. Before she'd been a shithead to Gabe and Messina. And before they found out what she'd done. Back when she felt like the girl who'd hiked three hundred miles through the wilderness.

You're still that girl, a voice said, and she didn't know if it was Val's or her own.

"But what if they don't forgive me?" She squeezed a handful of mud as she thought it, hard, until it squished out from between her fingers.

They might not.

Lottie waited for more of an answer, some kind of encouragement, but it didn't come. *They might not* was all there was. She had no choice but to face it.

"We're going back in the morning," she told Val. Lottie picked her up and hugged her tight to her chest, mud smearing over both of them. She was scared of what was ahead. Scared and alone. She took out *Wild* and opened it to a page. At least she wasn't scared of the book anymore. Now that everyone knew what she'd done, she didn't have to worry about it spilling her secret.

Cheryl Strayed's words, underlined in red by Val, found her eyes—*Nothing bad could happen to me, I thought. The worst thing already had.* She repeated them to herself over and over, a prayer that she hoped with all her heart was the truth.

82

MESSINA

Her flashlight was losing life. She hadn't been hiking long before the sun sank, turning the sky a blood red from all the crap the fire was spitting into the air. The darkness swallowed up the world around her. But she'd been too busy thinking about Lottie to let her fear in—until her light coughed its last breath and she was fully in the dark.

She stopped and closed her eyes, trying to get them to adjust. It helped marginally. A half-moon hung in the sky, clouded by haze. She could just make out the trail in front of her, and silhouettes of plants at the edges of her world. She felt off-balance. The darkness was disorienting as well as frightening.

"I am strong. I am brave. I am strong. I am brave." Messina chanted the words from *Wild* out loud as she walked, her pace slower now. "Nothing can vanquish me. I am strong. I am brave."

She climbed the ascent. A tug at the back of her skull urged her to turn around every few seconds for fear there was something stalking her. But turning only made the fear worse. *Let them stalk me*, she thought, not knowing who the *them* was but knowing the fear wasn't going to stop chasing her. She was going to have to live with it.

It didn't change anything anyway, her fear—the world was no more dangerous when she was afraid, nor was it safer when she felt brave. So, she kept moving. The soles of her shoes crunched against the dirt and rocks beneath them as she pushed herself up the ascent. When she reached the top, she found light, a flickering glow at the edge of the darkness. But it didn't bring her comfort, only the knowledge that she was moving toward the fire.

83

LOTTIE

Sunrise was wrong, glowing like Mordor instead of morning when she opened her eyes. White flakes floated down through the smoky air, but Lottie knew better than to think they were made of snow. She caught one on her hand. Ash.

She sat up and shoved Val into her pack, her lungs already burning from the smoke in the air.

"We've got to get out of here," she said to Val.

She found the trail and started at a run the way she'd come the day before. The air made her dizzy, but she pressed her legs as fast as they would go, ignoring the burn in her muscles. The world was something out of a sci-fi movie, all tinged the wrong color, with so much smoke she couldn't even see which direction it came from. She hit a tree root and went down face-first in the dirt. A searing pain shot through her ankle. A taste like salty pennies flooded her mouth. She spit blood onto the dirt, wiping her chin with shaking hands. Strings of red-stained slobber clung to her skin. She raised herself to a standing position on one foot and tried to put weight on her ankle. Pain like knives shot through her, but she could stand on it. She just needed to get back to the road she'd crossed yesterday. She'd find help there.

Wind slammed against her, throwing smoke and dirt and debris into her eyes and sending clouds of ash raining down on her. It refused to blow in a single direction, coming at her from what felt like all angles, threatening to sweep her from the mountainside. Her ankle screamed at her with every step. It swelled, looking like she'd stuffed half an apple into her sock. And it made going downhill more difficult than going up—loose dirt now turned treacherous beneath her unstable steps. Ascending was still painful, but at least she felt balanced.

The air was suffocating. She wished she'd brought water from the river with her. The sky was darkened with smoke, like night. Its edges glowed in every direction. Lottie turned on her flashlight to help her navigate as she choked on the black air. *Just get down to the road,* she told herself. *There will be help at the road.*

A wave of fear swept over her. What if there wasn't help at the road? Or what if she couldn't find the road in all of this blackness? She slipped in a wash. Her ankle snapped as she went down, loud enough for her to hear it above the howling wind. Blinding pain slammed her. She rolled over in the dirt and puked. It came out with a sound from deep inside her, a wail of grief and pain and despair. Tears and snot ran down her face. She didn't try to get up. She lay back in the dirt, not moving, as more tears seeped from her eyes. The pain was as blinding as the smoke. She knew by the contorted angle her foot was bent at now that there would be no more standing on it.

She was going to die out here.

She thought of the words from the book she'd repeated yesterday, that nothing bad could happen because the worst already had, and felt a crazed urge to laugh. *No*, she thought, *things can always get worse*. Worse was a pit of unfathomable depths. Worse had no limits.

She pushed herself onto her stomach, sticking her hand in the muddy puddle of her own puke, and began to crawl down the descent on her hands and knees, her foot dragging limply behind her. The road couldn't be that far now.

She had to be close.

84

MESSINA

She'd never again be scared by the promise of hell—this was it. Embers floated through the air, igniting the dry brush where they landed. The whole world was covered in fire. The air was black and unbreathable. Messina's shirt-collar covered her nose and mouth, but it did nothing to help. She kept moving forward in search of Lottie. There wasn't any choice now. No matter which direction she chose or if she tried to turn back, the outcome was the same—she wasn't going to make it out of this alive.

She tried not to think about it, about if it was the smoke that would kill her or the flames. She just kept marching. *I am strong. I am brave. Nothing can vanquish me.* She spoke the words only in her mind now—her voice was burned out by the smoke quarcels ago.

She ducked as an ember soared toward her, threatening to set her hair on fire. Tears seeped down her cheeks—not from fear, but from the smoke. She was afraid, of course. But it wasn't the kind of fear that made her cry. It was a different kind, a kind that made her strong. She was surprised by it, to find that she was still here, still moving. And that she wasn't a zombie. She was a terrified girl descending a mountain in search of her friend. She wondered if they'd die together, like they'd always imagined.

85

LOTTIE

She crawled. Her palms and knees bled, ground into burger meat, dirt and pebbles lodged in them. Behind her, her gnarled foot and ankle dragged, the bones grating against each other.

The road was below her. She could just make out the yellow line of it through the smoke and ash. The trees on its other side smoldered. She belly-crawled the remaining yards, bleeding and choking and exhausted. Her throat was so raw from the smoke it felt like she'd swallowed sand. She lay there at the side of the road, waiting for help. She clenched her flashlight in her hand, ready to wave it like a distress signal to passing cars.

She waited, talking out loud to herself to keep awake and alert. But no one came.

Embers like hellish rain fell around her, glowing on the pavement beside her face.

That was when she knew that no help was coming. That the reason there were no cars passing was because the fire department didn't let cars drive down roads that looked like this, lined in flaming trees, embers flying. They would have closed them off hours ago.

No one was coming for her.

She coughed against the smoke. Her insides were black with it. With a half-grunt, half-whimper, she twisted herself out of her pack and lay down against it. She put her head over the spot where Val was.

"I'm sorry," she whispered. "I'm so sorry."

86

MESSINA

A wall of fire sped toward her, engulfing the trail and everything else in its path. It roared and hissed, louder than she knew fire could be. She bolted downhill off the trail to escape it, running with everything she had in her. High brush clawed at her face. She tripped in its brambles, slamming against the ground so hard the air was ripped from her lungs. A horrible, grating sound came out of her as she tried to find a breath again. She forced herself back up and kept going, stumbling, but staying on her feet. She didn't stop until the downward slope did. Being down felt safer than being up.

She looked behind her, up the mountain. She'd come farther than she thought. The fire moved above her, flaming fingers that stretched out and consumed everything they touched. She coughed and spit into the dirt at her feet. Sweat ran down her face. When she wiped it, her hand came away coated with ash and soot, a gray and muddied mess.

There was nothing breathable left in the air. She uncapped her water and emptied the last of it into her mouth. It felt like it all evaporated before it even hit her tongue. Her body was spent. She wanted to lie down in this creek bed and surrender to whatever was coming, but some force inside told her to keep moving.

She ran along the creek bed, knowing she was completely lost now. Even if she managed to escape the fire, without the trail, she was in the middle of nowhere with no water and only a day's food. The last of her hope drained from her.

A deer charged in front of her, down the bank and up the other side. It didn't even look at her, running for its life, the same as she was. She wondered if she should follow it up the other side, or if she should keep low, like she'd planned, sticking to the creek bed. Another deer thud-thudded past her, a stag with massive antlers, so close she could hear its breath. She made a choice and followed its path up the other side of the bank, away from the creek bed. The air was worse up here, the ground thick with brush. Her feet tangled in it. She'd lost the deer now. Her shirtsleeve snagged on something thorny, stopping her progress. She ripped herself free, cursing the lack of a path. The deer had probably just pranced right over all of this brush.

She turned around, resolved to go back to the creek bed where she could actually walk, and saw it consumed by fire. She moved, pushing through the brush while it clawed and scratched at her, finally freeing herself. She climbed at a run, not daring to spare time to look back. There was nothing left in her, but somehow, her body still moved. She crested another ridge and saw the bright yellow line of a road below her. She ran for it. At least the pavement wouldn't burn—she could keep a few feet away from the fire on either side.

She reached the road and followed it the way her gut told her to go, using her instincts, like the deer, not stopping to second-guess if it was the right way. She ran as fast as her body could manage, hoping to pass a car or an emergency vehicle. The trees smoldered on her left.

Messina realized she wasn't running anymore. She was barely walking. No cars came, no flashing lights. Her knees gave out, and she dropped down in the middle of the road. Ash drifted out of the sky like clumps of snow. She felt a strange kind of peace, but it was probably just delirium from lack of oxygen. An animal scurried off from the side of the road, a coyote or something. Or maybe that was part of the delirium too.

Next to where it had been was an ash-covered lump the size of a person. Messina squinted at it through the smoke-filled air. She made her way toward it, crawling with the last of her strength.

It was Lottie.

She was bleeding. Her foot was cocked at an angle so wrong it sent a surge of nausea in Messina. She had to look away from it to keep from vomiting. Lottie didn't respond when Messina shook her, but her chest still rose and fell with breath. Messina lifted one of Lottie's eyelids and watched her eye roll around in its socket with no one to steer it.

A rustling sounded in front of her, and she saw the thing that had scurried off watching her from the edge of the tree line. A fox.

She tried again to rouse Lottie, clapping her hands and shouting, but all she managed to do was scare the fox. It darted away down the road behind her, just as a great roar barreled toward them. Messina threw herself down over Lottie, thinking it was the fire. But the squealing that followed wasn't made by a fire. It was the sound of tires slipping against pavement. Tires that were trying to stop against the roar of an engine.

87

LOTTIE

Lottie cracked her eyes and saw cages. Sounds that made no sense exploded around her—squeals and whines and barks. The world spun, and she shut her eyes again. The air stank of antiseptic. She tried again to open her eyes. Val's fox lay dead and caged beside her. Lottie pushed herself up, fighting the dizziness, and touched the fur of the fox's paw through the bars of its cage with a bandaged hand. Tears ran down her cheeks, but she let them fall. They splattered in little gray-tinged drops against the concrete floor.

"She saved our lives." Messina came into her view. She was wearing an oversized T-shirt covered in purple paw prints that said **MAKING FRIENDSHIPS THAT LAST FUR-EVER**. "They said they would've barreled right past us if she hadn't jumped in front of the truck."

"Is she dead?" Lottie asked, still stroking the fox's paw. Her fur was dirty, but soft.

"No, just sleeping off the anesthesia. She's got three broken ribs and her pelvis was dislocated. The vet came by and fixed her pelvis, but she said the ribs will take time."

Relief washed over Lottie, tears blooming in her eyes again.

"She set your ankle, too," Messina said. "The hospitals are all overwhelmed."

Lottie looked down and saw her ankle wrapped in a strange-looking cast. She remembered the way it had snapped on the trail and felt dizzy again. She lay back down. She was on some kind of makeshift bed on the floor. "Is that where we are? A vet's office?"

Messina shook her head. "Animal shelter. They were heading back after trying to collect some of the pets people had to leave behind when they passed us."

The little black dog in the cage next to Val's fox barked every half-second, a high-pitched noise that rang in Lottie's ears. Her head hurt from trying to understand Messina's words. Nothing made sense. "But how were you there?"

"I came looking for you after you left camp."

"Why?"

Messina frowned, like she didn't understand the question. Or maybe she hadn't heard it. The dog's bark was incessant. Lottie reached her fingers through the bars of his crate. He licked them furiously, smashing his nose and face against her skin.

"Why would you come after me?" She repeated the question.

"Because that's what we do. We take care of each other."

The tears came in earnest now, like they'd given her some kind of dog medicine that was screwing up her emotions. "But I don't deserve that. You know what I did to Val. You can't take care of me anymore."

"Sorry, Lot," Messina said, coming closer and squeezing her hands. "But you're stuck with me." She didn't let go. She held

Lottie's hands tight and looked in her eyes. "And I think it's time for you to stop that now."

"Stop what?" She felt so confused by everything that was happening.

"All the stuff in parentheses," she said. "It's messing you up." She reached into the dispenser on the wall and pulled out a brown paper towel, handing it to Lottie. She wiped her nose and face on it. It came away smeared with black ash. "I don't care if we don't matter to the world. You matter to me. You saved my life out on that trail and a hundred times before then by being my friend. And you did the same for Val. So I don't want to hear whatever you think you don't deserve. You deserve better than you've been giving yourself."

"But it's my fault."

"No, it's not," Messina said. "Yeah, you did something selfish, and some shitty dominoes fell. Do you think I haven't thought about that night and everything I could have done to make it turn out differently? Do you think Gabe and his dad haven't done the same, driving themselves crazy? We all should have done better by her. We all let her down when she needed us. But using that as an excuse to say 'fuck it' to everything she showed you on the PCT is a dishonor to her memory. What we found in ourselves out there was real, and she'd be proud as hell of both of us. Don't throw that away because you feel guilty. Val deserves better than that, and so do you."

Lottie shook her head. She wanted to accept this, to believe Messina, but she wasn't sure she knew how to. Even though somewhere inside, she knew it was the Truth. It was like there was a black hole inside her that was trying to swallow it up before she could grab hold of it.

Messina watched her, like she knew, like she could see the battle going on inside Lottie as she tried to hold on to the words.

"Knock knock." Gabe stood at the door to the room.

"I'll let you talk," Messina said, finally letting go of Lottie's hands but giving her a look of *I mean it* before she left.

Lottie looked down at the paper towel that had turned into a blackened wad in her hand. It was too hard to look at Gabe for more than a second at a time—she was feeling too much all at once. "Did you hear all that?"

Gabe cracked a smile. "Only the true parts."

"I'm so sorry." Lottie wiped her face again with her paper-towel wad.

Gabe sat down on the floor beside her. "Lot, I already knew."

Her stomach dropped at the words.

"I've known for weeks. Tristan's not the kind of guy who keeps that stuff to himself. He told some of the guys in the locker room. The day of the party."

"Do you think she knew . . . that it was me?"

Gabe shook his head. "I don't think so. She wouldn't have let you walk around the party that night without confronting you if she did. That wasn't really her style." He let out a breath that was almost a laugh, but not quite, his eyes lost in some memory Lottie couldn't see.

"Why don't you hate me?" The question half-caught in her throat, like it didn't want out.

"Can I ask you something?"

She nodded.

"Would you hate Messina or me if one of us had been the one to screw around with him?"

She didn't answer. Gabe raised his eyebrows like *well?*

"No. I don't think so."

"Then why are you so convinced you have to hate yourself for it?"

The little black dog whined again. Lottie put her fingers back through the openings in its crate. "You don't understand."

"Then help us to, Lot. You don't have to endure everything in life all alone."

His words reminded her of Val. The way she'd softly clunk her head against Lottie's. *Tell me what's in your brain right now,* she'd whisper. *We can share the load.* But Lottie could never figure out how. How to share it, how to turn her pain into words, how to say them without feeling like the effort would rip her in two.

"But what if . . ." She stopped. She hated how hard it was. She closed her eyes and tried again. "What if I don't know how?"

The door opened again, and Messina popped her head in. "Your dad's asking for you," she said to Gabe.

Gabe stood up, but he held Lottie's eyes. "You try anyway."

Messina helped Lottie hobble to the bathroom, keeping her weight off the broken ankle. Her body was destroyed. Her knees wept through their bandages. When she saw herself in the mirror, she hardly recognized the face staring back, blackened and streaked with ash and soot, puffed and swelling along the right side of her mouth, eyes reddened by the smoke. She looked like someone escaped from hell.

She wiped herself clean as much as she could with damp paper towels and changed into one of the shelter T-shirts that matched Messina's. She gulped water from the sink, half-choking on it, but she didn't stop.

"Hang on," Messina told her, leaving her clinging to the sink, standing on one foot. She brought her a plastic cup. "It's easier this way."

Lottie drank two cupfuls. It was a different kind of thirst than she'd felt after the desert, like the smoke had coated her insides, like she needed to wash them clean.

Messina helped her out to the front lobby and dropped her down onto a row of plastic chairs, leaving her marooned there while Messina helped to feed and water all the animals.

Gabe's dad chatted to someone outside on his phone, while Gabe stood by, his face serious. Lottie wondered who it was. The air outside still looked bad, but wherever they were, it wasn't as bad as where they'd found her.

The phone behind the desk rang. An older woman with graying, dirty-blond hair rounded the corner and answered it. "Lone Pine Animal Shelter . . . As soon as they lift the evac orders . . . I can't give you information on specific pets right now, we don't have the staff at the moment to identify them all . . . Yep, absolutely . . . You're welcome."

Lottie couldn't figure out why the name of the shelter sounded so familiar—she didn't even know where Lone Pine was. Messina brought her a bag of chips and a Coke.

"Where'd these come from?"

"Vending machine in the back," Messina said, grabbing a rag and a squirt bottle from the front desk and disappearing through the door again.

Lottie was licking salt from her fingers when a familiar form passed Gabe and his dad and pushed through the glass door, bringing the smell of smoke and a gust of wind with him that kicked up his long hair and beard. Lottie blinked. Craig was standing in the entrance carrying a pair of beat-up crutches.

"Think these will work, Mom?" he said to the woman at the counter.

"Ask her yourself," the lady said, motioning to Lottie.

A clatter erupted as Messina stepped into the room and dropped one of the metal bowls she was carrying. Lottie recalled how the last time they'd seen each other, Messina was convinced Craig was going to murder her.

"My friends!" Craig said, splaying his arms wide, a crutch in each hand. "I'm glad you're both safe. Is your other friend okay too?"

It took Lottie a second to realize he meant Val. "She's just fine," Lottie said.

Craig turned to Messina. She stared at him, wide-eyed. "I'm so glad you made me take you back that night I gave you a ride," he told her. "I had a huge blowout on the way home. It spun the car clear around. The passenger side got completely crushed by a tree." He twirled screws on the crutches while he talked, raising their height. "Heading back to the trail probably saved your life. Or at least a lot of broken bones."

Messina looked at Lottie, shock hanging from her face. Lottie looked back at her like, *See? Your gut was right.*

"Oh, speaking of broken bones—here." Craig held out the crutches to Lottie. The pads on the top were yellowed and misshapen. The posts had little dents all over them—they looked like someone had used them for sword-fighting. "They're my daughter's from a few summers ago, dance injury. They're not too pretty to look at, but they get the job done."

Lottie took the crutches. "Thank you," she said. "For everything."

He held out a fist to her. She bumped it. "Us wildlings gotta stick together," he said.

He went into the back and came out carrying her fox friend in a crate.

"Where's she going?" Lottie said.

"Wildlife rehabilitation center in Arcata," Craig's mom said, leaning over the counter to grab some papers. "She needs time to heal up and get used to being in nature again instead of a cage."

"Then what?"

"They'll release her into the wild, once she's ready."

"Can we tell her goodbye?"

"I suppose so, since she saved your lives."

Val's fox was still asleep from the anesthesia in her system, but Lottie was sure she heard her whisper *thank you.*

88

GABE

His dad drove them up to the Three Sisters Wilderness in Oregon. They listened to his Saturday Morning Donut Mix in the car. Elton John's "Levon" played over the speakers while Lottie and Messina sang from the backseat, slaughtering the lyrics but getting the tune right, at least. The tires hummed against the road beneath their voices.

The air was clear here, no trace of the fire. Lottie walked as far into the wilderness park as she could on her crutches, hobbling along the trail until she tired. Gabe piggy-backed her farther in until his arms and back started burning, and they all stopped. His dad carried Val in his arms. The mountains that gave the park its name, the Three Sisters Peaks, jutted up out of the horizon in front of them, severe and beautiful. A little patch of graying wildflowers stood next to them, fighting to survive the dryness of summer. It was a more beautiful place than Gabe could have imagined. A warm breeze blew, making the flowers dance. They all stood in the quiet of it, of the wild Val so loved to be in.

"I think we should let her ashes go here," Gabe's dad said. He wiped his eyes with his sleeve. "This is where she belongs."

"But the urn is sealed," Messina said.

Gabe's dad shook his head and twisted the urn's lid open easily. They each took a handful and let it go into the wind that whipped over their heads, into the sky and toward the peaks. It filled Gabe with a sense of peace he hadn't thought was possible anymore.

"Fun fact," Messina said. "The Three Sisters Peaks are volcanoes."

"Did Val tell you that?" Gabe asked.

"No," she said, pulling the pamphlet from the ranger station they'd passed through from her pocket. "But I think she would have liked it."

Gabe smiled, sad and happy at the same time. After a while, he said, "We'll head down the path a little and give you guys some time with her. Just whistle when you need a lift," he said to Lottie.

He started down the path with his dad, who put his arm around Gabe's shoulders. "I'm sorry I've been so out of sorts lately," he said. "I know you've needed me here."

"It's okay, Dad. You've been through a lot."

"So have you," he said, and Gabe knew he was right—he'd just been trying not to think about that part. "And you needed me. I won't leave you again. I promise."

"I won't either," Gabe said. "Promise."

89

LOTTIE

They didn't talk. They sat side by side on the ground with nothing but the sound of the wind for a long time. Lottie knew Val was in that space, in the quiet and the wind and everywhere all around them. She could feel her presence as tangibly as she could feel her own body.

Still, she missed her. She wasn't sure the ache of it would ever fade entirely, but at least now she knew where she could find Val. Lottie wished there was a way she could tell her thank you, and that she was sorry for letting her down. She hoped Val could feel it.

Lottie leaned in against Messina's side. Messina's arm wrapped around her shoulders.

"We used to do this all the time," Messina said. "Lean on each other." Lottie could hear in her voice that she meant more than just how they were sitting. "I can't remember when we stopped. Or why." Messina turned her head to look at Lottie. "I've missed you."

"I've missed you, too." The words brought a rush of feelings that swelled inside her, threatening to carry her away like an ocean tide—she was just getting Messina back in her life, right as Messina was about to leave for good. Lottie would be going back without either of her best friends. The pain of it terrified her, but she let herself feel it. She didn't run away or self-destruct or zoom out. She didn't want to be afraid anymore.

She sat with her feelings, her sadness. She let the warmth of Messina's body next to hers bring her comfort, even though she knew she wouldn't be able to take that comfort back home with her. She picked up a twig from the ground and scratched at the dirt with its tip. She drew a little outline of a fox. It wasn't a good picture, but Lottie thought Val liked it all the same.

"Do you think she's happy? And safe?" Messina said.

Lottie nodded, feeling sure of the answer. "I think she's finally home."

The breeze kicked up a little, whipping past them. Messina tilted her head back, eyes closed, letting it ruffle her hair. She opened her eyes and smiled at Lottie. "Me too."

90

MESSINA

The drive to Brookings went too fast. It felt like it floated by in minutes. Messina's insides were still all tangled up and knotted and terrified. She wasn't sure she was ready for this.

She and Lottie had used Gabe's phone to look up Anna Collins on the community college page on the way to the school. Her photo was there. *Anna Collins, Professor of Fine Arts.* Her eyes looked kind, the way Messina remembered them.

The parking lot was mostly empty, but not completely. "It's summer. She probably won't be here."

"Don't a lot of schools have summer classes?" Lottie said. Messina's heart banged in her chest so hard she was sure it was bruising.

She stared out the window and counted cars. She stopped when Lottie squeezed her hand.

"You okay?" Lottie asked.

Messina wasn't sure—she half thought she might puke. She should have come up with another plan. It felt like there was no way this could work out the way she was hoping. She was terrified to ask for help again and watch as the world turned its back on her. She didn't know if she could do it.

She dug around inside herself for strength, thinking of the words that she'd repeated to herself through the fire—*I am strong. I am brave.* They weren't just a hope anymore, something she wished to be true—they *were* true. She'd been through a wildfire, and three hundred miles of the PCT, and survived Jeffucker. She was strong. She was brave.

She looked at Lottie. "I'm okay. I think I'm ready." She opened her door.

"Want some company?" Lottie said.

Messina smiled at her. "I'd love some."

"Three-o-two B, three-o-two B." Messina repeated the room number they'd been given as they made their way down the art wing. The door was open. A class was gathered inside, students working at easels arranged in a large circle around the room. Lottie and Messina waited in the hall together, far past the door, where they weren't visible to anyone inside. They sat on the painted concrete floor, leaned against the brick wall and each other.

Anna's voice carried out into the hall as she taught. It was unchanged from Messina's memory of it from years before, tugging at feelings long buried inside her. Hearing it made her realize how much she wanted this, how much of her heart she was risking by being here. She chewed her nails, each one to the quick and then past, so they stung, tender even to the touch of the air. She bit one too deeply and it bled. She put it in her mouth. Lottie took her other hand and held it tightly.

The clatter of supplies being packed up filtered out into the hall, followed by students. Most of them were young, college-age, but a few were older. When they'd gone, Messina and Lottie lingered outside the door. Lottie gave Messina a little shove, pushing her over the threshold. Lottie didn't follow her in.

She walked in slowly, silently. She could see the back of Anna, the woman who'd been so kind to her, who she'd dreamt about. She scrubbed containers in the sink, using the spray nozzle so a fine mist of water floated up into the air around her.

"Anna?"

She turned, and her eyes locked onto Messina's. Messina knew instantly that she recognized her, the way her face changed. Neither of them moved. Painful seconds ticked by, and nothing came out of her mouth—no *oh my gosh what are you doing here?* or *it's so good to see you* or anything. Nothing at all.

"I'm sorry," Messina said, turning to go. "This was a mistake." She bolted toward the door, acid and choked-back tears and vending machine food all trying to come out of her at once.

"Wait, Messina!"

She stopped. Everything in her was terrified.

"I'm so sorry—I was just surprised." Her hand touched Messina on the shoulder. "I'm so glad you came."

91

LOTTIE

She hung around in the hall for a long time. She was trying not to eavesdrop, but she needed to make sure Messina was okay. She wanted to be there in case she needed her.

When Messina finally came out, she was with Anna. Both of them were smiling.

“You must be Lottie.” Her eyes were kind, just like Messina said. Lottie wasn’t sure why it felt like her own heart was breaking when she was so happy for her friend.

“Let me know when you’re ready,” Anna said to Messina, giving her shoulder a little squeeze before leaving them alone.

This was really going to be goodbye. That was why her heart was breaking—it had just realized it before her mind had a chance to catch up.

The two of them sat in silence for a long time.

“I need to know that you’re going to be okay,” Messina said finally.

“Of course I will.”

“No, I mean *really okay*.” She held Lottie’s eyes. “Lot, you left us and ran into a fire.” Lottie saw a flash of the future they’d almost had, both of them dead. "I need to know you're not going to keep running into the fire. That you'll talk to us, whatever it is. That you'll say you need help."

"I will," she said. Messina looked at her with unsure eyes. "I promise."

Messina's eyes didn't let go. Lottie knew she was searching, trying to see if it was the Truth.

The truth was this: Lottie wasn't sure if it was true or not. But she hoped it was.

The car ride back was lonely without Messina. There had still been a part of Lottie that thought she might turn around, like she always did, but she'd finally made it out. Lottie wished the happiness she felt for Messina would take the sting out of missing her, but it didn't. It didn't make it any easier to be going back to her trailer in La Conchita with both of her best friends gone now.

She had Anna's phone number so she could call Messina and see how things were going, once Lottie got a new phone. Messina was still promising to pay her back when they'd finally said their goodbyes, but Lottie wouldn't have it. "Stop ruining the moment," she'd said, smashing Messina in an off-balance hug that had nearly toppled both of them.

The moon shined silver against the ocean, making the night outside look cold. Lottie laid her head against the window and watched it follow them.

They crossed the tracks into La Conchita, and Gabe's dad pulled to a stop before the turnoff to Lottie's. Gabe turned around in his seat. "Do you want to come to our house?"

"For the night?"

"For as long as you want," Gabe's dad said. Lottie saw his eyes smile at her in the rearview mirror. "We've got the room, and you're practically part of the family."

Lottie pressed her lips together. "I'm okay. I think I'll just go home tonight. Thank you though."

"The invitation's there, whenever you want to take it," he said. He flipped on his turn signal and headed down her street.

The lights were off in Lottie's trailer. Gabe walked her to the door, carrying her pack for her while she used her crutches up the steps. Only the dim glow of the streetlight and the moon made it light enough for her to find the spare key.

"Are you sure you don't want to stay at our place?"

Lottie leaned on the porch support and pushed the key into the lock. "Yeah." Gabe's eyes were on her. "What?" she asked.

"It's been a lot. I just want to make sure you're okay."

"I am."

Truth: She wasn't sure.

"Okay." He brought her pack in behind her and flipped on the light switch. It lit up the room, everything stained a dingy cigarette-yellow. It smelled like decades of misery. Gabe set her bag on the couch. "I'm always around, if you change your mind."

She nodded. "I know."

He closed the door behind him.

Lottie dropped onto the couch and turned on the TV. She

turned it back off again, sitting in the silence. But it wasn't like the silence of being on the trail. It pushed in on her, every awful memory this place held, the hurt of it, how small it made her feel. Like she was nothing.

She wasn't okay.

She lay back against the couch with tears seeping from her eyes. Grimace wasn't even here to comfort her. She was more alone now than she'd been before they started the hike. Only now she could really feel it. Messina's words flashed through her mind. *I need to know that you'll say when you need help.* She smashed her eyes closed, and more tears rolled out down her cheeks. It wasn't going to get any easier, but she'd gotten stronger.

She grabbed her crutches and made her way across the block to Gabe's house. She felt silly for being so scared, but the feeling was there all the same. She tapped on the door with a soft fist. Gabe opened it.

"Hey." He looked exhausted, but he still smiled at her.

Her heart was pounding too loud inside her chest, making it hard to find the words she was looking for.

"Are you okay?"

She shook her head. "I think I need a friend."

Gabe opened the door wide, and Lottie crutched inside.

They watched *Raiders of the Lost Ark* on VHS, with Chicken lying between them and Grimace on Lottie's lap. "I'm glad you missed me," Lottie told him, scratching his ears. He purred and nuzzled his nose into her hand.

"Fun fact," Gabe said. "The frequency of a cat's purr can heal bones."

"Really?"

Gabe nodded, smiling. She could see on his face that he was remembering Val. One of those little bits that was just his. She liked how they shared them with each other, each getting to know pieces of her they hadn't known before.

"Want some popcorn?" Gabe asked.

Lottie nodded. "Always."

They left the lights off in the kitchen, only the yellow lamp above the stove glowed, but it was enough to light most of the room enough to see. Lottie hopped up onto the counter while they waited for the popcorn. The fake butter sizzled, filling the room with its scent. Lottie picked up the stack of papers next to her.

"What are these?" She could see they were real estate listings. What she meant was *What are these doing here?*

"My dad's been looking at new houses for a few weeks now."

"Oh."

Gabe looked around at the kitchen. "There are a lot of hard memories here. Plus, you know, the unstable hillside."

"No, yeah. Of course you'd want to leave."

The microwave beeped. Neither of them moved to get the popcorn. The last dregs of it still popped around inside its paper bag.

"We actually put an offer on one the other day, when we were at the animal shelter. It's a house in Carpinteria. They've accepted it."

Lottie stared down at the countertop. "That's great."

"Lottie."

She picked at a hardened spot of melted cheese.

"Lottie." Gabe stepped in front of her, moving his head between her and the cheese spot so she had to look at him. "There's a room for you too, for as long as you want to stay. It's a three-bedroom."

"Oh."

He watched her, waiting, his eyes somehow bright even in the dark kitchen. "So, what do you think?"

The idea made her head spin. "I think it feels like you're doing that thing again, where you want to be nice, but it's too much, like you're trying to rescue me or something."

He shook his head. "It's the opposite, Lot. I kept thinking *you'd* rescue *me*."

She laughed.

"I'm serious. I've thought it since I first got a crush on you, that you were this magic person, like no one else, and if I could just convince you to love me, it would fix everything and take away all the pain from my life." The thought seemed so absurd to her, that he could have been looking to her for help all this time. "I know you're not going to fix my problems. But I think we could still be there for each other, like we used to be. Like family."

His eyes held hers, waiting for an answer.

"Well? What do you think?"

Lottie shook her head. "I don't know what to say."

"Say yes." He had a look like she was being silly, like she was making everything harder than it had to be, like always.

"Okay."

"Yeah?"

"Yeah." She smiled, letting herself feel it, the goodness of the moment. It was strange and wonderful to sit there in it, soaking it in without running away. But she still needed something. “Gabe?” She wondered if this part would ever get easier, asking for things, letting herself feel vulnerable. “Can I have a hug now?”

In answer, he wrapped his arms around her, pulling her tight. She breathed it in, this new feeling, accepting help, accepting love. It didn’t make sense that it was such a hard thing to do, even though it was. She was glad she was trying, though.

“There is one thing,” she said, speaking into Gabe’s T-shirt where her face pressed against him. He pulled back and looked at her. She kept her eyes serious, hiding her smile. “I’m going to have to talk it over with Grimace.”

92

LOTTIE

She handed the blue slip to the office attendant.

"Ms. Sipes called me in?"

Ms. Sipes popped her head out from her office and waved Lottie inside. Lottie sat down in one of the mauve chairs in front of her desk.

"I asked you in so we could discuss your college plans. The last time we spoke, you were planning to go to a community college, either here or in Oregon."

"Yes."

"Since then, the essay you submitted won several awards, along with scholarship offers. Everything from Cal State schools to some colleges up the coast." Lottie nodded. It had all come as a surprise over the past few weeks, and she was still trying to process it. "Has that changed your plans at all?" Ms. Sipes sipped from her giant plastic cup and watched Lottie through the red-rimmed glasses that were new this year.

"I don't know," Lottie said. "I'm visiting a friend in Oregon this weekend. I'm going to talk things over with her and take some time to think about it, to figure out what I want to do with my future."

"Smart girl. You've got a couple months at least. That's a good amount of time to explore your options. Come talk to me once you've made up your mind."

"Okay, thank you, Ms. Sipes." She stood to go.

"Just out of curiosity," Ms. Sipes said, "what inspired your essay?"

Lottie thought back on what she'd written, how she'd poured herself into it, shedding light on so many parts of herself she'd tried to hide for so long. "There were a lot of things," Lottie told her, "but mostly a trip I took this summer with my friends. And a book called *Wild*."

"Well, you've done a great job. And it's good to see that you're taking care of yourself."

"Thanks. I've got some really good friends to lean on," Lottie said. And she knew it was the truth.

ACKNOWLEDGMENTS

This story took root in me a long time ago. It's lived in so many different forms, growing with the stubbornness (and pace) of a California oak. It was born out of what I needed, and what I hoped might matter to anyone wandering through similar feelings. I have so many people to thank for helping it get here.

Jim McCarthy, thank you for believing in this book. It was missing so much when it came to you, but you saw its potential, knew I could make it better, and helped me get it there. I feel so lucky to have you in my corner. Thanks for believing in me, for always having a solution, for being so coolheaded and warmhearted, and for generally just being the best ever.

Kristin Allard, thank you for loving this book so fiercely, for your brilliant insights and guidance, and for not letting me give everything away right at the start. Thanks to the entire team at Norton Young Readers for your support and for cheering on this book.

Nicole Chiarella and Natasha Buran—my genius writing witches. Thank you for your friendship and for years of word-making meetups, coffees, gluten-free snacks, and unwavering encouragement. And thanks for still being there when I finally crawled out of my writing cave.

Anna Jarvis, for pirates (obviously), for millions of texts that have encouraged me, made me laugh, and kept me going. And for always asking to read the words way before they're ready but still loving them anyway.

Myra Spence, for sending me that mental emergency kit when I needed it most.

Gaby Marquette, for your language expertise and encouragement.

Amelia Leicht, for countless nights of bacon tater tots and good conversation, and for being the smartest person I know and letting me pick your brain any time I ask.

Theresa Biskup, for your keen eye and knowledge of slang, for giving me advice even when you don't have time, and for listening to my rants while you drive. Also for keeping up the hug quota around here when I'm all tapped out.

Thank you to Cristin Terrill, for helping me find the plot when all I had were characters. And Beth Revis, for the kindest tough love on early pages forever ago when I didn't have any idea where this story was going. I'm so grateful to you both, and to the whole Wordsmith community.

Corey Ann Haydu, who taught me years ago to stay In Scene, something I've remembered in everything I've written since.

Ms. Farrell—thank you for *seeing me* all those years ago, when I was an angry, hurting, eighteen-year-old who never got her work done. You met me where I was and never stopped trying to inspire me. You were the best teacher. Thanks for making me read *The Catcher in the Rye* and helping me find a love of reading that would transform my world.

Lindsay, thanks for being the one I could talk to about it all. I know you can see all the Truth that's in these pages. Thanks for being my friend and for letting me put pieces of us here. I love you, S.

Thank you to Johanna, for teaching me to give myself grace. This story's journey couldn't have happened without your guidance.

Louie, for being the coolest boss ever and for being so supportive of my other job. You're an amazing human, and you make the world a better place.

Hayley, Bailey, and Quinn—this book couldn't exist without all the hours I stole away to the library to write and hone my craft back when I was juggling younglings. Thank you for giving me that time and space, and for helping me hold on to a part of myself I needed more than I knew.

Thank you so much to Cheryl Strayed. Reading *Wild* was life-changing for me. I wished I could go back in time and share that book with a younger version of myself, who desperately needed it. Writing this book was my way of trying to do that. Thank you for sharing your story, for inspiring me and so many others.

To Mom, for pushing through all the hard parts to find what we have now, and for believing in me. Kris, for love, hugs, encouragement, and for calling me Sam. Dad and Vicki, for always knowing I could do it, and being so proud when I finally did.

To my family—Team D—thank you for your endless support, love, and patience. And thanks for helping me get rid of the stuff in my own parentheses. Gregg—my partner through every wild adventure—you saw the magic in me before I could, and you never stopped reminding me it was there.

Finally, to my readers, thank you. While this book is a work of fiction, so much of it comes from very real places inside of me. Thank you for letting me share it with you.